The Bend of the Road

~

Tiding Westward

Also by K. R. Brehmer

A HERITAGE SAGA

The Way Back Home ~ Finding Rose

The Bend of the Road

~

Tiding Westward

A Heritage Saga

K. R. BREHMER

ꓘB

Published in the United States of America by K. R. Brehmer.
First Printing, 2020

ISBN 978-0-9864340-3-7 (softcover)
ISBN 978-0-9864340-4-4 (ebook)

Cover and book design by the author.

This is a work of fiction. All characters, organizations, events, incidents
and dialogues are either products of the author's imagination or are based
on the historical and personal record, both long past or more recent.

You can go wherever you wanna go
Go wherever you wanna go
Fly up to the moon and say hello now
You can go wherever you wanna go

Patty Griffin, *Go Wherever You Wanna Go*

PROLOGUE

—

THE GREAT STORM

Wadden Sea, Duchy of Holstein, October 1634

Old Johann rested his hands on his hips and tilted his head back as far as it would go, steadying wobbly legs to look up at a cloudless sky; then he straightened his arched back, closed his eyes and let out a long breath of a job well-done. The weather, for once, had been exceptionally fine during late summer and the first few weeks of early autumn. After three years of rain always at the wrong time, haying season and harvesting of other crops had come and gone without a hitch. Finally, dry, mild days were upon them—exactly what had been needed. The nearby sea had played an important part too, yielding up a plentiful catch of herring, cod and a variety of other fish. Storage sheds near their small peasant farmer dwellings, as well as barns attached to the ends of the largest houses scattered throughout the countryside, were brimming to the top, filled with grain, smoked fish and meats, more so than they'd ever been during the past few years.

At last! It was a good feeling that rippled through his rickety body. Recent years of half empty larders had meant

1

half empty stomachs. Now there was enough fodder for livestock and food for themselves to carry them through the approaching winter months without the usual struggle. It felt like things had finally turned around and fallen into place for the Reither family and their neighbors in the fairly isolated communities of the Wadden Sea region. Still, life was always a challenge in the intertidal area of the *Wattenmeer* stretched along a section of coastline within the larger confines of the North Sea.

Johann Reither, one of the oldest of the elders in the community, walked a few paces and leaned against a fence post as cracked and crinkled as his own windblown skin. Puffing sharply on a small clay pipe, he squinted up at the pale glare of a washed out sky before the feathery touch of a blue butterfly alighting on his forearm brought his eyes downwards again. It was a typical kind of day for his home on the north coast flatlands during the autumn months, before winter's claim turned it to dreary shades of slate gray instead. But now daylight was ending, when the sun goes to beer, as the locals say. He chuckled to himself when he thought about their peculiar expression for a Dithmarschen sunset. It was strange how one good harvest could create a sense of well-being among inhabitants in spite of all of the hardships they faced. A successful season should be enjoyed when it could. It was a special kind of camaraderie they felt at moments like these, a welcome diversion from the constant warring of nations and unexpected blows nature often delivered.

***

Turmoil had been raging across Europe since 1618, the

year when it had all started by a seemingly minor event so far away. Sixteen years had passed since a group of Protestants had literally thrown two Catholic councilors out a window in the Prague Castle, the incident that had ignited long-lasting hostilities. It was as if all it took to make new enemies everywhere, including in their own small corner of the world, was a physical brawl in a far-flung land! These religious-based, philosophical conflicts were still showing no signs of abating. They had become an integral part of the fabric of everyday routine, almost like they were a normal state of affairs, if the destructiveness and carnage of war could ever be said to be normal. Even old Johann's Dithmarschen—a republic remotely situated on the western edge of the European continent in which they lived and adjacent to its grander neighbor, the Duchy of Holstein—had not been spared from serving as a frequent battleground.

The Duchy of Holstein, defined by and squeezed between the North Sea to the west, the Elbe River to the south, and the meandering Eider River to the northeast, seemed to be a valuable prize for the taking. So many conflicts had been fought across the marshlands of Dithmarschen, conflicts having for pretext religious and political differences among rulers from other countries. In essence, they were battles for power and supremacy through land expansion objectives of distant governments. Lutheranism against Catholicism, duke against duke, king against king, countries often divided within themselves as to where allegiance should be owed. Johann often wondered to himself when would selfishness on such a grand governmental scale marked by year-after-year turbulence ever come to an end?

For those families like old Johann's who had for

3

generations lived near the sea in the marshlands of Dithmarschen, or inland populations who made their home on the *geestland*—the higher and rockier moraine formed by glaciers long ago—these nationalistic disputes and internal differences had never been experienced with such frequency as in recent decades in collective memory. To the contrary, a long-held spirit of cooperation and independence had prevailed among the peoples of Dithmarschen up until the middle of the preceding century when, after losing a major battle against the Danish, their autonomous peasant republic was forced into dissolution, their long-held sense of freedom suffering a major blow as a consequence. As a result, their council-based form of self-governance and reliance on self-defense from Viking and other intruders, predicated on egalitarian social solidarity and ties of kinship, had been replaced overnight with oversight by the sons of the King of Denmark. From their distant seat in another country to the north, they served as absentee dukes of both Schleswig and Holstein duchies.

Dithmarschen had been officially incorporated into the territory of an expanded Holstein and adjustments had been made. In view of the Protestant Reformation, Danish policies enacted in 1524 had changed by decree the official religious practice from Catholicism to Lutheranism. Long-standing free peasant or tenant farmers with small land holdings in Dithmarschen contrasted with both those farm laborers who were hired by and owed allegiance to their landlords on larger estates, and even more so with the memories of serfs bound to their masters in the almost bygone feudal society. In the former system, prevalent in many countries such as neighboring Denmark and Sweden, laborers were housed, received food rations and grew potatoes on a corner of land, the farmer's wife often milking the cows. Even children were put to work on the estate. While Dithmarschen dwellers might also contribute to the welfare of demesnes in addition to maintaining their own farms, it was not the added responsibility that pressured their families, rather it was the burden of dues in the form of taxes and other obligations that decreased the possibility of sustainable living as they had in the past; there were simply less resources to go around for each family.

Loss of independence to the Danish throne had been fought with as much ferocity as could be mustered, their resistance holding fast for a number of years. Ultimately capitulation became inevitable, culminating in the slaughter of most of the inhabitants of Meldorf in 1559, the most prominent and populous of Dithmarschen towns during the middle ages—even once the capital—by a more numerous and better armed Danish force. Acceptance and adaptation to whatever form of subjugation the Danes thrust upon the Dithmarschen people had been their lot and their only path to survival when basic existence was precarious enough.

There would be changes to get used to: Danish for one, at least as a second language to their native Low German, a new political system for another, and fundamental cultural differences. On the positive side, Danish rule would be from afar, and an enduring peace might finally put an end to the threat of further conflict. There was also the realization that administration by any of the other competing countries might have been even a worse alternative. Formalities imposed by a new regime would strive to change mindsets to gain loyalty and erase previous ways of living. Be that as it may, change wrought by a superior military force could not stamp out the memories of freedom they had enjoyed as a peasant republic. Unaccustomed to subservience to overlords since the 13th century, the period when obedience to noble rulers had ceased and farmers had enjoyed greater political freedom, they had been for centuries, and still remained, a close-knit society with clan-like family structure; it was an ethos strongly rooted in working together to ensure at least a subsistence level of existence for almost everyone. No more salient example of this spirit of cooperation could be found than in efforts to protect themselves from their biggest threat—a force even greater than an overwhelming army of soldiers equipped with the latest weaponry: **Water**.

Drainage of swamps had begun centuries before, and dikes had been built to stem a sea ever-eager to steal back and submerge the tidal flats and lowland bogs extending inland from its shores. Danger from water inundation was something present inhabitants and their ancestors had sought to manage since the very first settlements—but never to completely subdue. In recent years worries over the control of water had been reawakened with even storms of moderate intensity breaking apart and streaming through old and frail earthen dikes. Old Johann, with the voice of longevity, had frequently spoken up about what was needed but was met with shrugged shoulders and blank stares, as if it should be obvious nothing could be done under the unsettled circumstances of the times. Battles fought in and around the marshes of their homeland had taken precedence and left necessary dike repair undone. And, unwittingly, death on an unheard of scale from plague spread across Europe in 1602 had also diverted attention from the constant natural foe of flooding. Already creaky dikes on the densely populated island of Strand in Frisia northwest of Dithmarschen had been heavily damaged—some giving away completely—by raised sea levels caused by drifting ice floes reaching the Wadden Sea some ten years before, in 1625. It should have served as a warning.

By now, well-aware of the weakened condition of many of the Dithmarschen dikes, the duke himself had finally issued orders for their repair. Perhaps he had actually taken notice by listening to the words of Johann and others like him, elders who were intent on making the likelihood of an impending disastrous situation crystal clear. But up until now these commands had also been mostly ignored. However, even weaker storms of the just past summer had caused problems. Now that food supply for both people and animals was secured, it was time for villagers and townspeople to begin again in earnest in forming a plan to fortify the ageing banks and canals. This was the customary way it had been done in the past and how it should be done now in spite of changing authority. As always, it fell upon the local community to get the job done themselves.

***

Old Johann had attained such a venerable age that not only did his own family but his neighbors and other visitors called him *Opa*, the informal term for grandfather. He had outlived all of those with whom he grew up, including the longest-lived and much-loved horses on the farm. He took being addressed as grandpa by the community both as a sign of respect for his years and as a way to dispense with formality in showing his approachability, especially by the younger generations. They needed guidance and there was no better way to impart it than by listening to his stories in which advice was often carefully embedded. His ears always perked up when he heard someone asking for Opa Johann. It gave him much satisfaction when either the young, or even the middle-aged, plied him with questions to which he was able to provide sage answers. On many a winter evening, he regaled his whole family with stories of the past. Listeners didn't seem to mind if he embellished them a little by a fervent imagination.

But horses were really the main love of his life, his steadfast loyal partners in the work he had accomplished. To him they were almost at the same level of importance as his own family and they were treated as such. In turn they seemed to reciprocate in their own way. In fact, it was joked by some that Opa Johann must be part horse himself; his whistle let them know when he was coming and by the time he arrived ears were well forward on heads turned towards him, waiting to exchange greetings. Sounds of whinnying could be heard from a hundred yards away when he had brought carrots or apples to nibble on. Afterwards they were like putty in his hands.

Yes, Opa Johann thought he had seen and done it all in his years.

Clouds of light gray color had been slowly gathering in several parts of the eastern sky during the early morning hours of the 11th of October 1634. Riding on the accompanying slight breeze, they were a sure indication rain was coming their way soon. It was not an unwelcome sight since the recently cut fields could use the moisture to dampen down dust and post-harvest stubble remnants and of hoof-trodden pastures cattle had left from grazing. The earth was indeed dry and thirsty after its hard work during the growing seasons. The oncoming storm slowly moved from east to west, passing over a wide expanse of land and the Baltic Sea before reaching Dithmarschen; an appearance of normality raised no concerns over dike conditions. By evening, though, the clouds had darkened, nearly black and quite menacing. Then the smaller groups of clouds became one, amalgamating into a single enormous black mass in the eastern sky.

Even more alarmingly, a second storm had formed, coming from a different direction, out of the northwest. At first it seemed for an anxious few minutes countervailing winds had neutralized each other, and there was a standoff resulting in a strange calmness. But soon the wind picked up again slightly then blowing harder and harder until it became a major force to reckon with. Locals brave enough to face the fury of the first blasts head on were scrunched over, one hand holding tight to the tops of their hats, the other out in front as if leaning on a wall. Walking with the gusts at their backs was a different challenge in trying to plant legs to brace themselves from the flurries pushing them suddenly forward and side-to-side in unintended directions. Rapidly churning legs at times were sometimes not enough to prevent them from stumbling into a heap on the ground or into a fence. Just trying to stand in one place without moving, took all the strength one had.

By seven o'clock there was no doubt in anyone's minds this would be no ordinary storm. Howling winds were creating havoc with weaker structures, tossing patches of thatch from worn roofs hither and thither. Sheets of rain pelted their houses unmercifully and with such might that they almost expected to see raindrops driven through walls, piercing them like powerful arrows shot by a formidable enemy, as they huddled together for both warmth and support in front of glowing peat fires. With the promise of a long night ahead until morning light, sleep was nearly impossible to come by even for the youngest among them.

As for Opa Johann, he was too old and tired to let even a raging storm steal away his need for rest, though he knew before his eyelids closed tight it bore all the signs of one for the ages. But as soon as his eyes shut he fell into a restless sleep. His slumber was invaded by pictures of days gone by: childhood friends so long ago now; blue butterflies of springtime darting about in flowering woodland patches; when families worked side-by-side in the fields; battles between colorfully garbed soldiers; the many mistakes he had made in his life; reinforcing the dikes; those who were no longer there; and, of course, the horses he had known. One of his proudest moments had been when his horsemanship skills were called upon in joining the dike riders on another very stormy night. Even when mounted on an unfamiliar horse, he was among the fastest and most observant of the riders patrolling up and down the dike, splashing across drenched fields and jumping across canal waters grown wider and faster to save time when a rescue was at hand. Both steed and man kept their composure, riding with confidence in abysmal conditions; there could be no hesitation or panic when dealing with such tempests.

It was the same this night; everyone had taken shelter indoors by now if they could. The exception was the small contingent of horsemen whose responsibility was, as it had been his when Johann was a young man, to check on the state of the dikes during the course of a major storm. And this storm

10

was fast becoming one of them. Were there signs of dike failure—fine cracks running north to south, dark blotches of penetrating dampness, bulges where there shouldn't be? Were there breeches in the dikes, even as much as a minor trickle, or the sound of water pounding the banked earth beyond resistance, or inhabitants in immediate danger who should be alerted in order to seek higher ground for themselves and their animals? Making matters about as bad as they could be was the simultaneous advance of a storm-whipped incoming tide. The unbroken winds blowing off the sea, when coupled with high tides, were a certain recipe for flooding once again.

In a community reliant on mounted riders to monitor the situation, a patrol had been hastily formed to examine dike after dike before moving on to the tidal canals to do the same. All through the night until the breaking of dawn, the dike riders continued their watch and passed out warnings to those threatened as the surge grew in coverage and strength, ripping mud and thatch shelters apart and sending those closest to the shore scurrying from their dwellings to find shelter elsewhere. Relentlessly moving inland, the surge caused the same pattern to be repeated for farmers living in vulnerable positions further from the sea. Thinking incorrectly they would be safe, many were forced to seek refuge under the roofs of heavily beamed manor houses of the well-to-do.

On the following morning, by the time the villagers came out from wherever they had spent the night, the landscape had altered. Many small houses with weak or no foundations nearest to the coastline embankments had completely disappeared. These dwellings, some on recently cleared marshland, were no match for the destructiveness of this storm. Unstoppable flood waters had swept over the lowland taking with them all in their way, including the very land itself. It was as if the sea was making a powerful pronouncement in taking back the topsoil it had lost when the outer dikes were built: "Beware of my might! You see what I can do to your marshland if I want. It belongs to me when the tide is in and you will be left with only tidal flats, vast muddy wastelands, when it is out."

The sea had indeed struck a heavy blow, winning the battle this time around. Dwellers would have to regroup swiftly to deal with the vanishing of some of the most prized marshland under plow at a time when increasing population was in contention with a shrinking arable land mass. In the days afterwards, one of the ways the devastation of the storm was calculated, besides the loss of precious land, was in deaths of those who could not or chose not to escape elsewhere; a second measure was the bloated bodies of drowned livestock. The impact on mind and spirit would soon have to give way to pragmatism, for the physical damage from the flood waters had wiped away food supplies so confidently stowed away not long before; supplies thought to have been more than enough to survive the winter months ahead without the usual worries.

Perhaps it was the right time. When they went to wake Opa Johann from his night's reveries, the gentle shaking of his shoulder met with no response. Looking closer, they found a colorless face and hands cold to the touch. His demise at such an age could not be taken as a shock. But it was strangely disquieting that his peaceful, time-worn face in the morning light could be in such contrast to the ruinous storm that had passed across the land during the hours of darkness. There would be no more events to experience, no more actions to advise, no more stories to add to the long list recounted during his life. Maybe it was just meant to be that Old Johann had missed this story.

News soon travelled southwards of the aged and even more badly maintained dikes having been pierced through by salt waters on Strand to the north, the island where the storm struck first and hardest. Besides dikes giving way to tidal surges, the network of canals had also overflowed, the banks collapsing under the deluge of runoff rainwater. So severe was the damage, the island was no longer intact as a single entity—flood waters having divided the greater part of it into two halves. The tops of the remaining land that had once been the highest points had been transformed into a string of small islands on the perimeter. On Strand, loss of life had been catastrophic when compared to the mainland, not counted in hundreds but in thousands.

No, the great Wadden Sea storm of 1634 was one they would not soon forget. And neither would they forget Opa Johann.

OPEN DOOR

Central Coast, California, June 1992

On a trip to the San Francisco Bay Area to visit my brother, and about to leave from his house to return home, he stopped us before getting into our car. "Hold on a minute, you might be interested in having this." Then he handed me a thin, black binder while saying it was about our ancestors and had been given to him by one of our aunts a few weeks previously. A quick glance at a few pages before we got into the car revealed it contained neatly typed and carefully organized information on family history—ancestors, descendants and relatives—relating to our father's heritage, the German side. It would not be until many months later before I took the time to look more closely at the details it held. The focus had been placed on family members in America rather than those ancestors who had preceded them in Europe, and the starting point was my immigrant great-grandparents, both of whom appeared to have been born somewhere in what is now part of the state of Schleswig-Holstein in northern Germany.

The bulk of the binder covered the descendants of each of the nine children of my paternal great-grandparents, all born in the United States, one of whom was my grandfather, John. A rather poor quality photocopy of a family portrait photo, almost looking like a thin, see-through newspaper, showed all eleven well-dressed family members with corresponding names and dates under each of the unsmiling faces. It was my first encounter with my grandfather's eight brothers and sisters, all born over a fifteen year span from 1871 to 1886. Including my grandfather, the siblings counted five males and four females, most with very German sounding first names like Emil, Otto, Ida and Sophia, even though all were born in America. A tenth child, it was later learned, had died in infancy.

Interestingly enough, all of the children had been raised in Scott County, close to the city of Davenport on the eastern boundary of Iowa where it meets the state of Illinois. Some of them had even married there, but all of them eventually moved to another Iowan county. O'Brien County, about three hundred and forty miles away on the western side of the state, was the place they lived out the rest of their lives. It seemed like an awfully long distance to have gone for the times. What could have been the reason behind it?

It was striking how thoroughly family members had been traced and how up-to-date the coverage was given there was probably little internet searching assistance available at the time it was compiled on a typewriter. Photos gathered from living relatives and obituaries from newspaper clippings had been collected the old-fashioned way and effectively incorporated into an outline paragraph format of births, marriages and deaths for descendants of each of the nine children. All this was done without using a family tree computer program to create and spit out a genealogy report. In the end, what at first glance appeared to be a rather primitive presentation was easy to understand and certainly a credit to the time-consuming rigor required in producing it even if a few, mostly typographical, errors were later to be discovered.

The untimely deaths of some of my father's brothers during the 1940s were shocking to read about. It appeared only one of the brothers had died in Iowa so there might be much more to learn about what had happened to the others through archived newspaper databases and other resources. It is hard to imagine what it must have been like for their parents and other family members in the midst of already gloomy times of World War II. Obituaries and achievements of my grandmother and grandfather were also among the binder's contents.

But it was the very first page that held the information most enticing to me for discovering more about the European origins of our ancestors. While I knew almost nothing about the families of my paternal grandfather's siblings in America, it was not that which piqued my curiosity rather it was the allure of the deeper past, where generations of ancestors had lived in the old country that I wanted to know more about first. On two different occasions when I was a child our family had made the long drive from California to Iowa where my grandparents lived and their children had grown to adulthood. On the second trip, to celebrate their golden wedding anniversary, relatives from all over the United States had gathered together. So many people had come that it required one of the older grandsons, a cousin and Navy cook by trade, to put on an apron and bake more cakes as the long summer afternoon extended into an evening lawn party at their home. A few years older on this second visit, well-cemented memories of them were set forever in my mind as well as images of the area in which they lived. And seeing the three remaining siblings of my father together in one place for the first time made for a greater awareness of how we were all interconnected.

Nothing was said to me on either of those two visits by my grandparents about our German roots. And my own father either knew little about it himself, or simply never got around to saying what he did know. Looking back, I could only remember him mentioning his ancestry was from Holstein, which was somewhere in modern Germany, and the place where a well-known breed of cattle originated. So when that very first page of the black binder noted my great-grandfather had been born in Dettmarschen and his wife, my great-grandmother, near Marne in South Dettmarschen in Germany, my reaction was a mixed one. Okay, Germany seemed to be confirmed but what about this Dettmarschen? Where was this odd-sounding place? And Marne? Wasn't Marne the name of a place in France where a major battle was fought during the First World War? And what had happened to Holstein? Nowhere was it mentioned.

At the next opportunity, at a library known for its strong international collections, I headed over to the atlas case to see if these strange places could be found anywhere on maps. Neither Dettmarschen nor Marne could be located in Germany in consulting the indices of the modern, comprehensive world atlases. Perhaps they were just too small to warrant acknowledgement. Scrutinizing the actual maps of Germany to see if a place with a similar sounding name but spelled differently might be spotted also ended unsuccessfully. However, the library had many other types of atlases including several of the historical variety, one of which comprehensively covered the lands now comprising Schleswig-Holstein, the northernmost state of Germany. Still unable to sight the two places on large scale, detailed maps, another approach was taken by consulting a world gazetteer volume. Finally, after looking alphabetically for the place name of Dettmarschen, something much akin to it appeared. It was close enough that it could be the same place; it was a place called **Dithmarschen**. Rather than a town per se, it was described as a region in northwest Germany; **Marne** too was listed, and it looked as if it could be one of the main towns in the region. The gazetteer provided the latitude and longitude coordinates, and with these in hand a narrow portion of the historical atlas could be zeroed in on.

Stretched out over a north/south distance of about forty miles, covering a printed map page length of about eight inches, was the word Dithmarshen. And near the most southerly part of the area, not far from the river Elbe itself, and close to the letter "n" at the end of the name, the town of Marne itself was spotted.

In searching additional resources, it turned out the same region was sometimes denoted as Ditmarsh by English speakers. Also, the letter "h" in Dithmarschen was silent when spoken making the pronunciation of the first two syllables the same as the truncated and anglicized Ditmarsh. Apparently, the spelling of Dettmarschen as noted in the binder had been done in error, probably based on a guess from hearing the word spoken and not seeing it written down in its properly spelled form. True, it was not far apart from what the area was called in Latin, Detmarsia, yet another version found later on a 16th century antique map; so maybe there was justification for the variant spelling after all! If the size of the print on the historical map was any indication of magnitude, the largest nearby town, less than fifteen miles from Marne as the crow flies, was the coastal town of Cuxhaven. It was about twenty-seven miles away when reached by a combination of road and ferry. Since it was at the mouth of the Elbe River but on the other side from Marne and in the northernmost part of German Lower Saxony, it was neither a part of Holstein nor the Dithmarschen region.

Going back in time, contact and collaboration between the two places must have been limited only to fisherman in boats since no bridge passage existed due south of Marne where the waters across the Elbe were at their widest from bank to bank. Instead, the inhabitants of Marne must have found their natural geographical association to be with neighbors in other villages and towns within the area of Dithmarschen itself, both to the north and east, even though these communities were of comparably small size as well. What was determined with certainty, though, was that Dithmarschen had been part of the Duchy of Holstein during the first part of the 19th century and under Danish rule, before it was joined with Schleswig, its northern neighbor, to become the province of Schleswig-Holstein.

A corrected version of the place names along with the copies of the maps I had found were sent to my brother so there would be no future confusion for those researching our paternal roots in Holstein. Satisfied with what I had learned so far, the updated black binder was put aside to gather dust, lying untouched on a shelf for the next few years. But the door had been opened a crack. Without realizing it, the first steps had just been taken on a long road ahead.

WURTEN

Dithmarschen, Duchy of Holstein, September 1855

"C'mon Johann, get up. Time for catnapping is over. The fields won't cut themselves." There was no movement. Older brother, Hinrich, resorted to nudging him with his foot instead of wasting his time repeating himself, reaching down to tousle his hair, but not too roughly to avoid any recurrence of another scuffle between them. He had been through this before and knew not to go overboard with his teasing, potentially provoking a temper outburst which negated age and size differences in its ferocity. When Johann closed his eyes in the middle of the day after having eaten some dried meat and cold beans and after swallowing thirstily and often from the water jug to offset the sweltering heat, words alone were not enough to get a reaction from him. He had drifted off into his own dream world becoming almost unreachable by voice.

After working since dawn, and before picking up their tools to begin again until late evening, a routine followed now for several days in a row while the fair weather held, a weary body was resistant to rousing off the ground. So when a strong enough but non-antagonistic push with a foot rolled him half way over, it caused his eyes to open drowsily without any sign of rancor in them. He could not be angry with Hinrich who rested a scythe on one of his broad bare shoulders as he peered down at him. Even though at fifteen he almost matched his older brother in height—both of them slim and tall and of raw-boned build—as well as in strength, there could be no mistaking who was the boss. If Hinrich said it was time to get back to work, then it was time. Proper deference must be shown to his senior sibling in most things. So, Johann, shirtless as well, raised himself up with ease, slapped his cap back on his head, and followed his brother back to the corner of the long and narrow field they had been mowing before taking a welcome break from their labors.

It was not that Johann was lazy—far from it. How could he be? Inheriting the good name of Johann as he had from a continuous string of Johann and Hinrich-named ancestors down through the generations, he felt it had to be borne with the utmost respect to safeguard the reputation of those who had gone before him. No shame would he allow himself to incur. In fact, he had been up even earlier than the rest of the family again, well before dawn, to tend to the beloved horses stabled at the manor house. This was not part of his regular farm duties. And though it meant an even longer day, it was the highlight because he liked being with the animals as much as they seemed to like seeing him, and much more than he liked bending his back to toiling in fields of barley, flax and oat. So, as with other namesakes of his forefathers, Johann was the one in his family who had inherited an affinity to all things horses. Any chance he got, he would spend time with them.

Although the houses of large property owners were often referred to as manors, life in Dithmarschen for the most part had not been subjected to a formal manorial system; the inhabitants were not considered feudal vassals in any shape or form. As small farmers, the Reither family worked the few acres of the land they occupied while also giving over a portion of their efforts to caring for the farming needs of the largest landowner up on the hill, additional work without which they would not be as well off. In the past, the demands were much more onerous, but now it was somewhat easier to feed and care for a family, unless other factors intervened, which they often did.

But the family had survived so far, all five children along with both parents. Cathrina was the eldest child by five years. Next in line was Hinrich followed by himself then the two youngest siblings, Peter and Anna Christina. The Reithers, past and present, had worked the same small farm now for generations, at first in hereditary tenancy and afterwards, when large farms had been broken up and parceled out, as small landowners. The continuing relationship with their former landlord, the large land owner above them on the highest ground, had evolved over time, although they still made compensatory payments for their mortgage. If a family proved its worthiness, was dependable and stayed out of trouble, it was a common practice to go on the same way, an arrangement beneficial to both parties.

Their ancestors hadn't always been on this same plot of land. Johann's father had once mentioned to them that in the last century, sometime during the decade of the 1730s, the Reither family had moved from the small village of Helserdeich, less than two miles away, to where they lived now. He had no idea of the reasons for why they had changed farms at that time when he thought about it. It was just too long ago and the answer had been lost in the mists of time.

When the day was finished, the brothers shook out the straw and dust from their pant legs and mopped the dirt-streaked sweat from their brows with tattered handkerchiefs before shoving them back into deep pockets. They walked back towards their small home made of clayish sod walls and wood planks with a roof of thatch to top it off. It was no different from the others on the estate, no better or worse than hundreds of others throughout the area where they lived in Dithmarschen. And like the others, it was situated on a Wurt, a man-made hill built so long ago that no one knew when and by whom.

These elevated dwelling mounds, called Wurten in the plural, were the key to survival for man and beast, protecting them against the all too frequent flooding of the lowlands. As they approached their dwelling, walking up the slope of the hillock a little more slowly to home, Johann looked back over his shoulder at the grassland and the fields belonging to them and their neighbors. He thought to himself that safety from encroaching waters was, perhaps, not the only reason for living higher up than the rest of the plain-like landscape. Taking in the lay of the land as far as the eye could see gave him the feeling of having a little more control over natures whims—and for some reason a sense of importance too. On a clear day, the shapes of other village mounds, tree-lined much like their own, could be seen in the distance forming a slanted row towards the horizon, rising above the flat expanses which lay in-between each one.

During the evening meal Johann continued to let his thoughts wander to how they had come to live right here, on this land. He was old enough now to think back about the changes even he had witnessed. Already in his short life there had been food shortages and other hardships to endure. His father noticed how preoccupied his son appeared.

"Are you among the living, Johann? Why so quiet and with such a long, serious face—is there something bothering you?"

"No. Nothing at all, really. I was just thinking about how we happen to be here, on this piece of land…why our ancestors moved from the village of Helserdeich all those years ago. I mean it's just down the road and seems as good a place to live as this village. Maybe it was something like the potato blight we had when I was younger? I can still remember everyone talking about that; and that awful smell and sight of the mushy, blackened leaves. It seemed like the world was decaying before our very eyes and our hopes with it. Or then again maybe somebody or something forced us to move?"

"I don't know either what it was, but I don't think it would have been the blight. The last time the potatoes rotted was after the long rains in 1845, just a few years ago when you were six or seven, Johann. It spread to all the farms, but it wasn't the end of the world for us. No, it probably wouldn't have been a reason for leaving Helserdeich. Even when weather conditions in the following year spoiled both the grain and potatoes again we managed to survive somehow. The sun shone again and we had the best season for crops the next year. It wasn't like what we heard about across the sea in Ireland. They were relying on a single crop for food and only a single variety of potato; the failure there caused so much more starvation and grief for those people. But let's talk it over more after we finish our meal and clean-up."

He made sure to meet the eyes of all the children sitting across from him so that they understood the discussion was over for now at the dining table. Resuming it later would make for a very special evening they knew. Inwardly he was smiling at the curiosity of his children as they all rose to pitch in to make table clearing go more quickly, each one tall and slender for their age; a Reither family trait.

Later, when they all sat together near the hearth to listen, they heard more than they hoped for—more about the past than their father ever talked about before. He had been showing his age of late, his step a little slower it seemed to their young eyes. Stiffer in motion and stooped in posture, he took his time in making his way outdoors at the crack of dawn these days. For good or bad, it was as if the time to talk about the past had finally arrived, as if he wanted them to not forget where they came from—as his own father had passed on to him years before. He started by telling them more about the circular hill, a mushroom cap, on which they were now living, since it was what Johann had said he was wondering about the most. As far as he knew, some of the *Dorfwurten*, or large village hills, were made in the time before written records were kept, when prehistoric tribes roamed and competed for land. Certainly, many were already there when the Romans settled in the salt marshes along the North Sea coast. They had been quick to recognize their safety value and had proceeded to construct even more of them.

"Even before the Romans were gone, abandoning their settlements altogether, new tribes were migrating to the region, including our forefathers, the Angles," he told them. "The population grew again during the Middle Ages requiring more artificial hills to be built or raised in height. They continued to be the one tried and true protection against the threat of inundation. Year-after-year, century-after-century, using the same time-honored technique of layers of livestock dung and clay sod, sometimes with the addition of burnt wood, the elevations of pre-existing hills were increased to counteract periods of rising sea levels. Not all of the man-made hills were meant for human safety. Some of them were intended for livestock—for cows, sheep, horses, asses and pigs—when grazing on the lower grassland pastures became too dangerous."

"But why bother with building more of these hills to keep safe from flood waters? Why not just make more and stronger dikes instead?" Another son, Peter, had spoken up, interrupting his father's train of thought with his own eagerness to understand.

"Although there have been dikes for a long time, they weren't always here in such numbers, son, and as strong as you make them, powerful storms like they had in past times will surely revisit us again. We have learned from the lessons of our ancestors, often the hard way. There was too much water seepage from the inland marshes, and the practice of cutting of peat for salt production was way overdone, leaving the ground without natural drainage and susceptible to pooling. At particularly wet times the ancient canals couldn't handle the runoff and the water spilled over. This made times of flooding even worse for our farmlands. We know better now."

"Still then if…why not just move inland where the land is already higher? Mound-building wouldn't be necessary there."

"Ah, but that's a long story and I could go into the many reasons, but two of the main ones are that the marshland, close to salt water for fishing and an abundance of fresh water for growing food for ourselves and for livestock, is better than many of the inland areas. It's simply more fertile and more productive land. That's the first one. The other is the dikes themselves. Even though they don't hold up sometimes in the worst storm surges, or because they have aged without maintenance, by constructing dikes in the right places we can contain and control the richest salt marshes by pushing the sea water back a bit and thereby expanding the land on which our people can plant crops. Our numbers are growing steadily and we need more land for the villagers to cultivate and to build on as well."

"Is that like Kronprinzenkoog, then?" pitched-in Johann. It was the swath of land nearer to the sea than Marne on which he often found himself crossing to reach the sands of the seacoast.

"That's right, Johann. It was over hundred years ago when that good land was created from the seabed. And you all know by now, I'm sure, there's talk of making more polders, as our neighbors the Dutch call our Koogs, by reclaiming land which the sea has stolen from us over the years—maybe even gaining new land for cultivation which was never before dry as far as anyone knows."

"But what's the use if these new fields can all be washed away again at any time by the next devastating storm?"

"That was the way many people thought long ago, but you see Kronprinzenkoog is still there through many storms with families settled on it for ages now; and so is the more recent Friedrichskoog, carved mainly out of the island of Dieksand just two years ago and already with plowed fields and family dwellings. You see, we've learned to build better dikes now, dikes that can withstand even the biggest storm surges. With strongly built dikes protecting our koogs, there will be more of the best kind of soil for growing, and enough farms and food to feed all of the people living here."

Hinrich, Johann, Peter, Claus and Cathrina posed many more questions as the evening drew out. Ultimately, the one which needed answering the most was how their family had come to live on a hill while others did not.

"Shouldn't everyone live in the safest place?" asked Cathrina whose soft voice was barely audible. It was a question answered by explaining the need for more land on which to make homes for large families, and of the trust in the security system provided by the dikes. Many towns had experienced substantial growth, too, such as Marne had done in the last fifty years.

"More people need more land, more buildings. Not everyone can find a place to inhabit after the fashion of the past." Hinrich reminded them of their good friends who lived in Diekhusen on the other side of Marne. This village was not situated higher up on a hill like their own; instead it had been settled by the overflowing population of the ancient, nearby Wurt of Fahrstedt that wanted to maintain close proximity.

"And don't forget our cousins, the ones who live a bit further inland, to the east in Sankt Michaelisdonn—their home is on low-lying land as well."

Times had indeed changed. Dike construction had evolved since the time when it had been necessary for everyone to live on Wurten if they were to avoid having water coming through their front door, a fear that had always been in the back of minds. It was easier to sleep at night now when winds toppled grain stalks and rains made ponds in the fields.

ARCHIVES

Central Coast, California, Summer-Autumn 2007

Fifteen years had come and gone since the first time the black binder had landed in my hands. Retirement from working five days a week had liberated time to put towards new endeavors. So the binder was pulled from its resting place on a small shelf in a back room, dust blown off, and opened up once again. After so many years of solitude it needed to be studied from scratch; this time with a careful eye to the smallest of details. The names of my great-grandparents were revisited along with where they supposedly had come from within present-day Schleswig-Holstein, Germany.

Maps that had been copied from the library years earlier triggered a reminder of the importance of the Dithmarschen place name. Diekhusen, a small village near the town of Marne, had been noted as the place where my great-grandmother had lived, but only the broader regional location of Dithmarschen had been typed beside the name of my grandfather, leaving his exact place of birth unknown. To identify where he had once lived on an up-to-date map of Germany, and to learn if the place name information attributed to my grandmother was correct, would be the next nuts to

29

crack in tracing my German roots.

First efforts in starting this long-delayed quest were spent at the local Latter Day Saints family history center. A single film for Holstein was ordered containing a range of births that included years 1840 for my great-grandfather and 1850 for my great-grandmother, the two dates noted in the black binder. After waiting nearly an entire month, the film finally arrived. Containing the parish registers of baptisms, marriages and deaths for Marne, the handwriting was difficult to decipher.

Quality of the images was good, but the letters of the words in the handwritten entries were almost unrecognizable even for someone who had two years of high school German, including study of old script styles. Realizing it wouldn't be long before both my eyes and patience wore out, the proverbial towel was thrown in. Carrying on with the struggle would have been an ordeal for none but the bravest with limitless imagination and time on their hands. As it turned out no one else at the family history library was able to read old German writing in this kind of antiquated, perhaps just plain bad, penmanship either.

What other choices were there to release the ancestry information contained in the old Marne baptism registers? Perhaps someone else in our local community could be found who would have the uncanny ability to understand and take on the challenge of making sense of what was written on the film. However, before trying that angle, I started to explore the internet, eventually landing upon a seemingly very promising, no nonsense type of website offering genealogical research in situ, that is to say in Schleswig-Holstein itself. Rates were reasonable with flexible ways of making payment from overseas to a researcher actually living in close proximity to the area of focus. I immediately decided to try to make contact and gauge the response, if there was one, for its ability to tackle the task. A series of emails were launched back and forth:

My apologies for writing in English. I know a little German but not enough to write a message.

First, I am wondering if you are still doing research on German ancestors from Schleswig-Holstein. My great grandparents emigrated from the Dithmarschen region, great-grandmother from a village near Marne and great-grandfather perhaps from somewhere else in the region, but not certain about this.

I can provide their names and dates and general place of birth but that is all that I know about them. I would like to obtain their parish baptism records, the names of their parents and their baptism records, including place of birth, as well. I would also like to know when they emigrated from Germany to America, including from which port they sailed and where they arrived in the U.S.A.

Danke schön.

A reply came back the same day from Lutz Peters, a good sign a serious, business-minded person was on the other end:

Dear Sir,

Yes, I am still doing genealogical research in Schleswig-Holstein. My fee schedule and business conditions are online and can be found on my website.

If you want to get the text of the church records in GERMAN together with a translation into ENGLISH, the payment will not be charged on an hourly rate, but per record found. Please send your known information about your ancestors by email, and let me know how much research work I shall do for you (monetary limit).

Thank you.

Rates still seeming fair, and definitely preferring to have dual language versions of the same records, I immediately responded the same day. It looked like this was someone who was ready to begin as soon as we finished exchanging the necessary information:

I would like to proceed on a per record search basis. As I mentioned, I am presently most interested in church or civil records of baptism/birth for both my great-grandparents showing the church names and their locations in which they were baptized, and giving the names of their parents and any other information that may be on record. If the names of their parents are found, I would also like baptism records for them as well, if possible.

It would also be great to have their emigration request records, or at least know which port they sailed from in Germany to the U.S.A.

Great grandparents with anglicized first names:

John (probably born Johann) REITHER
Probable date of birth: 13 March 1840
Birthplace: Dithmarschen

Mary (maybe born Maria) Magdalena PEERS

Probable date of birth: 21 May 1850
Birthplace: Diekhusen by Marne, South Dithmarschen

I believe they were married after immigrating to America, but will let you know if I find out more and this is not the case. As for monetary limits, it seems like this would make a maximum of six records, if all are found, plus the payment fee. In addition to your travel fee, do you think one day is sufficient to locate the records, if they exist?

Four days went by without hearing back if Lutz had enough information to begin the research in Germany. Wanting to have an answer sooner rather than later to avoid losing momentum, I wrote a follow-up email, mentally prepared to have to begin again in looking for another in-country researcher if his answer was negative and he declined taking on the job. Two new details which had come to light during those intervening four days were included to help guide his research, should he choose to do it. I had learned through another source the birth date I had given him for my great-grandmother appeared to be off by two years—it seemed to be 1848 instead of 1850. And my great-grandfather had indeed married in America, in 1869, three years after emigration from Holstein with his surviving parent and siblings in 1866. Before he even had a chance to consider this additional data in his research, a message was received from Lutz the next day:

I did your research this week (limited to six church records). The given birthday of **Maria Madalena Peers** was incorrect by three years. She was born on 21 May 1847 and she was not married in Marne.

I have the baptismal record of your great-grandfather,

Johann Jacob Reit(h)er, born on 13 March 1840, the marriage of his parents, your great-great-grandparents, the burial of your great-great-grandmother—but did not find her husband's burial record. The "h" in parenthesis indicates this surname was found spelled sometimes with it and sometimes without it.

And going one more generation back, I also have the marriage of the Reither ancestors who were your three times great-grandparents, as well as the burial of your three times great-grandfather.

So, total, I now have six church records.

Regards,

Lutz

The initial impression I had gathered from his clearly laid out website had been validated. In acting on my previous signal to go ahead with the research, Lutz had already made the fairly short journey from his home to the city of Schleswig to visit the *Landesarchiv Schleswig-Holstein* to search for and gather together baptism, marriage, and burial records in the Archives matching the limit set forth. All except one of the records concerned my great-grandfather and his ancestors. And that single record established the true birth date of my great-grandmother once and for all. But it was paternal lineage Lutz had decided to focus on first. Although I wouldn't be able to see the specific German language register transcriptions and their English translations until advance payment was made, trust in his professionalism had been gained. When combined with my eagerness to know more as soon as possible, a decision was made to ask him to go

forward, actually backwards in time, to search for additional
Reither records in the archive's microform holdings:

> Wonderful news and great work! You're right Mary
> Magdalena was married in America in 1869.
> Is it possible to add two more records to your research if
> you can find them? It would be very interesting to know the
> date and port of departure, i.e. passenger list for my great-
> grandparents emigration from Germany to America as well
> as their date and port of arrival in the United States.
> If finding passenger list information is too difficult, I
> have also read that in order to emigrate, an application to
> leave Holstein needed to be filed with the authorities. Would
> you be able to obtain either the passenger list information or
> the applications that were filed requesting emigration?
> One additional question: is it possible to make any
> assumptions based on the surnames Reither and Peers as to
> whether the ancestors of these families originally came from
> Denmark?
> Whatever else you are able to find, just add it to the bill
> and let me know the total amount to pay.
> We are tentatively planning a trip to visit the Schleswig-
> Holstein area in the next couple of weeks via a flight to
> Hamburg and look forward to seeing where my family came
> from, especially if the rain eases up a bit!
> Thanks again for your quick work.

Up to this point, I had not made a concerted effort to
check online passenger lists, thinking it might be easier for
Lutz to do so from his in-country location not far from the
German embarkation points and access to native records. Or
he might be able to at least narrow in on when they left
through the application to leave the country process. This was

not to be the case however. His reply said he did no research of passenger manifests personally. But he did have a colleague living in Hamburg who could take on the assignment, if wanted. As for the country exit approval by the government, there was no application of emigration for my ancestors available. Applications only became mandatory under Prussian law in approximately 1868, a date which was after their probable departure from Europe.

Denmark having played a strategic role in both duchies of Holstein and Schleswig over many centuries, and with the family surname appearing in present-day phone directories in both Sweden and Denmark, I wondered if there was more than just an administrative connection to Scandinavia. Could it be that the Reither surname actually originated in the Nordic countries and then had trickled down to Holstein through regional migration? There were many instances of the family name appearing north of Hamburg, but it was not prevalent in any other area of modern Germany beyond Hamburg southwards.

But Lutz cast doubt about obtaining an easy answer to this question; he indicated only further research could show if the surnames had Danish or Scandinavian origins, however his inclination was they did not. However, there could be no denying coexistence and continuous interplay between Danes and ethnic Germans in the long-term history of Schleswig-Holstein, with Danish surnames and place names especially prevalent in Schleswig, the northernmost of the two former duchies. The Danish kings, in extending control to cover both dukedoms from 1559 until 1864, had occupied territory of the German Confederation for over three hundred years.

Extremely pleased with the first batch of records found by

Lutz, but not knowing how many more records of interest were available, another email was dashed off:

> Would you be able to continue researching past generations of the Reither family from where you left off? Another eight records would be a good stopping point for this next round. Birth/baptism dates are of particular interest.

Once again, trust in his competence was not misplaced. A rapid reply thanked me for my new order and noted he would continue the research as soon as the archives reopened in mid-August which was only a few days away. This was soon followed by two more messages; one indicating more records had indeed been located, the other describing the difficulties associated with unraveling relationships in much older and less descriptive church records as well as the approach taken to overcome them:

> I worked on the research this week and have now eight new church records at home. I am able to continue the research next week, as we still miss some of the baptismal records.
> I am back in time until a marriage in 1734, but to continue this research we have to research the baptismal records of all children of this couple. I need the names and locations of the Godparents. Do you agree to this?
>
> Lutz

Then a second message arrived:

> I was not able to continue with more research until

today.

The "early" records list only a limited amount of information. And around the 1700-1715 timeframe there were three Reither marriages in Marne. I am not able to tell you which one of these three marriages is for your ancestor. To locate the "right" one, we have to look at the baptismal records of the children of these three families. And maybe we have to look at the baptismal records of all children of the family in the last report, to locate any brothers or sisters as they may have been godparents then compare these names with the baptismal records of the three from 1700-1715 Reither families. That is the way every research has to be done if more than one family (all three husbands have the same first name) live at the same time in one church parish.

Do you understand this?

Lutz

Thrilled with receiving the results of his first two forays into my Holstein ancestors, the first limited to a set of six records as an initial test then followed by eight additional ones, Lutz was given the green light to push the research back as far as it would go. Another message was duly sent expressing that exact intention:

I would like to continue the research you've done on the families from the Marne area of Dithmarschen in Holstein. Could you now try to find church records for my Reiter/Reither relatives as far as you can into the past? I think the church records begin in around 1667?

I believe you mentioned that the archives where you do research reopened in August so I am hoping you will be able to begin the research as soon as possible.

Godparents played a particularly significant role in distinguishing families having identical surnames in the Evangelical Lutheran church registers. This was something I was unaware of until Lutz brought it to my attention. Back then, being asked to be godparent and consenting to become one appeared to be even a more serious role than it is today. The usual obligations pertained, such as acting as a sponsor at the child's baptism and assisting in the child's upbringing, especially in the event of the loss of both parents.

But during the times of these 18th century records there were additional responsibilities, including making sure the child stays true to the faith and the provision of consistent moral support. At least one of the godparents was supposed to be member of the same faith and, since it was not uncommon for both parents to die before children attained adulthood, it was customary for uncles, aunts, nieces and nephews to serve in loco parentis. And by carefully tracing the family tree connections between generations of these "periphery folks", the proper family line can be usually discerned—or not.

Lutz agreed to continue to dig further into the past, but because of intervening events on both sides of the sea, the process slowed considerably. He had again made it evident the quest for even older records was becoming more complicated, requiring perusing through more associated records, resulting in increasing costs which he tried to control as much as possible. It wasn't until the first part of October before I heard back from him after sending him a short query: "Have you had time to look for the *earlier* generations of Reither ancestors? And any luck in locating the *right* Reither marriage yet among the three possibilities?" His reply came back soon: "Yes, I have continued the research and I guess that I have the *right* marriage now. I will send the report in the next few days."

One thing led to another and my eyes did not set sight on the report until another month had elapsed. But when it did arrive, it had been worth the wait; eleven additional baptism, marriage and burial records! And with these new records, giving the names of the villages alongside the name of each sponsor, the relational geographical boundaries in Dithmarschen were fixed. Up until now it had been hard to get a sense of how far away relatives might live from one another and still be part of an interactive extended family when transportation was limited to animal and human foot power, but now a circle could be drawn enclosing all of these small places where kinship was noted. And a second benefit surfaced; misleading map distances and unforeseen natural barriers were no longer a troublesome issue to ponder over.

Another attempt was made by Lutz to take us deeper into the past that culminated in the exchange of these messages:

I am very sorry, but I was not able to complete the translation of the new report today. But I will continue the translation on Sunday evening and send the report to you on Sunday late evening or Monday evening.

There are many Reither records in Marne from approximately 1665 to 1750, but your ancestor was a native of a different neighboring church parish earlier on in time. I will be able to continue the Reither research in the records of that parish, if you are interested in a new research.

A different parish involved only heightened my curiosity:

Thank you for letting me know you will send the new

report on Sunday or Monday evening. I am really looking forward to getting it.

Yes, please continue the research of the Reither family in the records of the neighboring church parish as soon as you can. Go back to the earliest records, back as far as you can in time. Will you be able to do this research in a different parish in November?

And then one last message came from Lutz, regretfully acknowledging that he had gone as far as we could go:

I am very sorry, but research on the family Reither cannot be continued. The village Grossbüttel is located in the church parish of Wöhrden (former name: Oldenwöhrden). For this parish the church books of baptisms, marriages and burials start in 1732. No other church books are available.

You see that the Reither families have always used the first names Johann and Hinrich. But because we found no Reither godparents in the baptismal records from 1709 up to approximately 1750, we cannot link your family to the other Reither families in the church parish of Marne.

For the parish of Marne, where various Reither families lived the rest of the time, a list of thirteen Reither burial records from 1666 to 1700 is attached.

With this conclusive statement the paper trail of vital German records came to an abrupt end. To have reached back into time to the latter part of the 17th century was more than I had ever thought possible. A direct-line for Reither ancestors had been established, but questions about their lives and about my great-grandmother's family still remained a mystery.

MARIA-MAGDALENEN-KIRCHE

Marne, Dithmarschen, Duchy of Holstein, October 1855

Walking along alone on his way to Sunday service, Johann let thoughts ramble freely through his fifteen-year-old mind. Morning chores were over, but the extra time he had spent with the horses at the manor house had delayed his departure. His parents, brothers and sisters had all left before him and he had given his word he would either catch-up with them before reaching the church or join them inside at the pews on the right where they usually sat.

The distance from home to the Maria-Magdalenen Church in Marne was not much more than a mile when shortcuts were taken, so he knew full-well his youthful strides could make up for lost time if he wanted to but had chosen not to try instead. It was seldom he had the chance to just let his legs proceed ahead without having his arms, back or head burdened with tasks assigned by others. For a precious few minutes he could drift along in whatever direction he pleased and at whatever speed he chose to take, and this is what he wanted to do now.

After all, he did have a reputation among his siblings and friends as a bit of a daydreamer, able to shut out the present and seemingly float along within his own world at times. So why not live up to it? Some within his family blamed escapes from reality on the amount of time he was found with his head buried in a book. What was on those pages between two leather covers that caused him to so often curl up in a corner to read by himself, they wondered? Whenever he had a little time left over for himself in an evening, and when there was enough daylight or candlelight to see by, a volume of some sort transported him on a new adventure in which he joined the lives of the characters on the pages.

The latest work had been lent to him by Claus, the son of the large landowner next door, as had been most of the other books he had read before. It wasn't that common for simple rural farmers to be seen reading books in the first place, but Johann was fortunate in having the library in the big house at his disposal because of his close friendship with Claus. It was the same farm where he had an open invitation to visit the four-legged equine friends in the stables whenever he wanted, and often he would combine the two passions—horses and books. A book he had recently started was particularly unique because it was written by a local author whose renown had already spread well beyond local community attention.

Since its publication five years ago, *Immensee*, the length of a novella or a long short story, written by local author Theodor Storm who lived in the harbor town of Husum some forty-five miles to the north of Marne, had gripped him not only for its atmospheric accuracy in portraying daily life, but even more for the way it had captured the role fate had to play in relationships. From the very first page of *The Lake of the Bees*, or literally *Bee's Lake*, he caught a glimpse of what an undesirable self image could be like, and he promised quietly to himself to never lead the kind of life of the protagonist,

Reinhard, who had lost his sense of reality somewhere along the line. Johann liked to dream all right, but he knew when it was time to stop dreaming and deal with real relationships as they presented themselves.

In fact, relationships were exactly where Johann's freewheeling thoughts now led him as sure as his feet, step-after-step, mechanically carried him towards the church door. Sometimes he found the sermon to his taste and paid strict attention—actually remembering parts of it later when he got home. But for the past two months his attention had been diverted elsewhere, and the words of the pastor fled almost as fast as they came out of his mouth.

And this Sunday was no different as he was again eager to see the girl who had caught his fancy ever since he had met her at his uncle's house in Auenbüttel, a village a short distance to the southeast of Marne. Maria was rather compact of stature, unlike Johann's own tall and lean profile. And she was not the epitome of beauty; at first glance, most would probably consider her to be rather plain looking, if truth be told. But what had brought him around was the natural warmth of her personality he felt during the short amount of time they had spent together. Her clear blue eyes were like a magnet drawing him in and left him wanting to learn more about what was behind them. The way she carried herself, perfectly upright without any off-putting rigidity that says keep your distance, and the confidence in her step suggested a person who was sure of herself. When you added it all up, even though it was only their first meeting, she seemed to be a person of steady character with a strong dose of gumption thrown in for good measure.

Afraid that she might not see him in the same light, he had

not said another word to her since that visit. Too shy and unsure of his own worthiness, he had lacked the courage to approach her after the service was over on the past few Sundays. Nevertheless, he thought he had seen her blue eyes looking his way across the aisle on more than one occasion before quickly shifting his own eyes back again towards the altar. And the same pair of glowing blue eyes sometimes met his in the middle of the night somewhere between sleep and wakefulness.

As the image of her returned to him, his leisurely pace sped up, the distant spire drawing closer as the last parishioners entered the building. There would be a few more still to arrive, stragglers who had overslept, or some who had encountered unexpected delays, or those who just were hard-pressed at making it on time to any appointment. He quickly found his way to where the rest of his family sat, quietly waiting for the sermon to commence. Up front, near the altar, his friend Claus sat with his family in the section dedicated to families of substance. They looked for each other and when Claus saw Johann, he gave a small wave, receiving a similar reply in return. Next, his eyes searched the pews where Maria and her family always sat; they were still empty. But by the fidgety movements of parishioners who always sat on the benches surrounding these vacant seats, it seemed as if they were expecting them to come at any moment. Every minute or two he looked over again—still the seats remained untaken; then the opening words of the sermon were delivered and his stomach dropped to his knees.

Johann leaned over to his older sister and, pressing her arm, whispered: "Where are they?

"Where are you looking...who are you talking about?

45

Cathrina whispered back.

His head jerked swiftly towards the empty seats across the aisle, but before she could reply, their father's withering glare abruptly brought an end any further talk between the two of them.

On the way back home, expecting a reprimand to come at any moment, the silence was broken by Johann instead. By taking the initiative, he was hoping to head off a longer lecture.

"It was my fault, father. I promise it won't happen again...the church...I just forgot where I was for a moment. I asked Cathrina about the Peers family who never showed up. You remember I got to know them a little when I was in Auenbüttel a few weeks ago. Since they've been sitting in the same place every Sunday, I just wondered what happened to them—you know why they weren't there today."

"The two of you, I am so surprised by this kind of behavior, especially in a place of worship. You know better than that, you've been taught better than that. If it was your younger brother or sister who had behaved in such a way, that's one thing. But at your age, one grown-up and the other not far off, it's shameful that I have to worry about...to have to remind you of your manners, no matter what you were talking about."

Looking downwards, Cathrina wisely had kept her own counsel in letting Johann do the talking for her too.

"I am sorry, father," Johann continued. "This was the first time. As I said, it will be the last one too."

"I should think so." With these four words the conversation abruptly ended. Brief as they were, they were enough and had been taken to heart when spoken with the no-

nonsense look in their father's eyes.

Silence restored, all of the children, except for Hinrich, fell back to walk together, letting their parents lead the way home; Johann, duly chastised with eyes trained on the ground in front of his feet. The separation between family was sufficient for the youngest, Peter and Christina—the latter preferring to go by her middle name instead of Anna, her true first name—to begin chatting with each other.

"Do you think we should tell him, Peter?"

"I'm not sure if we should bring it up again right now. Johann looks rather glum and Cathrina may not want to hear anything more about it either."

"But I know he's still dying to know despite everything else. I think it should be okay to tell him now. I do."

"All right, but let's say it both together then. That way if he does get angry because we said something he really doesn't want to hear at the moment, we can defend each other."

The two of them moved apart from each other, placing themselves one on each side of their older brother, taking his two hands into their own. Angling their eyes upwards to catch his:

"Can we say something to you, Johann?"

"Not now, Christina. I'm not in the mood for listening to anyone." The pinched frown on his forehead emphasized his distress, but the children were not to be so easily dissuaded.

"But we know why the Peer family was not in church today. You forgot they also have children who go to our school in town."

Chiming in, Peter followed on Christina's opening: "And the teacher announced they would not be at school for a few weeks at least because the whole family has gone to help out at the house of their mother's sister in Saint Michaelisdonn."

Before Johann could object to any further explanation, Peter went on:

"Her husband has taken ill and she needs help tending to their farm before the winter sets in. She has to have someone to look after the children when she's out in the fields. He's so sick and weak he's unable to do a thing except rest in bed. It's a pity because he was almost finished with the new cabinet he was making for a neighbor. That won't happen for a while now. I wish I could be there to lend a hand with that instead of being in school. I'd much rather be doing woodwork. I know enough now that I could finish it myself with only a little guidance from his bedside."

Christina, amused by Peter's penchant for bringing up the subject of carpentry whenever he could, now took control of the story. "So if you had just asked us instead of Cathrina, we could have told you about why they weren't there. But you were nearly late getting there so there wasn't any time before the service began."

"So that's it," Johann muttered half to himself and half out loud as his eyes grew rounder with the news. Then his body straightened from a drooping posture, a slumping spirit revived as well. So that's where Maria Peers has been. But more importantly, nothing was wrong with her and she would be coming back. And when she did return from her aunt's place, he promised himself he would no longer let shyness be an obstacle in holding him back from speaking to her wherever they might next meet—except for inside the church during Sunday service!

Christina and Peter were delighted their news had such a positive effect on their brother. Their hands, which had been squeezed so hard by John that they felt partially numbed, were still painful to the touch when crushed fingers were finally unclenched. After he had released them, so cheered as he was by their story he bent down and wrapped his arms around their shoulders in a big brotherly hug. As the two youngest, it wasn't often they had chance to be recognized—to shine a little in an older sibling's eyes. They both felt they had grown a notch in stature and might very well be treated a little differently from now on. Skipping off ahead, they passed their parents to take the lead back home.

EVIDENCE OF EXODUS

Central Coast, California, Winter 2007-2008

Traditional family research had been turned slightly on its head. The common practice of working backwards step-by-step using genealogical records and oral histories from the most recent generations was reversed. The black binder had held so many details about the Reither family after they arrived in America in the 1860s, covering all the main United States descendants up until the early 1990s, there was no compunction in skipping back into time—to the generations in what is now the country of Germany. Back then, almost up until the time the family had boarded a steamship and embarked for New York, their home had been part of Denmark's external domain for more than three hundred years; in 1864, Austria, teaming with Prussia brought Danish rule to an end.

Sufficient basic data had been given to the Schleswig-Holstein researcher to be able to locate birth, marriage and death records for Reither family members for a period of about one hundred and seventy-five years—all the way back to the 1690s. But there was a gap. Lacking was proof of where they had lived, and when and from where they had left

Germany in transiting to New York and on to Iowa where the Reither family had settled. And there was the even bigger question of learning possible reasons of why they left Holstein at the very time they did. Hopefully, at least one of these questions could be answered.

The German researcher had a colleague who specialized in finding passenger list records from departure ports in Germany. But these types of records are also available for searching in several online databases and it was decided to try that direction first. The main ports of departure in their vicinity around the time the Reithers left were only two in number: Bremen/Bremerhaven and Hamburg. Since Hamburg was some seventy miles closer to Holstein, it seemed more probable they had travelled to that harbor to embark. But if they had decided to leave from the port of Bremen/Bremerhaven instead, there would be almost zero chance of finding a German ship manifest since all but a handful were intentionally destroyed at the hands of the Bremen Archives. The reason given was insufficient storage space for the records at the time. Losing records to fire or other disasters, which so often has occurred throughout history, is bad enough, but human historical shortsightedness is even worse!

Using the passenger list database of Hamburg departures required knowing more precise date information than had been previously gathered. Up until then only a very rough idea of when they had departed, the decade spanning 1860 to 1870, had been surmised. This date range was too wide to handle expeditiously, one which would involve hours of browsing through records with no guarantee of a successful outcome before patience gave out. However, 1866, the date noted in the year of immigration column of the 1900 United States federal census, would serve as a starting point, albeit without high expectations. From past experience, reported immigration dates were often inaccurate, often varying from census to census by as much as five years or more. The two-step German-side process, where an online handwritten index was searched first before accessing images of actual passenger list records, made the task even more cumbersome.

In the end, it was decided to forgo searching German records for the time being and turn to the much easier to consult passenger manifests recorded at American-side disembarkment instead. The majority of immigrants from the European continent arrived in the port of New York and, if the Reithers showed up on one of these lists, the port of departure should be given in Europe. When coupled with the departure date and name of the ship, this information would serve to hone in on the exact records in the German database, which usually provided more information on previous place of residence—one of the keys to identifying the exact family— than American counterparts did.

A group of passengers bearing the name of Reither was found arriving in New York appearing to match the names of the group of four people with the same surname from the 1870 federal census form in Iowa. However, it was necessary to overcome an initial difficulty because the beginning "R" of the Reither surname had been incorrectly transcribed in the database as a "B", resulting in a good deal of floundering about in the wrong direction. Fortunately, there was enough peripheral data about them to formulate non-surname searches to eventually land on the right family. Later it would be learned the name of the ship was also recorded in error, misconstruing the letter "a" at the end of **Germania** for the letter "c", therefore, listing Germanic as the incorrect ship's name.

As expected, there was no town or village of origin included on the New York list to provide a clue about their habitation history. The scant data only gave Germany as the country to which they had previously belonged, and farmer was denoted for each of them in the occupation column. Just to double check that the data presented had been correctly understood, family name, exact arrival date and ship name was entered into the *Castle Garden* website database covering Port of New York immigration center arrivals from 1855 to 1890. Confirmation of names, ages, occupations and gender of the passengers gave further assurance of being on the right track. It was enough to go forward to the next step.

The Hamburg ship records could now be narrowed to the single year of 1866 and searched in the German index. It was still necessary to scan through several pages of non-alphabetized surnames beginning with the first letter of the Reither surname before landing on the listing appearing to be the family of interest. The index provided the specific page number in the manifest and this was then used in the companion Hamburg database to find the actual image of the Reither family listing entry onboard. And there it was, a family of four travelling together on the ship Germania bound for New York—Johann senior and his children Johann, Peter and Anna. Proof of having found the correct Reither family was confirmed in the *Landes*, or country of origin, column, which, in the typical Germanic propensity for detail, actually contained the exact village or town of origin for each of the passengers on the page. In their case, a very slightly misspelled of version of **Darenwurth**, a small village in Dithmarschen, was written in a bold legible hand, followed by Holstein.

So departure and arrival records had now been collected for both New York and Hamburg ports, and with these documents, precisely where the Reithers had lived was finally made known. The name of the small village before they left their homeland as well as the destination in which they were heading had been added to their life history for future generations to contemplate, and maybe even to explore in-person someday. Yet the *why* as to their reason for leaving at the time they did had not been addressed and became the next challenge to be tackled knowing full well it might be at best an educated guess scenario in the end.

Given the large number of passengers also leaving their homes in Holstein that were listed on other pages of the same manifest of just one ship, there were signs of a mass exodus taking place. From Brunsbüttel, Helse, Marne, Saint Margarethen, Meldorf, Wesselburen, Gensingen, Friedrichskoog, Winsdorf, as well as a raft of other villages and towns in the district of Dithmarschen, leaving looked to have been occurring in droves. None of these places in western Holstein could be considered sizable, although some such as Meldorf and Marne, with a few thousand inhabitants each, were sometimes termed cities in writing. Altogether, the total population for the combined duchies of Schleswig and Holstein was around one million inhabitants in the 1860s.

Political life in Holstein was a bit like a yo-yo during the nineteenth century. But even much earlier, long before it was converted to duchy status in 1474 by the then King of Denmark, this small territory and its northern sister, Schleswig were not spared from experiencing unrest. Charlemagne established settlements north of the Elbe dislodging Angles and Saxons from their homes around the year 800. But after raids conducted by Danes and Slavs were countered by Frankonian influence from Bavaria between 800 to 1100, a relative peace under the House of Schauenburg had been finally achieved for the next hundred years.

Danish interests regained ground when their king was installed as Count of Holstein within the realm of the Holy Roman Empire in 1460. Battles between Denmark and the independent-minded Dithmarschen population during the 16th century, the devastation of the Thirty Years War between 1618 and 1648 and even more wars in the early 18th century using Holstein as a battleground sustained a pattern of upheaval. Germanic and Danish interests continued to vie for rule of Holstein over the succeeding years with troops from Sweden, Prussia and Russia playing important roles in wreaking military havoc on Dithmarschen lands in the early years of the 19th century.

For Dithmarschen, whose peoples and their language derived from Anglo-Saxon stock, the increases in taxation and other encumbrances imposed by outsiders as well as undesired allegiances brought about by changes in political powers had changed a long-held independent and semi-independent form of governing. In 1569 their cause was ultimately lost when a major defeat was suffered at the hands of the latest King of Denmark. And in 1580, just a few years later, Dithmarschen was divided into two halves: *Süderdithmarschen*, under Danish royalist rule; *Norderdithmarschen*, headed by a ducal group. This separation of South Dithmarschen from North Dithmarschen was to remain in effect until they were reunited as one county again late in the 20th century.

In view of its own special history—marked as it was by day-to-day self-governance for centuries, even when it was within the larger scope of Schleswig and Holstein duchies later—it was not surprising that further attacks on deep-seeded identity might finally provoke mass uprooting in Dithmarschen should the time be propitious. Such a moment presented itself when war once again broke out in 1864 over the objective of again resolving the recurring question of who would control Schleswig-Holstein. No matter what the outcome, it was certain that more changes would be thrust upon the Dithmarschen peoples as a consequence, like it or not.

In 1864 troops from Sweden, Prussia and Russia were waging war to invalidate Denmark's attempts to definitively incorporate Schleswig through constitutional revisions. Denmark's efforts to force further integration, including Danish as the official language in the duchy, were inimical to Holstein where the majority of the population was ethnic German, and the same was true for the southern part of Schleswig. Only the ethnic Danish majority living in the northern part of Schleswig was supportive of tighter linkage to the nation of Denmark itself.

The *Danevirke*, ancient fortifications believed to be first emplaced around 500 AD by the Danes then expanded and used repeatedly by the Vikings, became a battle line again for this new conflict. Man-built earthen works made of stone and boulder walls, with wood and brick added at various stages over centuries, the Danevirke was relied upon by the Danes as an a formidable barrier to enemy forces coming from the south seeking to move northwards. Akin in purpose to the earlier built and longer Hadrian's Wall, which formed the limit of the Roman settlement of England and still serves as the dividing line between the countries of England and Scotland, the Danevirke system of ramparts and trenches was about twenty miles in length. It began on the outskirts of the city of Schleswig to the east and stretched westwards to the marshland bounded by the natural borders of the Treene and Eider rivers, forming an unbroken line of protection. It could be viewed as a belt cinching the waste of the land where the distance from east to west was at its shortest.

But the combined forces of Prussia and Austria were too strong for even the Danevirke to resist in the long run. The Danish defeat resulted in the division of the territory, with Prussia assuming administration of Schleswig and Austria taking control of Holstein, including Dithmarschen. This time even the mighty Danevirke had been no match for German forces who managed to work their way around and through it. In 1866, only two short years later, a brief Austro-Prussian War lasting some seven weeks found both Holstein and Schleswig duchies dissolved and consolidated into a single entity annexed by the Kingdom of Prussia. The larger Prussian army had ousted the Austrian administration from Holstein and Prussia was elevated to the leadership role of a new North German Confederation soon afterwards.

It was exactly at this juncture, when changes and new masters were occurring with such frequency, that the Reither family may have said enough is enough. Along with many of their Dithmarscher neighbors, they had decided to say good-bye to the land they had trodden for generations, good-bye to the dikes that had been built and rebuilt with local labor to protect them from the elements, good-bye to the new communities which had sprung up over the years on land reclaimed from the sea and good-bye to their friends and remaining relatives. They had thrown caution to the waters, so to speak, in searching for a better life in America across the sea.

The means for escaping local circumstances were already well in place by then and within relatively close striking distance for a steady stream of emigration ships departing from the port of Hamburg. So in 1866 Johann Reither and his three children travelled to Hamburg and from there set sail for New York. The immigration date provided in the 1900 federal census had been exactly correct. Of particular note: two of the three children listed were male—aged twenty-five and twenty-two—both of prime conscription age for the Prussian army.

With a host of wars fought on Dithmarschen lands in the near past, there would be no reason to trust that violence and carnage of the most recent battles for supremacy by foreign interests would not continue into the foreseeable future under subjugation to new powers. While ethnic Germanic peoples in Dithmarschen were certainly grateful to shed the yoke of years of foreign Danish administration, Prussian control must have been like substituting one oppressor for another. Could the threat of sons serving in the army of a new government have been one of the factors, if not the main reason, for their decision to leave when they did?

THE OLD DIKE

Marnerdeich, Dithmarschen, Duchy of Holstein, January 1858

Icy winds rippling over the straw stubble behind lashing rains had kept them closeted away indoors most of the time for several days running. Without the heavy gusts blowing off the sea it wouldn't have seemed nearly so bitterly cold. Penetrating seams and button holes, sneaking over and around collars and under coattails, there were never enough layers of clothing to stop the bone-numbing chill for long. Still, even in these frigid conditions no snow remained on the ground, an earlier dusting having melted away after a brief spell of warmer days the week before. But the locals were used to it, as were sheep encased in thick winter coats and Holstein cows tucked away in barns where they nibbled on hay while sheltered from winter's whims.

Unlike in summer, when sky and sea seemed to meld into one continuous washed out, pale blue painting, the heavens above displayed a range of colors. Clouds turned from turquoise to angry black then into blotches of white and gray as the sun fought to gain its rightful place in the sky among the gradient of wintry hues that zoomed by. Despite the cold these changeable conditions were still preferable to days of monotonous slate gray, those gloomy skies often settling in over the land this time of the year for days on end that left their depressing mark on the temperament of those living under them.

Johann had grown antsy and was pacing about their tight living quarters. His younger, brother watched him and waited patiently. Finally, he came to a standstill.

"What do you think Peter, should we check on the livestock then risk a walk down to the dike for some air?"

Peter's eyes immediately grew wider and brighter—it was usually a surprise but always a good thing to be asked by your older brother, even if it was mostly out of desperation to find a way around another dreary day. But he had read Johann's mind and had almost expected an invitation this time; it was obvious that Johann was feeling trapped indoors too. "I can be ready in no time; just let me put my shoes on."

They threw on their long coats as they stood in front of their mother who, heavily wrapped in her own warm coat to fend off the indoor chilliness, sat mending cloths in the corner nearest to a small turf fire. Anna Cathrina had been feeling the cold in her bones more than ever this winter. The effort needed just to stay warm seemed to be wearing her down. Her husband and children worried when she often looked weary, although she never admitted it to them if they asked how she felt; she just carried on with the household duties without complaint as she had always done. But she did so now without smiling nearly as much as she used to do.

"Mama, we won't be gone more than an hour or two. We're only going as far as the pond in Marnerdeich, and may stop in to say hello to Carsten too." The embanked pond on higher ground provided good fresh water for animals on farms in the local communities on the west side of Marne, the one closest to the sea. It was located within the dike system originally built in the 16th century, during the years when many others were constructed with the assistance of Dutch expertise. Over the years that followed the dikes had been reinforced many times with added earth and higher bank walls to protect reclaimed land from returning to the sea.

"I'm not sure you should be calling on Carsten. Father and I don't want you involved in any more shenanigans like what happened last year. You know we both agree he isn't the best of influences, with his tendency for getting up to pranks and other mischief. Remember, he got into trouble on his own long before you ever got together with him. After you met and had become friends, you took your turn at it with him too."

"He's turned over a new leaf since then, Mama. Besides, all we did was to take a ride on two mules needing some exercise after being left alone in a cold muddy pasture for too long."

"Those mules happened not to be yours to ride, Johann. No permission was asked, and when farmer Bonelmann found they were gone he thought they had been stolen. He told his wife to go to all the neighbors to ask if they had seen his mules or any strangers about. But the only people in that field were you and Carsten. I'm sure he put you up to it; but it was you who chose to go along with him in this foolishness."

"But we returned them to the sunnier field next to the barn. You know how I feel about horses and mules and donkeys. We wouldn't mistreat them—just the opposite. So when they looked neglected, we just stepped in to help."

"Yes, and if you hadn't taken them back when you did, you might still be in jail now!" his mother added before he could go on. "And what if one of those mules had injured a leg after stepping in rabbit hole? You would have been in debt up to your neck—and there might have been a prison sentence to boot. And guess who else would have been held responsible?"

"You're right, mama. We've both learned our lesson, though. We've promised not to do anything like that again in the future and we'll stick to it. You'll see. So don't worry."

"All right, then. I know I must trust you. Just don't let us down again—and don't stay out in the cold too long."

After a trip to the barn to make sure the animals needed no further attention, the brothers marched out the door with hands buried deep in pockets and down the lane towards Marne passing lifeless chocolate brown dirt fields on either side. They crossed through the center of town before walking past a few more equally bleak fields on the other side and reaching the small village of Marnerdeich. Carsten's home was also his father's workplace; a blacksmith's shed attached to one end of the house was strewn with tools dented and gouged, and a large anvil took center stage. On the other end, an overhanging roof sheltered animals nosing through the dirt for a stray piece of straw to munch while forever hopeful of a few more pitchforks of hay coming their way soon.

Carsten went to the door to answer their loud rapping. An ear-to-ear grin said it all; greeting friends at his doorstep was a welcome interruption to the doldrums of winter routines for him as well. He turned to his parents sitting across the room and gestured with his arms in the direction of Johann and Peter to indicate company was there. After first hesitating for a moment to evaluate the situation, his father motioned for them to come over to him. For an instant Carsten thought they would say no because his father had simply waved an index finger back and forth while shaking his head at first. But then, in an exception to ordinary discretion when speaking of personal matters in front of others, he spoke:

"I don't have to remind you of what we recently talked about, do I? We don't want to hear of even the slightest involvement in trouble of any kind. That's meant for all three of you. I know your parents feel the same, Johann and Peter." They nodded understanding immediately.

"Be back in time to feed the animals before dark, you hear Carsten?"

"I will father." Coat and hat were nearly in place before the last words came out of his mouth. Then out the door they went in a rush.

Despite the deep brown color of the large brown chunks of plantless earth recently upturned under winter plow, and despite the equally drab leafless trees with claw-like branches scratching at the feeble northern lit sky, and despite the ice-covered puddles that crunched and cracked under the pressure of feet, the three of them were happy to be escaping seasonal blues, even if it was only for a very short time. In and around Marnerdeich were some of the oldest man-made dikes in Dithmarschen. Although a small village in its own right, Marnerdeich still fell under the jurisdiction of Marne.

There were also other dikes, constructed even more robustly in recent times, protecting smaller villages nearby and lone dwellings set out on salvaged land. Stolen from a sea much closer to Marnerdeich, new plots had pushed coastal shores further out to the west. From north to south, Kaiserin-Auguste-Victoria-Koog, Dieksander-Koog, Kronprinzen-Koog, Kaiser-Wilhelm-Koog and Neufelderkoog, all of these recovered areas had created additional crop growing space while providing an outer strip of security to a growing population.

Amiably discussing a wide range of interests as they ambled along—from farming to schooling before touching on recent history of their own homeland—Peter and Carsten arrived at a resting point in the lee of the remnant of an old wall. It was from there that they caught sight of the figure of Ursula hurriedly passing along another section of the dike in the distance. Seeing their old schoolmate caused the conversation of the older boys to suddenly swerve to local girls of interest. Young Peter had been happy to be a semi-interested listener to the voices of his brother and Carsten, content just to be allowed to be in their company, up until then. But when girls were mentioned his ears perked up. Even though their voices lowered in volume to almost a whisper, his ears were sharp enough to overhear nearly every word they spoke.

"Have you seen Trincke lately, Carsten? I heard she didn't go to stay with her aunt and uncle in Sankt Michaelisdonn after all. Is that so? That's the town where my cousins live."

"You're right. There was a change of plans because...well, she just stayed at home instead. And I was able to see her last week, though only at the market in Marne. She was with her parents so we had only a short time to be together before she had to go with them. But it was nice to see her even for a few minutes all the same. What about you, Johann—any word from Maria Peers, the young lady you've had your eye on?

"I'm not sure that I should say anything, but I have a strange story to tell you that involves her. But before I do, you must first swear you'll keep it to yourself—to tell no one else about it. And you too, Peter. I know your hearing gets even better when voices are low so I can't stop you from listening in anyway, but you know what will happen if you say anything."

"I do know. You can trust me to keep my mouth closed if you let me hear what you're talking about. You and I have other things neither one of us want anyone else to know about. And I will keep this to myself too."

Since Peter had given his word knowing full well what happens to a tattle tale, he knew it would not be taken lightly. Carsten gave his promise as well.

"Good. I'm counting on you both," and so he began his story.

"My father sent me over to our relatives who live across town in Schmedeswurth and then onto those in the closer village of Auenbüttel a few days ago to see if we could trade a bag or two of our potato seed for other varieties they had planted last season. The thinking behind it was that it would be good for all of our families to have at least two or more kinds planted should there be another blight affecting one kind more than the others."

"It's true, spring planting will be upon us sooner than we think and it's good to be prepared well advance. But that doesn't seem so unusual so far."

"Hold on, Carsten. I've only just started. What I was getting to was what happened when I was on the way home on Tancred, our pony, after it had turned dark. There was not even a sliver of moonlight to see by. Tancred and I were taking our time, going slowly, picking our way as carefully as possible to avoid potholes or branches scattered along the small backroad that rose before us. We had just come to a place where the road bends when suddenly there was a flash behind my eyes, sharp and intense, sort of like a tiny lightning burst, as I remember it. And then there was nothing but blackness, blacker even than the moonless night. The next thing I remember when I awoke was seeing my clenched fists at the end of my arms, as if they were still gripping tightly to the reins as they had been before. I was on the ground and it was cold—very cold. Except for shivering, everything was so still, so peaceful, just lying there and not moving. The dirt was like a bed. I didn't want to get up. I didn't want to move a muscle. My head was throbbing a bit, but it was so comfortable being there in the quiet darkness I didn't care.

"Long afterwards I tried to figure out what had happened. The pony must have stumbled on something and pitched me off. Or maybe he just took a false step when we reached the bend of the road where the curve is at its sharpest and had become confused about which way the road was actually going next.

"I probably could have just lain there forever, maybe even frozen to death, but what happened next, that's hard to comprehend and amazing in a way. While still on the ground, on my back and looking up, the figure of a person floated above me. Not just any person, though; it looked exactly like Maria! It reached down and placed a hand underneath my shoulder and without sound, mouthed the words "Rise up". And because of the calmness of that voice, I did. As soon as I was standing with knees shaking, I ran my hands over the blood trickling down my forehead and felt the lump underneath; then I saw the rips in my pants and through them the fresh scrapes on my skin. Looking around, I spotted Tancred then ever so slowly made my way over to him.

Somehow I pulled myself onto his back. I guess I was lucky he had not trotted far off or gone home but had remained stationary only a dozen or so feet away.

"I know it sounds silly, and it was probably just because I was dazed from the knock I took on my head, but even if it was purely imagination, it worked to get me up on my feet and going again—to get me back in the saddle on Tancred and home."

During the telling of the story Carsten's mouth and eyes grew wider and wider still while his jaw dropped lower and lower. Peter had heard part of the story once before, but he too felt stunned, almost as much in hearing it a second time as he had when Johann had told him a little only a couple of days before.

"You should be grateful you are alive and still with us, Johann. We certainly are. I'm shocked. I think there really must have been some kind of guardian angel looking over you. It's surprising I haven't heard about this from anyone else."

"That was intentional, Carsten; that's the way I wanted it. I've told no one but you and Peter so far, and only you two because I know you'll keep it to yourselves, at least for the time being. Not even my father who was worried about my condition when he saw me afterwards. I couldn't keep it to myself any longer, though. But I don't want word going around that Johann the dreamer is now seeing imaginary things, apparitions, he thinks are real. I don't want to run the risk being taken for the village idiot!"

"Don't worry about me."

"Me neither," repeated little brother, Peter, shuddering to think of the punishment he would receive if ever he was found to have called his brother by such a description.

"You know one more thing that makes this such a weird coincidence is that Maria lives in Diekhusen, which is on the way back to our home. I don't remember, but I probably was half-way thinking about her in the darkness as I neared her village. So maybe that's another reason it was her likeness there above me. Nevertheless, it was...I don't know exactly what to call it."

They had been talking all the while as they marched along the top of the banks of the dike in the opposite direction. Reaching the old school footpath below the dike leading to Marne, they scampered down then turned around and headed back the way they had come, choosing this time to go along the bottom of the bank in trying to shelter more from the wicked winds. Hunched over to fend off the powerful blasts managing to find a way around the bank wall to remind them of the raw weather, they fell silent, each one left to their own thoughts.

DANISH CENSUSES

Central Coast, California, Spring 2008

Direct-line Reither ancestors documented through baptism, marriage and death records had been unlocked by Lutz, the Schleswig archives researcher, all the way back to the late 1600s. Oddly enough, the Christian name of every direct line male ancestor was recorded as either Johann or Hinrich. Johann, John in English, was a popular name throughout Germany and Prussia in the 19th century. The name Hinrich was popular as well, but primarily among ethnic Germans living in what is now northern Germany. In Schleswig-Holstein, north Rhine, Lower Saxony and Brandenburg and in the eastern part of the Netherlands, Plattdeutsch was the language widely spoken instead of High German dominant in the rest of Germany to the south; the name Hinrich itself was Low German for the more commonly found southern equivalent of Heinrich. Plattdeutsch and its Dutch dialects stemmed from Old Saxon, the ancient and medieval language spoken by inhabitants during the very early years of North Sea coastal settlement.

Many siblings of Reither family members were also noted during Lutz's research. By no means was it an exhaustive list of relations as they were primarily from death records where children of the deceased were sometimes recorded and sometimes not. No place of residence was given for any of the siblings. The villages in which direct ancestors lived had been identified, however, and had stayed surprisingly consistent, changing only once in over one hundred and seventy years during the period from the late 17th to middle 19th century. And even for a less mobile era, the move from west to east between Helserdeich and Darenwurth in Dithmarschen was minimal. When grouped together with the slightly northerly, third village of Helse, these three villages formed a farming community triad closest to the northern side of Marne.

To fill in some of the gaps and give a more complete picture of names and residences over time, there was available another set of yet untapped archives—microfilmed Danish census records held at the Latter Day Saints comprehensive genealogy library in Salt Lake City. At the time of access, these records could still be ordered for delivery at local LDS family history centers. LDS ended its film borrowing program by mail in 2017, but the very same records have now been scanned and made digitally available online, with clearer images and an easier method of viewing and saving.

Census-taking in Schleswig-Holstein had been conducted periodically by Denmark, Danish kings holding sway over the two duchies for centuries. The enumeration entries were written in either Danish or German, or both, depending on the year and the ethnic make-up of the district being counted. Marne, primarily a non-Danish, ethnic German jurisdiction in the South Dithmarschen district of Holstein, had extant census records for the years 1835, 1840 and 1845 compiled in German. Dreading the prospect of struggling to read old

German handwriting on film, Lutz was once again contacted to ask if he had access to the censuses. He indicated that he did, at a premium price and with the proviso there would be a delay of over a month in doing the research because of the normal summer closure of the Schleswig archives.

After weighing the pros and cons of waiting and the cost, it was decided to attempt doing the research myself even though it might take up to two weeks before the LDS films arrived. So census films were ordered covering the Marne vicinity, and the difficult process of deciphering the German script initiated. It actually proved to be easier than interpreting German writing from the much more challenging parish registers. Census takers must have been selected after passing a handwriting test, assuring a higher degree of legibility to the broader populace. Once the two variations of the arcane style of denoting the name of Reither were identified and established as correct by cross-checking them against the transcribed church records provided by Lutz, the embedded penmanship peculiarities provided a model for indentifying other Reither listings.

Since extended family listings during the ten year span of the three censuses were not limited to the village of Darenwurth as they had been for direct line parish records for the same period and much longer, relatives were discovered in several villages on the other side of Marne. The data revealed there were a total of four groups having either the Reither or Reiter spelling of the surname. Three of them were in easy walking distance to Marne: the villages of Auenbüttel and Schmedeswurth to the southeast and Darenwurth to the northeast. The fourth, Norderdonn, a rural section of the town of Sankt Michaelisdonn—sometimes abbreviated as Donn—

was further to the northeast.

Sankt Michaelisdonn, the size of a real town as opposed to the other three, was the most distant from Marne. For 1835 census purposes, including one end of the town known as Süderdonn or South Donn, Sankt Michaelisdonn had been lumped together in the Marne district with much smaller villages such as Diekhusen, Helse, Helserdeich, and about a dozen others. Even though it had a far greater population than any one of them, numbering some seven hundred and fifty residents, it was, in fact, not far off from a population of the one thousand forty-two people living in Marne. By the population standards of the time, it could well have been considered the center of another district in its own right.

Since the Reither name was a rather uncommon one in Dithmarschen, it was likely many of the local families with the same surname were related in some fashion. In matching family members named in parish death records to census surveys, it was possible to determine at least two families enumerated in other villages were definitely connected. With further analysis of the church records in relation to census records, it seemed likely other similarly-named families were related as well.

Danish census records offered a critical identification advantage over population records from many other countries because the listing for the female spouse of a male-headed household was given by first name followed by her maiden surname. United States census survey entries normally list wives by married surname only. Taking maiden names together with ages, it is sometimes possible to trace parents and other relations of both wives and husbands. Pursuing tangential relations adds to the richness of local places and names and broadens family scope. On the other hand, it also intensifies an already time-consuming endeavor through sidetracking excursions into female lines at the expense of the primary search effort. It was easy to be carried away in exploring families with surnames such as Detlefs, Dressen and Rund, among others, before turning attention back to the Reithers. In the end, it was striking how many female spouses also came from the same handful of villages and towns where the greatest distance between the two largest—Marne and Sankt Michaelisdonn—was only about six miles.

Occupation was also provided for each person in the Danish censuses. The Reither families in villages encircling the town of Marne were invariably noted as farmers in each of the three surveys. Indeed, most of the adults tallied were noted as farmers, as there wasn't much other industry aside from fishing in the area during the decade preceding mid 19th century. One exception was a small brewery located in Marne itself, established in 1775. A much larger, full-fledged brewery requiring a sizable number of employees to produce Dithmarscher Pilsener beer and other beverages was later founded by the Hintz family in 1885, well after the time of these censuses. It was in the same location as its earlier counterpart and remains in operation to this day.

The discovery of a number of other siblings and relatives who were related to direct-line ancestors was accomplished through these German censuses. And using the information gleaned from them was a much quicker way of learning more about their existence than having more parish records researched in an attempt to trace family members mentioned in death records. The places where other Reithers had lived around Marne were pinpointed on a detailed local map.

Uncovering the names of the members of these families would later prove to be critical in unraveling complicated relationships post-immigration to America.

Total population for the whole of the greater Marne district numbered some six thousand in 1835. Ten years later, the 1845 census established it had grown by five hundred individuals, a sizable increase of over eight percent in a relatively short period of time. The town of Marne itself grew by nearly two hundred and forty inhabitants. The villages closest to Marne showed increases as well, possibly attributed to a combination of birth rate change and local area migration to be nearer to advantages of town living. Additional land suitable for family farming had been under pressure for a long time in the small region of Dithmarschen—the creation of land from seabed mitigating the problem for a while—but in the long run there was still insufficient land for an expanding population to survive in an economy based primarily on agriculture and fishing.

Unforeseen to them was the coming of additional conflicts impinging on their lives, and along with them, the worry of changing taxation and living conditions once again. Plague, storm surge flooding, potato blight, multiple wars and land shortage had been their crosses to bear over centuries. Changing rulers and foreign governance had displaced clan-like social structure. Long-held freedoms had long since been relinquished, creating discord in traditional social structure. The next two decades would again affect the destinies of those in the Dithmarschen community and in the rest of the duchy of Holstein as well.

FIGHT OR FLIGHT

Marne, Dithmarschen, Duchy of Holstein, February 1858-December 1859

At eighteen years of age, Johann Reither's school days were over. In past years his physical contributions to the household took place mainly during the long hours of summer months; of course he had daily chores of shorter duration throughout the year too. At critical farming times during non-summer months, he was excused—like his schoolmates had been as well—from the classroom to become an extra hand in the fields or pastures. But by now he had become a full-time, non-seasonal year-round farm laborer, holding an equal responsibility with other adults behind the plow or tending to livestock. While they had only two cows for milking as well as a handful of sheep of their own, the family also lent a hand in caring for the animals of others—especially the Friesian cattle and the heath sheep so adept at clamoring out of bogs and even the deeper dangerous swamps much loathed by all of the farmers in their neck of the woods.

It had been only a few years since the latest military conflict begun in 1848 had ended. Resulting in victory by the Danes, it had reassured continuity of Danish rule of Holstein.

It should have meant life would peacefully proceed down the same path for many years to come. But this was not to be as other rival powers not content with the outcome continued to rattle sabers. Johann had been too young at the time of this war, however, to understand its real threat to their lives and livelihoods. But nowadays he made sure to learn about their history, and of how the lessons of the recent past might bear on what might be just over the horizon.

"Why do people seem to worry about Prussia and the German Confederation still? Wasn't it all settled when Denmark defeated the militants residing in Schleswig-Holstein along with their allies, the Prussians and Germans?" Their afternoon meal was over but the sun was still out, albeit sagging near the bottom of a winter sky. They had only a few minutes more to digest and to talk a little before heading back out to their last labors before darkness and chill brought them back indoors for the evening.

It seemed like the answer to Johann's question should have been a simple one when his father started to respond. He would soon find out nothing could be further from the truth.

"It's hard for us to grasp because it's been going on for so many years, way before the most recent war ended. And it's a very complicated story. As you know, our two duchies of Holstein and Schleswig are part of the Danish kingdom. They will still be when the current king dies and the crown passes down to descendants who will follow in his footsteps as our next rulers. By virtue of the current King's parents, there are connections both to Denmark and to the German Confederation. He is the Danish Duke of Schleswig to the Danish-speaking majority living north of the Eider River as well as to the minority who speak German in the southern part of that duchy. And he is also the German Duke of Holstein, which consists of mostly ethnic Germans like us."

"So then he should be happy to have the best of both worlds—he should be able to please everybody—instead of turning Holstein into a battlefield once again."

"As I said, it's not as simple as that, Johann. There are factions in Denmark wanting to integrate our homeland and Schleswig more tightly into the Kingdom of Denmark through government revisions. Our neighbors to the east, the German Confederation and Prussia, want to keep us within their sphere of influence by maintaining our Holstein form of government which favors German-speaking landowners even though we are technically part of the Danish kingdom. And there are even Danish citizens who oppose modifying the Danish constitution which could, by attempting to definitively incorporate ethnic German dominated Holstein into Denmark, lead to greater interference by the German Confederation in the Danish dominated duchy of Schleswig in the long run. So you see things are more muddled than ever and far from being settled. Even though we are off in the far western corner of the land, these other countries, all harboring control and expansion desires, seem to be unable to leave us alone here in our Dithmarschen. They may even be afraid we'd try to restore our past history of independent governance!"

"I think I follow you, father. It seems like the Danish king has the perfect ethnic background for placating both the Danes and the Germans. But for whatever reasons, he has decided he would like to bring us more into the Danish fold, on paper at least, to unite us more thoroughly, in effect, with the rest of Denmark. But we are German-speakers first!"

"You've said it better than I could, Johann. I'm glad to

see your schooling has paid off. What's more, we have been at..."

"And the German Confederation in league with Prussia would likely to do the same," he broke in, "to bring us more within its realm by emphasizing our ethnic and language speaking differences with Denmark and our natural affinity with German culture."

"That's right. That is my opinion too."

"It also seems to me these mighty powers should look for a compromise in some way, if they can't just leave us alone— maybe by letting Schleswig form closer ties with Denmark while Holstein does the same with its German-speaking country cousins."

"Wouldn't that be just the thing to do? But it's a way too simple and sensible solution. When based on past and present personalities of rulers involved, the duchies of Schleswig and Holstein are perceived as a package, to be treated in tandem, not to be either arbitrarily or logically split from each other in terms of governance. No, Johann, I'm afraid by the various pressures exerted it isn't going to end well for us. Things really haven't gone our way for a long time.

"But never will we, or should we, forget the Black Guard, those mercenaries hired by the then Danish ruler who, more than three hundred and fifty years ago together with the Danish military, tried to take the Dithmarschen soil right from under our pitchforks. That time they failed. Just like then, the next time we will still be the ones mopping up the bloody fields and the slaughtered animals, repairing our dwellings and counting the losses of our neighbors after the feuds have come to a stop—until the next round of fighting begins. And so it goes on like that.

"But isn't it time for you to work on the new fencing in the north pasture? Those replacement rampart hedges won't plant themselves."

"I'll only take the pickaxe and spade with me. The saplings are already there. It shouldn't take too long to get them in the ground. I'll be back before dark, father."

"Will you take your brother?"

"No need, I can…"

"He can manage on his own. It's just a few plants. I should continue working on fixing the feed shed." Hinrich interjected, who had been listening while sharpening a knife blade.

No more than a fifteen minute walk across the upper pastures was necessary before he arrived at the broken hedgerow with tools balanced on his wide shoulders. And before long he was nearly finished with the digging and planting, even managing to work up a sweat in spite of the cold.

Stamping down the final shovelful of earth to fill in around the base of the last plant, he was surprised when from the other side of the hedge a few yards away a thickly built, dirt-encrusted human form emerged. In his concentration on the work at hand, he hadn't noticed much else; but now he recognized it was the rumpled figure of Höbcke Vogt. Johann had not seen him since Höbcke had suddenly left school during the previous year. Although he had heard there was a problem in Höbcke's household which caused his early leaving, he had not been sad to see his face no longer in the classroom. To the contrary—it had been a great relief. For whatever reason, he had been a nuisance at school and wherever else they happened to run into each other, even when

Johann was with friends. It seemed Höbcke had selected Johann as the object on which to take out whatever was bothering him.

Although Johann was one of the taller among his classmates and was usually left unbothered because of his size, Höbcke had challenged him to match his meddle against his own through a head-to-head physical battle of some kind or another on more than one occasion. First there would be displays of strength or speed of movement intended to impress and intimidate. And there were also the accompanying taunting words, insults slung at Johann's reluctance to stand up to him. Johann had tried to ignore most of them, but in front of the schoolhouse door, just before he had skipped out from school for good, Höbcke had intentionally bumped into him, throwing an elbow into his chest for good measure. In a menacing undertone, Höbcke told him he had better watch out; that he would see him again somewhere to settle scores once and for all. Fed up with Höbcke's actions by now, Johann had shoved him back, catching him off guard and sending Höbcke sprawling down the school steps. He then walked nonchalantly back into the classroom as if nothing had happened.

Now Höbcke stood before him on the border of a field well out of eyesight and earshot of anyone else. "I've been waiting for this for a long time. Now you can't avoid me any longer. The time has now come to teach you the kind of lesson you can't learn at school. Put down that spade, you bookworm."

The suddenness of it all—the odd time and unexpected setting—in meeting up once again with someone who he had wished to forget all about left him a bit stunned. His first thought was to pick up his other tool, turn around and walk away towards home. But before he could act, Höbcke's challenge came again:

"Well, what about it, bookworm?" spat out the aggressive intruder with a scornful voice and curled upper lip. "Are you thinking that spade's going to help you? Are you afraid to throw it down and take your beating like a man? Or are you just going to run away like a scared rabbit?"

Strangely, he was almost glad for these words. He now realized Höbcke was not to be deterred; he would surely pursue him and persecute him whenever he could until he forced a showdown. So today, right now, was as good a time as any to get it over with. Johann dropped the spade, moved over to meet him face-to-face only a couple of yards apart, planted his feet and met the shorter, stockier lad's stony glare with his own.

Höbcke rushed towards him like an angry bull in the field. But Johann sidestepped him with the skill of a Spanish matador, using Höbcke's own forward motion to push him down to the ground. He rose back up quickly and launched a fist towards Johann's head which was deflected to the side with a forearm. Next, they found themselves tumbling to the ground again, intertwined in a wrestling match in the dirt and grass. First one was on top and seemed to have the upper hand then the other shook him off and it was his turn to be in control. There was no telling how much time went by, but finally the scuffling ended in two exhausted, scratched and bruised fighters hardly able to raise an arm to continue. There was no clear winner, but the look Höbcke gave Johann as he got up and straightened his shirt was no longer the usual one of scorn and superiority; there seemed to be more than a touch of respect in it now.

No further words were exchanged; but hands were proffered and taken for a long shake. And with that, just as suddenly as he had appeared, Höbcke walked back to the other side of the hedge and down through the field. Johann picked up his tools and went the opposite direction towards home, stopping only once to brush the dirt from clothes and face the best he could before he got there. He hoped his parents would be too busy with something else to notice his disheveled appearance. What had happened was personal, between the two of them only, and he was not of a mind to give an explanation to anyone else.

He needn't have worried, for their attention was indeed invested elsewhere. News had quickly spread throughout the community: the German Confederation had declined to admit the validity of the revised Danish constitution, leaving matters even more unsettled as to their future. His parents wore the preoccupied and glassy looks the announcement had brought. The grass stains, dust, scrapes and scratches on his person were all but invisible to them.

***

It was not long afterwards, in early autumn of 1858, that Johann's mother, Anna, first registered a change in the energy she normally devoted to daily tasks; up until recently, tiredness was little more than a foreign concept attributed to others, but lately she had begun to understand what they felt as lack of stamina was becoming usual to her as well. Still, it did not seem important enough to think anything could be really wrong. It would surely pass, just like a seasonal cold or a temporary bout of fatigue following a long winter. By the end of autumn she had realized cooking and other chores routinely performed for the household were becoming drudgery and causing her to fret. Excuses she had made for herself had ceased. Listlessness could no longer be ignored. She had always taken great pride in her role in keeping a healthy and happy family unit together in view of the travails of a sustenance farm household. But now when she tried to maintain a positive disposition in front of her children, she knew it was only a mask—she was pretending.

There was a future to look forward to but it was hard to focus on it. Her oldest child, Cathrina, was soon to be married to someone who was well-liked in the community. She hoped her daughter's wedding to be only the first with all of her other children to follow in time. However, as each day passed she was aware of growing weariness, sometimes now with irritability when even minor things didn't go exactly as planned. And with each succeeding month her temperament seemed to become steadily worse before the questioning and worried eyes of family members.

It should have been diagnosed sooner as a persistent malaise of some sort; but like for many others, there was a natural tendency towards denial. Finally, she was no longer able to ignore it for what it was: an illness that she could not shake. The urge to sit down to rest many times during the day or simply to lean on something solid when standing for a few moments to catch her breath had become normal. Instead of devoting hours after the evening meal to mending clothing or in sharing a few quiet moments with sons and daughter before bedtime, she chose to retire at an earlier hour to recoup sufficient force to be able to get up again the next morning.

Doctor Telsche from Marne was called in several times during the autumn and winter months but was unable to diagnose a precise condition. His best treatment advice to both her and for her family was to allow more rest whenever she felt it was needed. With more rest and time, her body may be able to fight off the mysterious ailment from which she was suffering. Whatever it was, it had been progressing slowly but always moving in the same direction—towards the worse.

Then a year passed since Anna had experienced the first symptoms, and 1859 became even less kind to her. She rarely got up from her bed now. Weakness had spread to her limbs and throughout other parts of her body, at times her neck barely able to sustain the weight of her head to keep it from drooping. Appetite lost, her shrunken body appeared to be nearly half of its former size. It was out of the question to try to make the trip to church on Sunday. However, that did not stop her from privately giving thanks to the almighty for the life and family she had been blessed with when nightly prayers were said. It was as if she knew her time was short and about to come anytime. And after the doctor had finished the latest examination of his patient, he stepped outdoors with her husband—out of hearing of the still keen ears of Anna— lowered his eyes towards the ground and shook his head, confirming Anna's own belief.

A hint of her once tenacious spirit could still be detected now and then when she managed a grateful look and smiling eyes again for a brief moment. In the midst of what should have been the most festive time of year, only five days before Christmas day, Anna quietly left behind the cares of the world with her husband's hand tightly clutching her own. The Evangelical Lutheran faith which had supported her through trials and tribulations, as it had done for generations before, shown in a face at peace; it was the same faith the others now turned to in their grief. Even the prayers of the pastor during his earlier visit to their home a few days before, dabbing oil with his thumb upon her forehead, hands and feet, anointing a person whose specific bodily ailment is undetermined, had not been able to stay her death for long.

Within arm's reach, the family bible still lay open on the table at her bedside.

FAMILY AFFAIRS

Central Coast, California, Autumn 2008

The discovery of the Reither family passenger lists from both New York and Hamburg ports provided significant answers but opened up new questions as well, including the most pressing one: Who were the actual members of the Reither nuclear family? While the two manifests matched each other as far as number and names of family members, they didn't perfectly match vital records found in researching the Schleswig archives. Listed were great-great-grandfather, Johann senior and three of his children, Anna, Peter and Johann, the latter my great-grandfather.

From the burial record for Anna Cathrina Reither, the spouse of Johann senior, it was clear he had lost his wife in 1859, seven years before the family's immigrant ship had sailed for America. The passenger lists ascribed no wife or other senior female person associated with the family, which made sense and seemed to confirm there had been no second marriage, at least during the period between 1859 to1866. But Anna's burial register had noted four children. What had happened to the fourth child named Cathrina? Furthermore, in line with the burial register, the 1845 Holstein census showed not only Cathrina but also a fifth child named Hinrich!

There seemed to be no record of their departure from Germany or arrival in America either before or after the rest of the family had moved on. And no answer has been discovered to date as to the exact disposition of these two children, but the most likely scenario was that both Cathrina and Hinrich had stayed behind in Dithmarschen. Cathrina, the first born, would have attained the age of thirty-one by the time the others had left for America. Hinrich, the second oldest among the five children, would have been about twenty-nine. Both of them would have been beyond the average marital age for that period. It could also have been equally the case that one or both of them had passed away before the departure year.

Likewise, there was no sign of their residence in any part of Iowa, the state where the other Reither relatives had chosen to settle according to federal censuses for 1880 and 1900. Cemetery and tombstone records confirmed great-great-grandfather, Johann senior, passed away in 1872 in Iowa. The last Iowa census recording for him in 1870 discloses no additional wife present, lending credence to the likelihood that he died a widower, aged sixty-two, having never remarried after arriving in America.

Of the three children who came with him, two of them married and had children, spawning a wealth of descendants. The third child, called Peter, appears never to have married. Johann senior had carried his original name to his grave in Iowa having only had the chance to enjoy his new home for six years; there would be no Americanization of his given name to John. His son, my great-grandfather, on the other hand, had transformed into John from Johann Reither by the time of the 1880 United States census. The Christian name of

John for future Reither ancestors continued to be a popular one in following generations for children born in America just as it had been in the old country both through tradition and by happenstance.

Iowa must have been earmarked well in advance of departure as the place to where Johann senior and his children would be heading straightaway. Statehood had been achieved in December 1846, some twenty years before they would appear on the scene. Their arrival was only four years after the passage of the Homestead Act in 1862, which was a huge draw for many to come to America in seeking free land if certain conditions were met. It might well have been that new immigrants who had submitted formal intention papers for becoming citizens may have heard of the lack of availability of homestead land in Iowa. Many parts of the state had already been snatched up by land speculators and others during the land rush interval of 1853 to 1858; in fact, the majority of public lands had already passed from public to private hands by the end of that period. Some of these acquisitions were thought to have been on the shady side, with hints of land-grabbing, and many were to pay a price in the global financial Panic of 1857 and the turmoil during and after the Civil War.

From the document trail he left, Johann does not appear to have become a homesteader. However he and his family may have benefitted from someone else having fulfilled the five years of living on and improving the land requirement before a legally filed homestead claim for a maximum of one hundred and sixty acres was finalized and the plot was theirs to keep for good. Or it could have been a land purchaser—often an absentee landlord who obtained land prior to the enactment of Homestead—from whom the younger Johann rented a farm of about two hundred acres, working it as a tenant for a share of agricultural production. Both the 1870 and 1880 *Selected Federal Census Non-Population Schedule*s quantified in detail crops and livestock produced, including their value, for the large farm that the two Johann Reither generations occupied. It was reasonable that land exceeding one hundred and sixty acres in size could have been formed from both a homestead claim and a supplemental land purchase before they became occupants.

A more probable scenario is one that finds Johann as a tenant farmer of one of the large owners intending to turn uncleared land tracts into actual farms. James Thompson, the president of the National Bank in Davenport was one of these Iowan land holders who had split a large tract into forty-four farms, building homes on many of them for farmers who rented from him for a production output share. Johann's family farm in a town nearby may well have been on one of Thompson's rental tracts. Later, great-grandfather Johann, now going by John, would be the first of the Reithers to relocate to the other side of Iowa, to the northwestern corner of the state, not far from where the state lines of Iowa, Nebraska, Minnesota and South Dakota converge.

Johann senior and his children would not be the first of the Reithers from Dithmarschen to choose the state of Iowa in which to settle, however. His older brother, Hinrich, at the age of fifty-three, along with two of his three children by his deceased first wife, Wiebke, and three more by Mathilde, his second wife, had emigrated from Holstein in 1857, almost ten years before great-great-grandfather Johann's family voyaged from Hamburg. Hinrich and Mathilde also farmed land near the town Davenport, about thirteen miles from where Johann senior and his children were to set up household in the same vicinity soon after arriving in America.

Vital archives records about the Reither family had identified Hinrich and Johann as brothers. But because Hinrich was not part of Johann's household, nor was he listed even in the same village at the time of the three German censuses, it was a mystery for a while as to where he actually had lived in Dithmarschen. Connecting Hinrich to Johann in Iowa first became the key to unlocking his exact whereabouts in old country records later. Once details were studied in United States censuses, including names and ages of his wife and children born in Germany, the German censuses were searched again and measured against the same information for any Reither families in the surrounding local villages within proximity to his brother's Dithmarschen residence. Before long, an entry was found listing a Hinrich which included the correct names and data for the rest of the family members living in the same household. Beyond any doubt, it was confirmed Hinrich was from Sankt Michaelisdonn.

But the mystery didn't completely end there. In a strange turn of events it was learned in putting together the bits and pieces about Hinrich that one of his sons, Peter Reither, who had also lived in Sankt Michaelisdonn, had married a woman in Iowa with the same surname as his own. Her name was Anna Reither who had also been born in the future nation of Germany. Next to her first name the middle initial of "C." had been appended; and the same record noted 1848 as her year of birth. In the 1880 federal census, the more precise birth place of Holstein was reported for her. For each of the other U.S. censuses in which she appeared over the decades, she was forenamed Christina rather than Anna, the wife of Peter

Reither. Combining the two names of Anna and Christina into a single person immediately set off an "aha" moment. I knew I had come across this exact name somewhere before! But where?

It was recalled that the 1870 U.S. census listed a child by the name of Christine as one of the three children of great-great-grandfather, Johann. It was Christine not Christina, though, with an "e" at the end instead of an "a", but it was close enough since either version was more distinctive than many other first names typically were. And the same census had also omitted the "h", noting the family name as Reiter instead of Reither found in more accurate successive surveys. It was also recalled this name was somewhat of an anomaly; for both Hamburg and American passenger lists from 1866, their arrival year in America, noted an Anna, daughter of Johann Reither, as having the exact same age as the Christine in the United States census. It now seemed almost certain these first names had been used interchangeably and referred to one and the same person: **Anna Christina Reither**.

The German records from the three censuses conducted over a ten year span from 1835 to 1845 would not be of any use in providing confirmation since she had been born three years afterwards. So the next and hopefully final step to be absolutely sure they were the same person would be to go over again the birth, marriage, death records found in the archives. Returning to the first batch of six records containing the most recent German ancestors in Holstein, the burial record of Anna Cathrina Reither listing her four children was reviewed once again; Anna Christina was one of them, the very same person as noted in the Iowan censuses!

With this discovery the family tree chart now became a bit

more unwieldy by virtue of the son of a two times great-uncle marrying the daughter of his brother, my two times great-grandfather. The marriage of first cousins was not illegal in any state before the American Civil War, however in the post-war years most states did ban it for various reasons. But during the time of Anna Christina's marriage to Peter it seems to have been a fairly common practice not only in Iowa but in other parts of the world as well. Iowa is now among the group of states that do not currently allow legal first cousin marriage.

Through their marriage, the fact that Hinrich was the brother of Johann had been unveiled by working backwards in time. So there was now positively a second line of close Reither relatives whose immigration to Iowa in1857 preceded direct line ancestors by nine years. But only two of Hinrich's three children by his first wife had been on the passenger lists in 1857. The third child, whose name and age was known from the German censuses and who was twelve years older than the next oldest child, was missing. Had he, yet another ancestor named Hinrich, stayed behind in Holstein? Perhaps he had already married and started a family there? Another story was about to be told.

EMPTY YEARS

Marne, Dithmarschen, Duchy of Holstein, January-April 1861

Their mother's death in 1859 was a crushing blow to them all, especially to her widowed husband. Johann's father, sisters and brothers all displayed their grief differently; one through spending long hours alone tending to farm work; another sitting next to her father for hours on end waiting for him to say something—anything; a third alone in complete silence.

Even as they had witnessed her decline over the past year, the weight of her presence had remained ever alive within their household. And even when she could no longer perform the tasks she had done before—when her usual endurance from dawn to dusk had all but vanished—the few words she spoke to maintain order in the home had been received with a no-questions-asked obedience. All of her children had accepted what needed to be done no matter how much it added to the burden of their workload. Although they all saw her physical powers fading before their eyes, her formidable influence in controlling the family's well-being had left an impression, albeit a false one, that things could return to normal again. It had given them hope, a reprieve from thinking the unthinkable.

On the evening after the light had finally gone from her eyes forever, Johann had sought solace from his favorite author. He had remembered a verse and wanted to reread it again now. It was called *Schliesse mir die Augen beide*, or *Close Both My Eyes*, by Theodor Storm:

> Schliesse mir die Augen beide
> mit den lieben Händen zu!
> Geht doch alles, was ich leide,
> unter deiner Hand zur Ruh.
>
> Und wie leise sich der Schmerz
> Well' um Welle schlafen leget,
> wie der letzte Schlag sich reget
> füllest du mein ganzes Herz.

* * *

> Close both my eyes
> with your beloved hands!
> Let all my suffering
> gain rest beneath your hand.
>
> And as gently the pain
> wave upon wave lies in sleep,
> As the last blow falls
> you fill my whole heart.

Dismal January gray skies opened the door to the New Year of 1861. Then the gray turned even darker still, and a wall of sleet pelted down on the land for hours on end. When it finally stopped, the temperatures tumbled even further downwards as did spirits already thought to be at their lowest point. For weeks on end there had been little talk between them about what had happened, about the question begging to be answered on all their forlorn faces: What were they to do now to restore a broken family which was badly functioning and in a state of disequilibrium? Over a year had passed since her December death and it was still as if the thought of planning how a family could proceed without her should be avoided, as if time had stopped at that moment. In mourning, their father was in a state of paralyzed inaction, an overwhelming lethargy had possessed him. The absence of his normal role as head of household and in setting an example for them to follow made the grief felt by his children all the more difficult to overcome.

Cathrina, the oldest daughter, had indeed married in December of 1858 as planned. At the age of twenty-four she had joined her husband on a small holding in a nearby village and was now only a couple of months away from the birth of her first child. She had told them she would come back to help until the family regained stability but only until her child was born. Hinrich, as the oldest, had readily accepted her offer in place of his father's mental abdication. Recently turned thirteen, Anna Christina, the youngest of the four children, had already assumed most of the cooking and housekeeping duties after their mother had become often bedridden, the watchful eye of her mother barely able to guide her daughter's efforts when she returned from school. Of her three brothers, two had already finished with their education and the third, Peter, nearly sixteen now, was nearing the end of his formal schooling as well.

On a late April evening with all of the family sitting down, Hinrich marshaled his courage to speak of the future. He had become the de facto head of the family and asserting himself at this time he thought to be necessary. Turning towards his father first, he plunged forward:

"It's time to think about how we'll manage from now on. We're all here together at one time for once so whatever we decide to do it will be a family decision. Cathrina will be leaving us soon to go back to her husband and get ready for a new family. But we've just started a fresh decade, yet things haven't changed for the better even one iota for us. We seem to be in a state of confusion. So I think we should talk about what we can do now while we have a chance—before things get even worse, or just stay the same."

His father raised his head up and straightened his back and shoulders from what had become a habitual slouch then slowly nodded his assent. But still he did not speak. So Johann filled in the gap.

"Hinrich's right, you know. Of course we'll never forget our mother, but we must start doing what's best for the rest of us before it's too late. Not only are we being bounced around between the whims of countries wanting to be our masters, but our very livelihoods are undergoing changes as well. We all know how the population has grown while the land hasn't, at least not by nearly enough. Good neighbors whose families have been in Dithmarschen forever have left their farms to go to the cities, or even further away, for both these reasons. When they leave, their farms are often joined together with a larger land owner's holdings. There's no place left for new tenants because farm machines are replacing what strong arms and backs used to do."

Peter and Anna Christina were all ears, wrestling to control their excitement before hearing what their brothers had to say before making-up their own minds afterwards. Cathrina kept quiet too but for her own reasons. She grew anxious when anyone spoke of leaving their home. Would her family be the ones going somewhere else next? She knew one thing for sure it would not be her husband or herself or the soon to be born infant that would be going anywhere. She was set on staying where she was no matter what, to continue to be part of the land her mother had cherished and where her grave would be forever. Others could give up everything—pack up a bundle or two and never look back—but she had no intention of moving to a city, or across the waters for that matter, to pursue enticing opportunities. She believed in her heart it would work out for them right here at home. They just had to be patient and keep fighting to improve upon what they already had, and learn to work around new impediments.

Hinrich knew and respected his sister's feelings although he would not allow himself to be deflected from what was best for the rest of them.

"You know it's been nearly nine years since father's brother, Uncle Hinrich from Sankt Michaelisdonn, went off to America. He was the first of the Reithers to leave with his two sons by his deceased first wife. His second wife, Aunt Mathilde, and their children were with him too, and they all sailed off on the bark Nordamerica from Hamburg to New York before travelling on to Iowa."

"But why did they pick Iowa as their final destination?" Anna Christina wondered. "Why not other places we've heard of, like Milwaukee or Saint Louis or Chicago, or even staying in New York?"

"You've heard of Iowa too, I'm sure, and its neighboring state of Illinois as well. These were the places chosen by many who decided to emigrate from Dithmarschen. They're two of the places having an abundance of open farmland to till, and where the lie of the land is supposed to be much like our own: flat. As for the climate there, well I think we'll have to get used to it. It's said to have hotter summers and much colder and snowy winters than here. But the soil is said to be quite rich so crops should do well. And if that's true, we can do well there too!"

"Is that what Uncle Hinrich does in Iowa?" continued Anna Christina, always the more outspoken between Peter and herself.

"Yes, they're farming," chimed in Johann, "but you know there's other jobs needed there as well. You know the Schlueters—the family that was always good with their hands before they left here—they've become barrel-makers in Iowa. Apparently, there's a big need for coopers to make enough containers to hold all the grain grown by farmers, especially because a large proportion is transported to other places. So you see there's room for skilled craftsman as well as farmers."

By now Cathrina had found her voice. "I know where this is heading—you and Hinrich have a plan in mind. I can already see myself soon waving good-bye to the rest of our family. I hope it's not so," her voice quavering a bit, "but if you're going...if it's what you really want to do..." Welling tears about to spill over became hard to restrain.

Hinrich gave a long, steady look towards his sister before answering: "Johann and I have been talking it over together for some time now. We're young and strong, and an opportunity ripe for the taking seems to be right in front our eyes. If it were just the two of us, we would set off right away—tomorrow would not be soon enough—but we're not. We're a family that sticks together. But we know what your situation is and how you feel about staying, Cathrina. We will always be family no matter where we are."

"I thought as much. I knew you'd be leaving here."

"Don't let yourself fret about it, Cathrina, at least not for the moment anyway. From what we hear, now is not quite the right time for us to go to America for several reasons. First of all, there's fighting going on there. A war has broken out between the northern and southern states.

"When our friends the Schlueters went to America, rather than going to New York like Uncle Hinrich did, they went first to the port of New Orleans in Louisiana then carried on from there to Iowa. Even if we wanted to follow the same route, which might be a little easier, it wouldn't be possible with the South fighting to separate from the North. No, the timing for starting over in America is not right now, not in the midst of another war with such upheaval going on. Why should we replace what we have suffered for so long here with the same thing there? That's all we need! No, we must wait until the war is over there and things get back to normal again.

"Secondly, we've also heard the talk of the starting of a program of land grants to farmers intending to settle in certain parts of America. This rumor has been going on for a long time but may actually come into practice soon. Also, there's yourself, Cathrina, we ..."

"We want to be here when your first child is born, Cathrina—to make sure everything is settled for you and Drees and your farm before we leave," added Johann, breaking in to finish his brother's thought.

And now tears welled again in the corner of Cathrina's eyes. But before they had grown large enough to fall, Anna Christina, the pragmatic one, added a few words:

"But what if there is no free or inexpensive land, how could we afford to buy anything? How are we even going to pay for the passage to get to America? And what would we do with all of our animals, equipment and other things we have here? What could we take with us, Hinrich?

"Stop right there, Christina; it's much too soon to start worrying about things like that now. Besides, there are always others here who would be happy to buy from us whatever we have to sell. Whatever happens in America, we have one thing that no one can take away from us— we know how to farm. We understand the way to work the land so it will produce enough to sustain us, and we know how to pull together to survive. You have to have faith in our family and in the almighty above that it will all work out when the time comes."

Up until then their father had remained silent as usual, showing little interest in the discussion. But now he spoke in response to the mention of religion. He had sought comfort in that direction often during the past year.

"Yes, we must have faith in the lord above," he emphasized with a vocal strength not heard for over a year, "and in the fortitude to persist our ancestors have passed down to us for generations. This is in our blood. I think it is time to shed the troubles here, time to take our chances somewhere else, time to reach out towards a new future. I do. America just might be somewhere where we will be able to regain the independence taken from us, the sense of freedom our countrymen once had by working hard and by working together as family and as a community."

Once engaged in the conversation, his urge to continue talking became unstoppable, like a runaway horse, animated at times, serious when needed—all to the astonishment of his children who had come to take his lack of interest in almost anything for granted. Many voices had circled around him for months without a peep uttered from his mouth, as if his ears had registered nothing in his brain as to what was being said. But now he seemed to want his voice to be heard loud and clear.

"You remember the words your mother spoke several times during her last days," he continued, "that we must die in the faith of our lord Jesus Christ and God grant that we may all meet again in heaven. I think whatever we do, wherever we go, whenever we leave, our family will stand by and look after each other. I agree with Hinrich. We should wait a little—but hopefully not too long—to see if the fighting comes to an end in America, and to see if land becomes available. And we need to be here to see Cathrina through birth of her first child. It shouldn't be that long, though, before we can follow brother Hinrich's journey to Iowa, if that's what we still want to do when it's time."

"Thank you, father." Hinrich turned to look at Johann then at each of the others, tight-lipped and with an otherwise expressionless face. Only those closest to him could see the sense of relief his father's words had given to him.

Feeling tired their father went to bed at an earlier time than usual. Afterwards, the young people exchanged a few more words before retiring themselves. It had a been an important evening for them; a milestone had been passed and they could now feel that all of them were ready to look to the future together whatever it might hold in store.

HINRICH AND JOHANN

Central Coast, California, Winter 2007

Hinrich Reither, oldest of three children of the brother of great-great-grandfather Johann, was an unaccounted for man of mystery. Along with his brothers, also bearing the now familiar forenames of Johann and Peter, he was a child of his father's, also named Hinrich, first marriage. A second wife produced three more children, almost the entire family arriving together on the same ship from Hamburg to New York in 1857. More children born in America would follow.

But the younger of the two Hinrichs, twelve years older than his closest sibling, was not among the names on the manifest. A difference of twelve years was a long span of time between children, particularly during an era when families were often quite large with children rapidly arriving one after another, sometimes on an annual basis. Perhaps there had been other failed births in-between? Whatever the circumstances, Hinrich would have achieved adulthood long before the rest of the family moved across the sea, which might serve to explain why he had not been travelling with them. It was already fixed from U.S. Federal and Iowa State Censuses that the family unit, save for Hinrich, had settled in the fast-growing city of

Davenport, Iowa.

However, further research uncovered another Henry Reiter—Johann had now changed to John, while Peter continued as Peter and Hinrich usually morphed into Henry among new immigrants—of young Hinrich's correct age living in Davenport in the censuses of 1860, 1870 and 1880. If this was truly the person of interest, he probably had managed to find his way to Iowa around the same time as the rest of his family but must have come separately by himself or possibly with another group of ancestors.

His census trail ends in 1880, and his demise is confirmed by the 1900 census, which notes his wife as a widow. But did this Henry Reiter really belong to the family of my great-great-uncle, aunt and cousins in Davenport? Passenger lists briefly searched for New York arrivals in the neighboring years did not find him listed. His census name was spelled Reiter, omitting the "h", unlike those relatives who came in 1857 and direct-line ancestors arriving the next decade who had held fast to the "h" after leaving Holstein. As for occupation, he was listed as a cooper, not as a farmer like most of my German ancestors had been both in Holstein and America.

Cooperage, as it turns out, was not as an uncommon type of employment as it might seem in mid-1850s river cities like Davenport. Goods such as pork—together with cornbread a staple diet of southern slaves—grain and milled flour were packed, stored and then shipped in barrels by steamboats going both downstream and upstream on the Mississippi. While Saint Louis was the largest market for products from Iowa before the coming of the railroad, shipments were also sent down river all the way to the port of New Orleans where they were then transferred aboard ocean crossing craft to supply other parts of the world. Timber harvested in forests to the north up river was floated on flatboats providing Davenport and other towns swelling with new immigrants with essential building materials.

Even before Iowa achieved statehood—carved from a huge swath of land in the heartland of the country that had once been part of the 1803 Louisiana Purchase from France and becoming the twenty-ninth state in December 1846—Davenport had already been a prominent settlement on the banks of the Mississippi. Situated on a wide bend in the river, it was one of the pre-chosen destinations for immigrants from Holstein and Schleswig as well as from other areas of what would later become Germany. It must have sounded quite tempting for those wishing to quickly establish themselves in taking up from where they left off.

Nevertheless, there was as yet no guarantee with any degree of certainty that this h-less Reiter cooper was the missing child of Hinrich senior. Additional evidence needed to be secured to make such a case. So another review of passenger lists was made, this time with a more open-ended approach to when he might have departed from Europe and to where he might have arrived. Once again, the online *Hamburg Passenger Lists, 1850-1934*, known as the *Hamburger Passagierlisten, 1850-1934* at research facilities in Germany, was searched. Only one passenger met the birth date range and broader time frame criteria for Hinrich/Henry Reiter/Reither. And it came as a surprise to see this person was noted as heading to the port of New Orleans!

At this point, I had never heard of another relative mentioned in the state of Louisiana. An abbreviated form of this passenger's first name, "Hinr.", supported someone originating in Holstein in contrast to Heinrich, the spelling used most frequently outside the Low German speaking regions of Germany. The fact that the last name was the more familiar Reither version rather than Reiter was viewed as a recorder's discretion—sometimes they wrote it down one way sometimes another way. Age was correct, which was in his favor for this person being a match. But what was much more significant was his specific place of origin in Holstein. In a fair hand was written *St. Mich. Donn, Holstein*, an abbreviation of Sankt Michaelisdonn, the very same place from where the family of the brother of my two times great-grandfather had lived before immigrating to Iowa in 1857. What was somewhat startling, though, was the year of departure; it was 1852, a full five years before the other Reithers had left!

There seemed to be almost enough evidence now to make him out as the missing Hinrich—but not quite. The Hamburg passenger list should be complemented by one on the American side, a New Orleans arrival list, similar to manifests consulted for New York or Boston; and sure enough there was one entitled *New Orleans Passenger Lists, 1813-1963*. Not much was expected to be different from the Hamburg lists, although an appearance on a New Orleans list would mean he had safely arrived and could also confirm name spelling and if ages matched. How wrong this expectation turned out to be. Instead of place of origin as noted on Hamburg manifests, in the destination column labeled "The country in which they intend to become inhabitants", Davenport was written!

There was much less doubt now that all of the family members had been accounted for, and the case of the missing child was closed. Or had it been? If Henry Reiter had indeed preceded the arrival of the rest of his family by five years he could be considered a forerunner, an advance guard in as much, of the family's displacement to a new land, and in doing so, laying the ground for the rest to join him. The choice of sailing to New Orleans instead of New York or Boston should not have been much of a surprise because by 1852 there was no railroad yet serving Davenport; it would not be until January 1856 that the first major railroad link running between Davenport and Iowa City was completed. A railway bridge over the Mississippi was built not long afterwards to connect the Iowa railway to the major Illinois line arriving on the other side.

Appropriately named the Chicago and Rock Island Railroad and finished only two years earlier in 1854, it started in Chicago and ended in the town of Rock Island from which Davenport could be seen just across the river. This long stretch of railroad, later shortened in name to the Rock Island Line, had become the main means of east-west transportation for both cargo and people and, when linked to the railroad across the water, opened up easier access to the fertile fields of Iowa. Before the advent of trains, new immigrants arriving by ship on the East Coast travelled overland by horse and wagon or coach in stages while those arriving in New Orleans boated up the long Mississippi waterway for about two weeks to finally reach Davenport.

Since the final destination of Davenport had been inscribed on the American passenger list, it was probable a ticket which included the price of the river trip northwards was purchased at an office near to Henry's home or while he was in Hamburg.

Disappointingly, Hinrich's possible role in family immigration history would not to turn out to be that logical. It was not the first time conclusions based on name similarity, birth and immigration data had led to incorrect assumptions as more information came to light. Once again the zeal to fill in a blank, to complete the picture by tying loose ends together whether or not they actually fit had got the better of me. For from a second passenger list provided by the Davenport Public Library, it was learned there were actually two possibilities for a Hinrich heading to Davenport during the same year, both of them arriving at the port of New Orleans in 1852; the first, spelled Reither, already noted, and a second one, listed as Riter. Yet again, another spelling version for someone whose occupation was also given as cooper!

The surname Riter, spelled just differently enough, had been missed in initially perusing the lists. But newspaper obituaries from the *Davenport Daily Leader*, the *Davenport Democrat* and the *Davenport Daily Times*, when taken together, left no question the second Henry Riter, cooper, was indeed the same person as the "h-less" Reiter with the same occupation noted in the federal and state censuses. The omission of an "h" in the Iowa censuses and the death notices had been no arbitrary oversight of the recorder this time. Moreover, his brother John, after serving in the Union Army during the Civil War, had returned home to join Henry in the cooperage business in Davenport before leaving Iowa for good to migrate to Nebraska. Clearly belonging to another family maintaining a different surname spelling, all the assumptions made with such smug confidence about Henry Reiter, cooper, had been wrong. He was neither the sought after missing third son nor a relation at all!

***

Johann Reither, one of two true sons of two times great uncle Hinrich and his first wife, on the other hand, had been positively identified among the passengers arriving together as a family in New York. Born as Johann Jacob Reither, not to be confused with my great-grandfather by the same exact name, he presented no difficulties in this respect. But tracing his course in America would not be without its own difficulties. In searching the 1860 census—the first one conducted after the family's arrival in 1857—he was unable to be placed in Davenport, or even within the limits of the state of Iowa. Oddly enough, after widening the search to nearby states, then to all of America and for all census dates, he still seemed to be non-existent, completely sliding under the survey radar for whatever reason. Census takers seldom missed accounting for individuals no matter where they lived in these earlier enumeration decades when the population was smaller and the collection method was in-person, door-to-door, and more thorough.

By chance, a lead was finally generated through a probate record for his father in Davenport. Following his father's death in 1887, this record listed a son by the name of John living in Indianapolis, Indiana! So focusing on that state only, Johann was finally tracked down in an 1896 record of marriage occurring in Marion County. This was no ordinary record, simply giving names of bride and groom and little more as was often the case for older records, or even one that was above average where names of American born parents of the bride and groom are included. Very rare indeed, the record gave the groom's father's name and the maiden name of his mother, the mother who had died in Holstein in 1843 long before John immigrated to America. It was certain the right person had been found. But what also stood out was that John's name included the middle initial "J", apparently a holdover from his birth middle name of Jacob and important enough for distinction purposes to have it placed on the official marriage document.

Having obtained verification that Indiana and not Iowa was his place of residence in 1896, shifting resource focus to Indianapolis was the next logical step. The pattern of using his middle initial "J" to identify him in assorted documents was instrumental in digging up more information and in separating him from others with the same first and last names. A link to a *Find A Grave* listing for John J. Reither from a secondary database produced the date of his death and the cemetery in which he was buried. There was no accompanying photo of a headstone, suggesting the information about him was probably from cemetery files rather than from the tombstone itself. Strikingly, the 1896 marriage record date was only one year prior to his death in 1897. It also indicated that he had been a widower when he had married in 1896, leaving open the question of the name of his previous wife.

As a next step, it was learned that the cemetery's website offered a genealogical search service of their records for a small fee. This approach might be able to supply an answer to whom his former wife had been and if they had any children. There was already a likely candidate since there were two persons interred in Crown Hill Cemetery in Indianapolis with the surname of Reither and they were both buried in the same plot. The person who shared the plot with John J. and had the unusual first name of America was also located on the *Find A Grave* website. But because birth dates were listed as unknown, it was impossible to judge ages of either person. And without ages, an educated guess could not be made as to what their relationship might have been; husband and wife or parent and child or cousins or even some more distant relative bearing the same surname? In placing an order for cemetery staff to research the owner of the plot—when it was purchased, obituaries or addresses of the decedents and possibly copies of death certificates included in their files—a picture might emerge of the relationships between these two individuals. Or not.

But before the cemetery documents arrived in the mail, an article was obtained from the Indianapolis Public Library on John J. Reither which had appeared in an issue of the *Indianapolis News* after his death. More than a brief obituary, the beginning of the second paragraph read: "The dead man was an industrious old solder, and lived for many years in Hadley Avenue, West Indianapolis." In this one sentence it was established this was indeed the same man repeatedly found listed in Indianapolis city directories at the same address over several years, and he was a military veteran. Curiously, the article's emphasis seemed to be on clarifying the circumstances of death; it reported he had died from natural causes rather than from a robbery assault. In a second article in the same paper, it was noted that he had been attacked by "footpads", the equivalent for highwaymen at the time, having been "sandbagged" while carrying a large sum of money from the recent sale of his home.

Arrival of cemetery records information and death certificate for John J. came close to putting to rest any need for further searching: the place of birth of John J. Reither was given as Germany and he was sixty-two years old when he died in 1891, corroborating other information. America Reither was forty-five when she preceded John J.'s death by six years, making them more likely to have been peers than at a father-daughter age differential. Furthermore, since John J. was noted as widowed at the time of his death, it was now clear that his second marriage had indeed lasted less than a year.

A lone military index card, giving only his name, abbreviations of regiment, company and service, military unit, date and name of the filing state, application and certificate numbers suggested the possibility to a path for acquiring more information about John J. If his pension file was available for purchase from the National Archives, military files could provide a wealth of details. This card was part of the *Civil War Pension Index*, further described as a *General Index to Pension Files*. Veterans of that war, or their widows, were entitled to pensions if the soldier sustained injuries resulting from their service or had died. Pension adjustments and increases occurred years later to support older veterans after a new law was passed basing the amount of payment on length of service and age.

What seemed peculiar, however, about the facts presented on the card was that the pension request was filed in Indiana, while John J. was invalided as a soldier attached to the *Kentucky Cavalry*. True, the state of Indiana shared its southeastern border with Kentucky and Indianapolis was only a little over a hundred miles away from Louisville, so it was plausible he had enlisted in that state. But could this be another case of mistaken identity in the end? Data normally

111

contained in the pension file itself seemed to be the best option for trying to confirm or deny the validity of this person so an online order to the National Archives for his record was duly placed.

The Civil War pension file did indeed explain the story behind John J.'s movements after arriving in America. Rather than going with his father and two brothers to Iowa, he was, for whatever reason, disposed to strike out for Kentucky instead—to Elizabethtown to be exact. But it was not on Kentuckian soil that he enlisted in the Civil War. Kentucky's governor had prohibited mobilization of Union forces on Kentucky soil, and, to show non-favoritism, proclaimed the same restriction regarding forces of the Confederacy. However, the state next door allowed the formation of Kentuckian Union regiments within its borders, thus his training took place at Camp Joe Holt in Clarksville, Indiana. John J.'s familiarity with Indiana from events and experiences at that time may have led to his choice to move there several years after the end of the war.

His wife was not mentioned in the pension documents, but because he was said to have been living in Kentucky in 1870, a census record was finally obtained for him under a corrupted spelling of his surname. This was the missing piece of evidence to show that John J. and his wife, America, who was a native Kentuckian, were indeed husband and wife; and it was augmented in noting they were the parents of two children as well. The oldest child aged three at the time, suggested their marriage may have occurred just after the conclusion of the Civil War in 1866 or 1867. A search of the online database of the Hardin County Clerk's Office verified this conclusion; April 1866 was their actual marriage date.

Two other record types appeared in family history databases, both giving limited snapshots of John J. Reither in Indiana. First, while he was found in one census only, a string of consecutive annual records solidified his long-term residence in that state. Listings from 1883 through 1892 in the Polk Indianapolis City Directories gave the same residence address of Hadley Avenue, West Indianapolis, occupation as carpenter also remaining the same. Like a longitudinal study on movement, these city directories were of significant value. And since he had called Indiana his home for such a long time, this state became a major concentration point for further research.

Conflicting with earlier newspaper reporting, an ironic ending seems to have been John J. Reither's fate. After surviving the rigors of war during a four year military stint ending in the Deep South, an Indianapolis obituary noted his death was caused by liver abscess and blood clot, which may or may not have been complicated by injuries sustained from the assault at the time of the robbery. Shockingly, it was also reported that he had been about to be married for a third time!

Not to be left out without mention, Peter Reiter, Henry and John J.'s other brother, had also served in the Civil War. Unlike Henry and John J., he was neither among the unaccounted like the former nor did he move to a different state as the latter did. But as with John J., he was of the right age to have fought in the War of the Rebellion, as the conflict was alternatively called, and it was found he had enlisted almost at its outbreak in 1861.

An unusual war-related document about him surfaced in another of the online databases; on a membership card crammed with his personal information from the *Department of Iowa of the Grand Army of the Republic* the name Reither, Peter appeared. Almost like a life story in a nutshell, his name was followed by: residence address, date and place of birth, date and place of death, including the name of burial cemetery and the numbered location of his gravesite, name of wife and children and war record.

Mustered out of the Union Army in Alabama in 1865 at end of the war, he had been promoted to quartermaster sergeant in October of 1864. The Grand Army of the Republic, or GAR, was a veterans' society of the Union Army chartered in 1866 in Decatur, Illinois. Membership reached a peak at over four hundred thousand in 1890. By then the organization had offices, called posts, spread throughout the United States. Instrumental in serving as a pressure group to create pensions for veterans, the *GAR* also was involved in charitable work, fraternal and memorial activities. The GAR's enduring legacy of observing the 30th of May each year as Decoration Day has been maintained ever since it closed its doors in 1956, although it is currently celebrated as Memorial Day on the last Monday of that month.

DECISIONS

Marne, Dithmarschen, Duchy of Holstein, January 1866

"If you bring it up one more time, you'll have to sleep in one of the cow sheds tonight," the thrust of a hand towards the door providing extra emphasis to his threat. Tolerance in listening to one of his younger brother's obsessions on something—whatever it happened to be at the time—usually ranked high among his attributes. But this time Johann's repeated anxieties about future plans of the Peer family was one too many for his own nerves to take and had finally got the better of him.

"But Hinrich, I just wanted to find out if you…"

"No buts about it; not another word, Johann." I've told you over and over all that I've heard is that they said they intend to emigrate soon as well. What they're thinking right now, at this moment, I'm still in the dark about, just like you. So you'll have to ask them yourself. If you can't wait any longer, why not make a quick trip over to their home? It's very cold out, but at least the wind has died down. You'll still have some light for a little while longer if you get going right away".

With the spell of bad weather they'd been having for the

past week, just trying to keep the animals sheltered and fed, along with themselves, had kept them pinned down in all too familiar surroundings. Until now there had not been even a glimmer of an idea about going anywhere else; their own farm needs had taken all of their attention. If his older brother was giving his consent for him to leave home for a few hours, who was he to object? He was already feeling his spirits buoyed by the thought.

It had been many years now, more than ten when you took time to count, since he had first found himself in her presence. It was inexplicable to him, but even way back then, when he was only fifteen and she not yet ten, there was something about Maria that had captured his interest. It could have been the way she carried herself even at a younger age—shoulders back, perfectly erect, looking straight forward and without a hint of uncertainty in her step. Or maybe it was how her eyes confidently met his. Her movements seemed to flow as naturally as the words she spoke. Afterwards, the attraction had been more of watching and studying her from a distance. But as they grew older and their friendship deepened, Johann learned one day she too had been keeping an eye on him as the years went by.

Although his brothers and sister had been long aware of Johann's fondness for Maria, they also knew she was seven years his junior—not yet even nineteen—while he had become an "old bachelor" of twenty-five. Her parents were adamant when speaking to their daughter that she was not yet of age to marry. They also had their own ideas of whom she should marry when the time did come, and it was not Johann Reither. Johann's father had married a woman with the same surname and it was their belief that another marriage between two related families would be one too many even though they were only distantly connected. Now, as plans were forming for leaving Dithmarschen, they hoped the whole issue would be dropped and disappear for good. It seemed to be already the case since they had not seen or heard anything about Johann for some weeks. Perhaps, he had finally realized it was not a match looked upon with favor, and without their approval had turned his attentions elsewhere.

Out the small window on the side of the equally small home in the village of Diekhusen, Maria's father could see a yet indiscernible figure coming down the road towards their gate. Then it drew closer, with coat collar turned high, and tall, thin body bending like a young sapling in the still powerful gusts; there was a familiarity to its profile and stride and his hackles began to rise. A firm knocking on the door and he was face-to-face with Johann Reither. His jaw immediately clenched and eyes hardened involuntarily, approaching a glare. Annoyed as he was after such a long reprieve from having to think about this man, village manners would not allow keeping his daughter from greeting him in such weather. They had not said as much to her about him but Maria was nevertheless aware of their opinions. And she could be a handful when she thought she had been wronged. If she found out Johann had been to their home while she was there and had been kept in the dark about his visit, there would surely be a forthcoming outburst disturbing to the whole household. It was much more prudent to keep a strong-minded daughter content for everyone's sake!

"Good day, sir. I hope I'm not interrupting your dinner. I've just stopped by to say hello to Maria. It's been such a long time since we've had a chance to see each other."

After a telling pause, he half-heartedly called out: "Maria, someone is here to see you. Could you come to the door if you're not busy?" Almost before his last word was spoken she was there at the door, having already recognized the voice of Johann from the kitchen alcove.

"Come in, Johann. Hurry! It is way too cold to be outdoors any longer. Father, why did you leave him standing out there like that? He'll be turning blue and into a block of ice if he stays out there a second more." Her father just lowered his eyes while motioning Johann to enter their home. Then without another word he picked up his hat and swung a heavy coat across his shoulders and went out the door himself.

As soon as he had gone and the door was shut behind him, Maria and Johann looked at each other and rolled their eyes in a "there he goes again" moment of understanding between the two of them.

"I know he doesn't want to see me here—or anywhere else for that matter. Whenever your father's around and finds us together he is obviously bothered by my presence. His reactions are getting more intense every time; one day soon I think he will explode and tell me to get lost. I'm sure he wishes I'd evaporate like a summer cloud, for good."

"Don't let that way of thinking ever stop you from coming to see me, Johann. He'll have to live with you stopping by and us seeing each other if he wants to keep me at home. In his mind he thinks he is protecting me from getting involved too soon with anyone, not just you. And there are other worries as well, most of them imagined. I've told him I'm won't be ready to get married until I'm older, but that doesn't mean I can't like someone now. I don't think he believes me. He'll get over it someday. He'll have to." So convincing was her support that, when taken together with the comfort of the warmth of being indoors, he started to feel the tension ooze out of his body.

"He really doesn't know me at all—it's like he's formed an opinion of me on something pulled out of thin air! I know he believes I'm too old for you, still I think there is a lot more to it than that. There's something else about me that seems to be bothering him."

Hearing their voices below, Maria's mother descended the stairs from the loft above to join them so they brought their conversation to halt.

"I thought it might be you, Johann, although your voices were so low I couldn't be sure. Can we offer you something warm to drink to take the chill off?"

Her mother was caught in-between her husband and Maria, but that did not stop her from maintaining customary civility to a guest. Besides, unlike her husband, she actually had a fondness for Johann. He came from a good family, was known to be a hard worker and had a likeable personality. Of course she knew how her husband felt about him; he had talked to her enough about his worries, even though Johann's family had links to her family. Like the Peers, generations of Reithers had made up part of the community with marriage between the families occurring in the past. So she remained guarded in her interactions with Johann. Not wanting to risk going against her husband's wishes and causing discord between them, she couldn't say how she really felt about him. It was a delicate path to tread since she also sensed the depth of her daughter's feelings for the young man.

"Thank you, Frau Peers. But no, I won't be staying that long. One of the reasons I came was because I wanted to let you know about our family's decision about going to America; it will be happening sooner rather than later, before the winter ends. Father and my older brother Hinrich plan on looking into booking a passage to New York as early as next month. We would like to arrive in America and make our way to Iowa in time for the spring season planting regardless of whether we are able to rent farmland or work on someone else's farm. You know my uncle's family has been there for several years now and they should be able to help us get started, I'm sure."

"We had heard a little about that a few days ago, Johann, from your father actually. He's aware that we've been thinking about when we want to leave too." Maria's eyes were fixated on her mother's face the whole time, hoping that she would say more. When she had said "our family", they had suddenly enlarged. Nothing definite had been mentioned to her or any of her seven siblings, some of whom had been in been in and out, upstairs and downstairs and starting to approach them only to be waved away with a sidelong glance of annoyance. She had accidentally overheard a few words spoken between her mother and father but not nearly enough to know what their thinking was for sure. It was fortunate now that her mother was in a talkative mood, Johann's presence and their common objectives opening up the faucet for a trickle of words to flow out.

"We think your family has the right idea in deciding upon a departure in March. With any luck, the worst of the winter weather will be behind you by then and there would be less risk of an unpleasant passage due to rough and stormy conditions. Arriving in America around the time of seeding season for summer crops would be a big advantage in giving you a chance to quickly get started in doing whatever you can.

You may have already heard, the Ehlers family has decided to go with us whenever we choose to leave. They said it's up to us and they'll be ready."

"The Ehlers? Which ones, mama? No one has mentioned them before and there are so many living around us."

"My father's brother. Your uncle, Maria, and his family, the ones living right here in Marne, you know—Claus Ehlers, his wife and their three children. They've only recently made up their mind to emigrate as well. I guess it comes down to being fed up of what's happened here, like for us and so many others."

"Didn't you say at one time, mother, there was an Ehlers relation who was a seaman? Are these Ehlers of that family?" Maria had recalled ages ago hearing stories about a seafaring man—not a fisherman who fished the Wadden Sea like so many of the locals did—but someone who sailed the oceans.

"You've always had a good memory, Maria, unlike some of your brothers and sisters. No, that family is, of course, related, but they're not the ones from Marne I was talking about. Captain Ehlers is the distant cousin who has been in command of the steamship Germania. His usual route has been from Hamburg to New York for the last few years. But he's gotten older now and may have retired. Your father has tried to get in contact with someone who might know if he is still making the voyage. If he is, maybe he'll be crossing the Atlantic to New York again soon and we can join him onboard his ship."

This was news to Maria, and for Johann a very interesting proposition. He had not anticipated learning so much, especially from someone other than Maria. The smidgens of gossip he had heard about others leaving Dithmarschen had just been shored up. Maybe it could be they would all be setting forth sooner than they thought. Even though no exact dates were mentioned, the main thing was hearing Maria's family would be going for sure. Up until this moment, he had often contemplated how he would tell his father and what his reaction would be when he said to him he would be staying behind if Maria's family had decided not to leave. Now he could exhale and breathe normally again.

"If you'll excuse me, Johann, I must begin to prepare the evening meal. It was nice to see you again and please give our regards to your father and family." She smiled when she left them to talk alone together for a little while longer.

"You see, Johann," Maria paused and grinned, "all of us will be on our way to America before you know it. I'm glad you came over; none of us would have heard what was happening from father probably right up until the time to leave was upon us. Your coming broke the usual pattern of silence around here about things important to us all. Father believes it's better for us not to get involved, to know too much, or we'll risk getting overexcited and worries about friends and old routines will begin to set in. And there's always the chance plans could change again. Then he would have to deal with the disappointment that would bring about."

"I've told you, Maria, before about my father—how long it took him to talk about anything after mother's death. This seems to be a common trait among our families. My brother Hinrich had to take over making decisions and do the talking for a long time. But father's much better now. It's Hinrich who's become tired of answering questions, especially from me."

The two of them continued to discuss the idiosyncrasies

of parents and other things for longer than Johann had intended. When a second look through a small peephole in a fogged over window pane caught darkness of evening almost upon them, the conversation came to an end. After wrapping himself up as snuggly as he could to fend off the frigid elements about to be faced again, it was a quick goodbye and out the door. A fast-paced walk home with the fleece-lined collar of his coat tightly pressing against his neck became more like a trot to help stay warm. Instinctively dodging every road impediment, his feet saved him from taking a tumble as if guided by unknown powers. He felt safe and secure; nothing could hurt him.

Family members were gathered together to greet him when he entered the door. Worry had begun to take over when he hadn't returned before night had fallen. In fact, Hinrich was on the verge of wrapping up and plunging into the blackness himself to fetch him home from whatever was detaining him.

"Here you are—finally!" It was said in a voice edged with both irritation and concern. Now that he was home and apparently unscathed, Hinrich's mood had shifted from concern to an upbraiding.

"It would have been common sense to come home before dark, you know. All of us here could think of nothing else but what had happened to you." But before he could continue his reprimand was wrenched away from him by Johann.

"I have news for you all," launching immediately into a diversionary tactic in hope of taking the edge off the start of a less than cordial welcome back.

"I think you will be surprised," it would be impossible, he thought, to resist the excitement his voice managed to contrive, "in what I have to tell you!"

SCHLESWIG-HOLSTEIN

Dithmarschen, Schleswig-Holstein, Germany, Summer 2008

Sufficient progress on research on family history in Holstein had been made to this point to stimulate a desire to see the places my ancestors had come from—to spend a few days around their former home surroundings and experience any cultural legacies firsthand and up-close. So without further delay, a summer trip was planned to visit the northernmost region of Germany. By now the villages and towns had been pinpointed on the map, the important dates nailed down, the location of the district parish office and church identified, and the major boundary defining rivers of the Elbe, Eider, Treene and Stör recognized.

Two late nineteenth century-built canals, the Nord-Ostsee-Kanal and the Elbe-Lubeck-Kanal, the latter replacing a medieval canal, provided cross-country goods shipment on waterways between the Baltic Sea—also called the Ostsee—and the North Sea, had also been designated as important landmarks. Descriptions and photo familiarity with a land and its features had reached their limit. It was time to walk in the shoes of ancestors, to take in the contours of the landscape, to wade in the waters of the Wadden Sea; and maybe even an occasion for meeting a few of the local folks.

A car rental from the Hamburg airport soon had us on our way north. The distance from the airport to the town of Marne, where we had prearranged accommodation, was under an hour and a half, if we made no stops along the way. Driving in good weather, we passed by the port town of Brunsbüttel by the North Sea mouth of the Elbe River before heading a few miles inland and arriving at our hotel without a problem. The city-state of Hamburg itself—like a bite taken out of the bottom of the Schleswig-Holstein map—an independent enclave whose northern borders were swelled by integrating villages once belonging to Holstein in the past—would have to wait until after we had finished visiting our primary target. Once in Marne we quickly settled into our room and left just as quickly to experience the long, lingering twilight of a season marked by warm days and nights. The hotel, chosen because of its easy walking access to the town and surrounding villages, was indeed perfectly situated, not that there was much choice; it may have been the only place to stay in Marne at that moment!

Although it was no longer the same church building of my ancestors' era and constructed between 1904 and 1906, the "new" church was still an impressive centerpiece of the town, just as its predecessor had been in its time. The old church had served its purpose for centuries, probably having been built sometime after the second Battle of Bornhöved in 1227. It was then that Dithmarscher natives, with the help of allied forces, ended Danish authority and established a free peasant republic for the next three hundred years, until 1559 when Danish predominance would return to rule once again.

Inside the current Maria-Magdalenen-Kirche, up front to

the left of the altar and opposite the old pulpit on the right side stood the ancient baptismal font passed down from one church iteration to the next. This primitive font would have been the same one used for baptisms of documented ancestors going back at least seven generations but going back much further than that to its origin in the 1300s. Held on the shoulders of three human figures serving as its legs, the substantially hefty, solid bronze receptacle with bluish-green patina appeared as if it would endure another seven hundred without a problem. Never to be forgotten, a model of the old church as it was in my immigrant ancestor's time lay under a glass enclosure providing a tangible image of times past as did the beautifully preserved wood-carved pulpit nearby, which had also survived the transfer from old church to new.

Again on foot from the hotel front door and down the block, our familiarization tour of the small town continued the next day. A visit to the *Evangelische Gemeindezentrum*, the Marne parish office, was the first order of the day. Situated just across the *Osterstrasse*, the small road in front of the church itself, the office appeared to be part of a multi-purpose building which included a community center. Despite having to contend with our very limited German, a welcoming and helpful staff member understood what we wanted to see and pulled a weighty church register from the shelf which included the year of interest, 1840. Hopefully, it would contain the original marriage entry matching the German transcript of one of the family records I had received earlier from the researcher and had brought with me for comparison. If the actual register itself held exactly the same information there would no longer be any doubts regarding the accuracy of the other transcriptions made by him—all taken from the microfilm images housed in the Schleswig archives and supplied in both German and English translation in email attachments. Once my brain had adapted to the worst handwriting style yet encountered, the register entry proved to be word-for-word identical to the transcription.

The urge to view original document evidence had been well-satisfied. But it had not happened without the assistance of personal research experience gained over the years. When the register was first opened to the correct date of interest with the aid of the staff member, the entry sought appeared not to be there; something was amiss. Allowed to sit down alone to look further into the volume's contents, it was soon realized the large volume was divided into three different sections: baptisms, marriages and burials, the dates repeating themselves for each section. And in the second section the marriage entry was found just where it should be. With most present-day research done using the microfilmed archives, it must have been unusual for someone to want to look at the oversized leather-bound volumes themselves. Parish staff in trying to be helpful had been unaccustomed to the peculiar arrangement of the old register.

Aiming to visit the cemetery next, directions were asked since it didn't appear to be in close proximity to the church. The answer was a let-down. While there was a sizable "new cemetery" out of line of sight behind the other end of the parish office, the original cemetery, which had at one time surrounded the old church when it was just across the street, was gone. The entire area had been paved over for a parking lot for both the current church and the *Rathaus*, the town hall only a few steps away. The graves had not been moved from the old to new cemetery so the names and remains of those who had been interred there were lost forever. Only two markers bearing the family name were located during a brief walk through the new cemetery, both of them with dates from the latter part of the twentieth century.

Our pedestrian tour led us next to the front of a well-preserved two and a half story building with the curious plaque embedded in the brickwork to the left of the entrance; *Marner Skat-Club. 1873*, it read, which meant nothing at all to us. A second sandwich board sign containing the words *Heimatmuseum Marner Skatclub* and standing nearby helped to clarify the building's current purpose as a local history museum. At its outset in 1873, the Marner Skatclub had been a private local historical society where members brought exceptional objects to be housed and viewed by like-minded historians. In 1928 the town of Marne took the museum over for the benefit of all citizens; later the building had undergone remodeling, including enhancements for special exhibitions or community events. Even marriage ceremonies were allowed to be performed within its walls nowadays. It turned out to be a diverse and fascinating collection of objects and descriptions, including explanations of the building of the polders, like the sizable Friedrichskoog, and physical cultural history in the form of furniture, household appliances, earthenware, porcelain and textiles as well as artifacts from the old Marne church.

As it was early in the day, we had the *Skatclubmuseum* almost to ourselves during the first half hour of our visit. The only other person there turned out to be a local newspaper reporter who was equipped with camera in hand. After a brief conversation with him in which we were found out to be American tourists on the trail of ancestral roots in

Dithmarschen, the reporter asked if he could take a photo or two of us while we were looking at the displays. Next morning, a photograph appeared in the *Marner Zeitung* accompanied by a caption about our visit. A day and a half in Marne and we had already made the news—and without getting up to any mischief! .

The remainder of the morning was spent wandering around the immaculately maintained town, old and new buildings alike in excellent condition, painted in bright but complementary colors. Town center roads attractively made of rose-colored pavers and narrow enough to keep low-level traffic moving at slow speed were designed to be favorable to pedestrian crossings from one small square to the next. A blend of benches, bike racks, handsome light poles, sculptures, flowers and trees combined to demonstrate an awareness of the importance of town image and artistic taste in making it a welcoming place to visit.

Afternoon hours were devoted to the ultimate quest. Map in hand just in case we went astray, we walked out of town northeast heading towards the hamlet where ancestors had lived for generations. The distance was short, about a mile and half of flat walking on a sparsely used roadway bordered by a mix of tranquil green fields and pockets of tree-fronted dwellings; it seemed almost like a quiet stroll down an oversized footpath. We knew we were there when we saw the street sign for the *Darenwurther Chaussee* and soon afterwards houses and barns grouped together on an elevated section of land—the small mounded village we had come to see.

The structures on the small hill were perhaps a dozen or so in number, some with rounded roof edges, some made of brick or plaster. But nearly all of them had low, single story side walls with large steeply pitched roofs, doubling the height of the buildings and providing upstairs, sloped living and storage space. Each house had windows on both ends where the walls were two-storied, and windows were also cut out of the roof overhangs on the sides as well for more light and a peek of a view. It would probably be a fair assumption that from appearances the majority of families living on the hillock itself—which could be circled at its base in less than a half hour by foot—were engaged in some way in common agricultural endeavors, perhaps sharing large storage facilities, a practice likely to have been done in bygone centuries.

Helserdeich, the second village that had figured prominently during earliest family history generations, back to the late 1600s at least, was the next destination of interest due west. Another mile and a half along an empty road and another seemingly self-contained hamlet, with large agricultural storage facilities attached. Turning southward for the return trip back to Marne, we were greeted by immense fields of bright green crops.

When we paused under a tree at a bend of the road to admire the expanse of the field, a young woman passing by on a bicycle stopped and asked: "Kann ich dir helfen?" An offer of help was immediately understood. Producing our map, we told her of our main purpose; experiencing the places where ancestors had lived years ago. She spoke English well and a friendly conversation ensued. We learned the crops we had been staring at were cabbage and that Dithmarschen was the largest cabbage-growing area in Europe. In fact, the German Cabbage Route extended for over eighty miles in the district. Our walk back to Marne sealed the cabbage notoriety of the area for us in passing green field after green field on both sides of the road.

Next morning began an exploration of greater Dithmarschen: the Wadden Sea, the dikes and water channels, other towns and villages. Seaside waters made for wading and swimming started at land's edge and continued to be shallow as far as the eye could see. Fine weather had brought a good crowd out to bask in the sun and cool off in the warm seawater, but numbers were in proportion to a small area and not at all overwhelming. The Schleswig-Holstein Wadden Sea National Park was one of three national parks along this special shoreline of the North Sea, the countries of Denmark to the north and the Netherlands to the south incorporating the other two coastal parks. The German and Danish segments, when taken together, have been designated a UNESCO World Heritage site.

Stretches of grass-covered dikes looping their way close to the shore were repeated inland. Following current contours of the seashore as well as old boundaries of past centuries before land reclamation, the dikes remain functional and essential to the well-being of the area today. On 18th century maps, dwellings could be seen almost pressing against the landward sides of the base of protective embankments, but modern times find them sporadically hugging both sides—even in-between dike bands—indicating a willingness to take risk because of the greater security from the danger of encroaching waters. Mechanized construction and stronger materials have improved flood control and created higher embankment walls; if a breach should occur, earthmoving machines could affect swifter repair compared to the past.

Canals to control rainwater and storm surges

complemented and sometimes mimicked curvature of dikes. Much more prevalent than the dikes, these water channels were also scattered in all directions throughout the marshland. Grazing sheep kept the grass on embankments and canal fringes nicely mown. Close by, wind turbines standing tall like stiff giants dotted the coastline. Catching the sea breezes to generate electricity, wind farms were abundant in Dithmarschen and were said to produce about half of its energy needs.

Dithmarschen could not be left without a visit to Heide, a town twenty miles north of Marne known for its cultural heritage situated at the crossroads and heart of the district. The market square, reputed to be the largest in Germany, was encompassed by long blocks on all four sides. One of the larger towns in the immediate area, Heide was full of activity, drawing local shopper and tourist alike to its walking-only streets.

Leaving Heide, the coastal town of Husum and its harbor carved out by storm tides centuries ago, was next on the itinerary. Finding a room in the afternoon in the middle of summer in this popular place could have been a nightmare even with its many hotels—and almost was. After walking from reception desk to reception desk in the town center and receiving the same no vacancy response, a staff member took pity on worried faces and offered a room down the street in an annex, albeit with a proviso. She warned that, since the room was not part of the actual full service hotel itself, it may not live up to expectations; to the contrary, it exceeded them in all the important ways: comfort, cleanliness, peace and quiet.

It was only a few minutes' away from our door to the *Husumer Hafen*, the inner harbor area where much of the town's activity took place. With a cloudless northern sky above where the depth of blue was strongest straight up and fades to near white on the horizon, we were lucky enough to be there on a day when a craft fair was taking place in the open market square. The local artisans had produced works in wood, glass, ceramics and other materials in exceptionally high quality and unusually creative designs.

The same good fortune could be said of the next stop at one of the restaurants overlooking the water offering special take-out meals through a side window for those who chose not to seek seating within. *Fischbrötchen*, fresh fish taken from the sea at their doorstep, then prepared in a variety of ways and served on a roll, was nearly irresistible to the passerby as attested to by the long lines of diners trying to find a place to sit. Fish served on bread can be found in Germany here and there, even one well-known chain seems to have branches in most cities, but any comparison to fresh *Husumer fischbrötchen* would be left wanting.

It was remarkable that in this fully booked small town with teems of people wandering the streets and harbor not a single other American was noticed to be there. It seemed to be similar for other nationalities as well; it was as if only Germans knew about this port town's attractions and found their way there.

We drove inland to *Friedrichstadt*, a town with much apparent Dutch influence in its origins, the next morning. Architecturally, many, if not most, of the houses had classic Dutch style fronts. The bridges crossing the many canals, and the Eider River itself alongside which the town was built, seemed to be all of Dutch-inspired design. Boats loaded with tourists plied the canal waters. Those passengers wearing hats

133

and caps shading their heads from the intense sun during what must have been a local heat wave were surely the happiest of the sightseers, for there were no roofs on the small crafts to provide protection. Meandering down paths and streets was a slow, sticky slog—you could almost reach out and touch the oscillating heat currents rising up from the pavement. Still, most of the faces in the crowds seemed content, their owners probably pleased to be sweltering instead of shivering when the season of warmth was such a fleeting one.

During the next two days we drove to the cities of Schleswig and Rendsburg, each with a population of less than thirty thousand. The largest cities of Kiel and the once opulent and powerful port city of Lübeck were skipped as they had been brief stopovers years before at a time when hitch-hiking through Europe was still in vogue. As we wended our way through the countryside between the cities and within them, it was encouraging to see separate bike paths even on the majority of the main highways. Cycling routes seemed to be firmly embedded in town and country planning, especially since the flattish terrain was well-suited to peddling by riders of all levels. Many parts of Germany were bicycle-oriented, but few places in Northern Europe could come close to neighboring Holland in sharing a love for this mode of transportation.

HAMBURG

Marne, Dithmarschen, Duchy of Holstein, February 1866

When Johann told his story of the emigration plans of Peer and Ehlers families to his brother Hinrich and the rest of his family, they were only moderately surprised. Both his father and brother had known these families were fed-up like their own, and nearing the point of making a final decision in choosing a date to depart as well. They were happy to learn, just the same, of the possibility they could be leaving around the same time as they had hoped to book passage. One thing that hadn't crossed their minds, though, was Johann's reminder of the vague recollection of a seafaring relative who might still be taking ships from Hamburg to New York.

The prominent Captain Ehlers had at some point in the past been mentioned as a family relation of the local Ehlers, but without Johann's bringing him up again the next idea would not have dawned upon them. If it could be worked out and he hadn't retired, why not try to arrange to go all together on Captain Ehler's ship? The journey often took close to two weeks and they knew what an agitated sea could do to the sturdiest of ships and the hardiest of passengers. To be in experienced and familiar hands would ease their minds a great deal; there would be that extra degree of confidence in reaching their destination alive and in one piece. They needed to talk with the Peers soon before it was too late to change plans.

Wasting little time after these revelations, Hinrich was dispatched to Marne to check if there was a ship captained by Ehlers leaving within the next two months. He immediately learned that on the 3rd of March the *Germania* was scheduled to sail from Hamburg and under his command. Catapulted now into making a definite decision for an exact departure date on the strength of an Ehler at the helm, the families came into quick agreement and passage was made for that date. Sailing ships still formed a significant portion of the slow to modernize German-operated fleet. But since the steamship Germania was of recent build, having made its maiden voyage only three years before in 1863 under the reputable transatlantic Hamburg America Line, their decision had been all the more simple to make.

Less expensive crossings were still available on older sailing ships. But would they really want to subject themselves to confinement for up to sixty days on an old-fashioned vessel blown by the caprices of the wind when they had a much more reliable and speedier engine-driven choice? It would have been starting off with backwards thinking when everything else was looking forward. It would surely be less than a handful of years before the last of the sailing ships were replaced altogether.

The Reither family sometimes at variance on possibly debatable issues was unified in their decision this time. There would be only one scheduled stopover on the way—at the English port of Southampton—the day after their embarkation from Hamburg. For those who wished, there would be a few hours to roam the bustling streets of that rapidly expanding city while the ship took aboard additional passengers. So on the following day, Hinrich, together with Johann, returned to the ticket agent with the fare money in hand. Thankfully, when the agent asked about small pox vaccinations, they had been prepared to answer that their father had been vaccinated in 1812 when he was four, and his children had all received inoculations around a dozen months after they were born, as prescribed.

Details concerning coordination with the Peers and the Ehlers families troubled the minds of the Reithers as they readied themselves for leaving. It wasn't the initial stage of the journey that gave them concern. Their relatives, who had farmed in nearby Sankt Michaelisdonn, had departed for good during the previous decade, travelling to Hamburg mainly by train without problem from the railway station in Itzehoe. The station had opened only the month before their departure in April 1857. Now it would soon be their turn to travel the first twenty-five mile leg of the journey to Itzehoe by wagon, perhaps with a group of fellow pilgrims to accompany them. And there on the banks of the Stör River they too would begin their rail passage southwards towards Hamburg.

Itzehoe was still the closest train station of *Die Marschbahn*, the Marsh Railway which had begun service in the mid-1840s. The trip would have been shorter by six miles for both their cousins who had left a decade before and themselves if the much-talked about extension of the railway to Sankt Michaelisdonn and more northerly points of Holstein had already been completed. Regardless of station distance, it would be no simple task to know with any certainty how the

137

other families might figure into their own itinerary on the day they were to leave. Each family would be taken up with the chaos of their own last minute preparations, obligations and unexpected impediments, not to mention that they lived on the other side of Marne from the Reithers. It was understood from experiences of others that while planned arrangements might be made with the best of intentions, passengers trying to rendezvous before boarding a train together might not be so easily accomplished. For Johann, any chance of uncertainty was unacceptable if he had anything to do with it.

"Should I go today," his eagerness to have a definitive answer again besting any self-restraint, "to make sure the Peers are meeting us at the same time and place that we'd decided before?"

"Not today, Johann. Don't forget you and Hinrich have to move the stored potatoes to the new community storage cellar just on the outskirts of the opposite side of town. We can't leave them go to waste after we're gone and maybe we will add a few coins to our pockets for our efforts."

He was adamant in setting aside as much money as they could to tide them over until they could get on their feet again in the new life that lie ahead. Small sums had already been collected from the sale of the few furniture items of any value; their livestock and farming equipment had been spoken for and payment already received for the most part. The extra funds would help when added to the little savings judiciously salted away for months. Like those before them, walking away would be with only a single case each containing clothes and perhaps a memorable personal item or two squeezed inside. Everything else unsold would be left behind and used by those who remained.

"All right, father. But you know there is only a little more than a week before we will be in Hamburg. What if we don't hear from them soon? How can we be certain they'll be on the same train if we don't take the time to check with them?" He tried to fight off visions of Maria separated from him, she on one side of the ocean and he left wondering what happened on the other.

"We have to get done what we can and let the Peers and Ehlers families do the same. Time is short for all of us. So we should let them be left in peace to attend to their own affairs. God willing, we will all see each other either here or at the station."

Johann slightly moved his head in acknowledgement. Some sign of agreement was an expected and necessary reaction when his father spoke his mind. And he could almost find sense in his words even if emotions had a way of trumping reasoning. But this time his meager response was only meant half-way. If a chance to meet with Maria again before going to Hamburg came up, he would seize it no matter what his father thought. It was unlike him to be disobedient to a parent, but it might be done without harm or consequence if his father knew nothing about it.

"Where's my brother—where's Hinrich got off to now?" He was anxious to get on with the potato shifting and get it out of the way.

"He's run next door to the Gimmini's to deliver rakes, spades and the other tools they wanted. He'll be back in a minute or two then off you two can go. I've got to go into Marne myself and you should be done before I get back."

Using the larger cart, the two brothers moved the potatoes in relatively short order. With their father occupied and the storage cellar almost halfway to the Peers home across town, it was as good a time as any to make a hasty journey. With his long strides, he thought he could easily make his way back home well before his father's return.

"Could you take the horse and cart back by yourself, Hinrich? And would you keep it to yourself that I went over to the Peers and not tell father? Make up some excuse about why I'm not with you that's believable if you run into him on your way back. I won't take long and should be back well before he is in any case."

Older and younger brother who were often at odds with each other over concerning mundane things—caught-up in competitiveness and petty jealousies—could usually be counted on to support each other, when it came down to protecting each other's interests from third parties who became involved, even if it meant evasive responses or stretching the truth a bit to avoid trouble.

And there was never any doubt from Hinrich's squinty-eyed grin and slight shrug of a shoulder aimed towards the town that he understood and would serve as rear guard this time as well. Given the go ahead and assuming a playful racing stance, he shot off like an arrow.

Maria was home when he arrived. Without any small talk, she reaffirmed their leaving plans hadn't changed. Hurriedly, they went over them again, to meet on the same train for Hamburg three days before the actual sailing date no matter what happened before that. They had just enough time for a few more words of assurance before Johann took off for home. He was holding his breath when he entered the door, letting it out only when he learned his father was not yet there; his idea had worked, his mission successfully accomplished.

Calm was short-lived.

Then Hinrich asked him to sit down for a moment.

"I have something I've wanted to tell you but didn't know exactly how to go about it so I hope you don't take it the wrong way now. It's been on my mind for several days, ever since Margret and I made up our minds. You know I've talked about her for quite awhile. What I haven't shared with you and the rest of the family up to this point is she and I have decided to marry, and sooner rather than later. It's still hard to say, and I would have said something earlier if we had been sure before—but I won't be going to America. Margret has no brothers. They need help with their farm, someone to take over working the land soon. You know, it's the one not far away in the village of Schmedeswurth. I'm older than you and more used to the ways of doing things here. It's harder for me to change when I'm sure of what I want to do where I am. And with the right person by my side, this is the place I want to be."

The shock of there suddenly being only four of them instead of the five leaving for America, the sixth, Cathrina, already staying behind with her family, left Johann stunned for a moment.

Hinrich continued, "I only told father the day I went to get the tickets in Marne. When I gave him just four tickets, he knew there would be no changing my mind."

Johann had only a minute more to digest the news before his father came in through the door. He wore a heavy frown, deepening the crinkles already lining his forehead; sullenly, he turned to Johann and looked him straight in the eyes.

"Marne is a small town, son, and you know what happens in small towns. When someone on a dead run passes by close

141

to where I am talking to blacksmith Harke and his shop door is open, it draws attention, especially when it turns out to be a person you're supposed to know well. "Where is the lad going now?" I asked myself. "Wasn't he supposed to be tending to the potatoes with Hinrich? What's he doing in town at this hour? And later in the afternoon when I meet Eckert on the way home, he mentions he has seen you going in the gate of the Peers residence.

"I am disappointed with you. I trusted your word to stay away from their place and take care of our own affairs. Your infatuation with Maria, a girl barely nineteen, seems to have gotten the best of you and clouded your thinking. This has come between us as a family and it's shameful. You have let her entice you away from your duties and your own family's reputation at a time like this. She is still too young and her parents will not let it happen. Her father feels the same way, I believe. By your behavior you're making me dislike a girl I hardly know anything about. What would your poor mother have said?"

"Maria is not enticing me or anybody else," he began loudly with a growing temper before catching himself: "I'm sorry, father. I just thought I had enough time to do both when I left, and knowing how you feel about minding our own business I didn't want to upset you. Instead, I've managed to do just that."

"But your word, Johann, you promised...we had an agreement."

"I didn't say I wouldn't go to the Peers. I said nothing, if you remember."

"That kind of ambiguous answer won't do; no, it won't do at all from a son of mine. I think you know quite well what was meant; there was an understanding between us. When you make excuses like that it makes my unhappiness with your conduct even greater. We must be able to trust each other in our family with no mother to turn to for support and guidance. I'm so glad we'll be leaving soon and there'll be no more of this nonsense from you, I hope. Once we all have to deal with what is ahead of us maybe you'll be able to occupy your own mind with something else besides the young Maria. I don't approve of your actions, or of hers either for that matter. Even though you are of age, she isn't. Remember you still live under my roof. As far as I'm concerned this is over between you both."

Johann was unable to verbalize a response. First his brother's news and now his father's reproach were too much to absorb at one time, beyond his capability in formulating a measured reply. Engaging the eyes of his father again for a split second with rekindled fire in his own, he turned and walked abruptly out slamming the door shut behind him.

***

Hamburg, German Confederation, March 1866

Black smoke belching from the engine's stack drifted backwards into faces leaning out the windows of the trailing passenger cars as the steam locomotive slowly pulled the train away from the Itzehoe station. Eyes riveted on scenery rolling slowly by for a last look at the familiar backdrop of everyday lives for so many generations were forced to blink over and over again. When the fumes and soot became too much to bear, a retreat back inside the carriage and window closing became the only recourse. It was the first day of March and the sky was overcast. The widowed father and his three children, Johann and Peter who were now young men, and Anna Christina, almost an adult and turning eighteen during the forthcoming voyage, were comfortably ensconced in seats across from each other. The train was full of other families as well as passengers travelling alone, all keeping a close eye on their belongings. The Ehlers had greeted them on the platform as expected. Mixed emotions shared with others experiencing the same feelings were welcome distractions, a chance to commiserate on what they were giving up without dwelling too much on their own misgivings, and to speculate on what the future might bring,

But there had been no sign of the Peers family at boarding time. Johann had tried to watch in every direction for them. Had they still been overlooked somehow at the station? Maybe they had arrived at the last moment and were installed in a different wagon. There was only one way to find out so he got up.

"I'm going to have a look around to see what there is to offer." He didn't wait for a response and instantly disappeared down the corridor.

Fifteen minutes later he returned to his seat and sat down quietly, gazing out the window without really seeing anything at all; not the landscape sliding by, not the trace of sun lingering low in the sky, not the few dwellings almost abutting the tracks, nor anything else. No sign of the Peers family had been found anywhere; they were definitely not on board this train. What could have happened to them? When he had spoken with Maria everything seemed to have been in order. His head was spinning and he didn't know what to think now.

Gradually, as the less than two hour journey to Hamburg noisily rolled by on iron wheels, Johann came back to himself, shaking off a feeling of helplessness. By the time they stepped off the train and onto the platform swarming with people at the Hamburg-Altona station he had collected himself enough to be able to assist with the next stage of their journey, not so much by choice but out of necessity. He was needed because within seconds after arrival the two families were beset on all sides by hotel room agents waving brochures under their noses while shouting out the advantages for emigrants to stay at their accommodations. At times it seemed close to breaking out in fisticuffs among the aggressive salesmen, so bent were they on trying to secure new clients at the expense of competitors. The language and cultural confusion that had existed before the cession of the Danish-administered Holstein city of Altona to Prussia in 1864 was now a thing of the past. But Altona, on the fringe of Hamburg, remained separate and a predominantly Jewish city. Ever since the duchy of Holstein had come entirely under Prussian dominion territorial divisions had been erased.

Along with constant pestering by hotelkeepers and coachmen vying for their business, money-changers and ticket salesmen provided additional harassment. Fortunately for them, the families had been forewarned against allowing themselves to be taken in by the hawkers, often making pitches that would later prove to be untrue. Johann had eventually spotted an actual train representative, unmistakably identified by the uniform he wore, the same as pictured in the official poster attached to the station wall behind where they stood. Aware enough by now to brush off the others as if they were annoying flies, Johann approached him.

145

"Can you assist us, please? We are in much need of your help. Our family is looking for a hotel, one that's safe and where we can reach the harbor without too much difficulty."

"Don't worry. That's what I'm here for. Follow me to the station office—just ignore the rest of these vultures around us. We will soon get you sorted out with a good proposition. It seems by your number you are emigrants, not migrants intending on staying in Hamburg? Our office can provide advice on what you will need to get started and it can also help with arrangements to get your family to your vessel on time for departure." His voice of calm authority in spite of the station's chaotic activity had obviously been well-honed in dealing daily with the same predicaments and anxieties facing new arrivals.

"Thank you very much, sir. We were told to expect to be propositioned but were not ready for such an onslaught. It was like being under attack by a swarm of angry bees!"

"We hope to put an end to this kind of situation soon. It's a nuisance and embarrassment in more ways than one. There are plans right now to ban hotelkeepers and other runners soliciting business from new arrivals from inside the station altogether. They will first need to be licensed to operate and then only outside the building in the future. This will buttress the benevolent association to protect emigrants that's been in place for a few years. As it is now, emigrants are still often lured to shoddy establishments on a verbal promise of special pricing. Without seeing a written price list first, they are led to a hotel only to find they will be paying more than expected for inferior meals and rooms lacking proper sanitary controls. This will change soon but not overnight. More laws to protect emigrants from being exploited are now in the works."

In his efforts to handle the train station mayhem it occurred to him that he was the one speaking up this time, not his older brother who usually was in charge these days since their father remained distant and listless. His brother's absence had unconsciously propelled him into taking responsibility for the welfare of the family. Chronologically speaking, he was indeed next in line behind his father in age now but still so much younger than Hinrich. So just as with Hinrich, when father had become son and son father, it was Johann's turn to do the same.

True to his word, the station representative provided a list of three reasonably priced lodgings in Hamburg to examine. Travelling by large wagon from the Altona station, they found the first one they visited to their liking and decided to forgo taking the time to look any further. It was on the edge of the old town, a desirable location away from the questionable suburbs of St. Pauli and St. Georg. And especially preferable to Veddel, the even rougher quarter surrounded by the harbor. Their stay in Hamburg for only three nights would still leave them plenty of time to shop for supplies such as utensils and additional clothing they had been advised to take with them on the voyage to America.

After they had looked over their rooms, Johann and Peter made arrangements with hotel reception to have transportation ready to take them to the Hamburg docks for the morning of the 3rd of March. The ship was not to sail until evening, but they didn't want to leave anything to chance. In any case, they were required to be at the port well in advance for health screenings, as well as vaccinations, if needed. Even though the conditions were fair at the moment, weather in March could turn nasty in hours, impeding even a short journey to the port.

On the following morning, the two brothers took off by themselves to explore the various quarters of the city. In front of a pharmacy on the first corner they passed there was a rack of newspapers for sale. Given the number of competing Hamburger papers to choose from, it was a wonder how there could be enough going on and inhabitants living there to support a local press with so many different titles. It didn't take them long to find out as they passed by large building after large building, shop after shop, neighborhood after neighborhood in what was beginning to feel like a city without end. Multistoried buildings had apartments or offices on the upper floors with shops below on the ground floor. Some of these stores looked very expensive, but overall neighborhoods of the city were diverse in appearance of affluence.

One of the most impressive building groups faced the *Aussenalster*, a lovely lake with large, handsome single family residences encircling it. They managed to complete a circuit of the lake before asking directions twice to find the way back to their hotel. Weaving through the impassive faces of the throngs, curiosity carried them through the *Altstadt* and by the front of the *Rathhausmarkt* then on from the central marketplace square to city hall before reaching the *Neustadt* section of Hamburg's inner city. All along what struck them the most was that no one seemed to recognize anyone else on sidewalks and streets, no one stopped to talk for a few minutes, there wasn't the slightest acknowledgement of someone's existence, save for an occasional "excuse me" in accidental brushing of arms; it was just a constant stream of impassive bodies trudging back and forth seemingly getting nowhere and knowing no one.

By the time they returned to their hotel they were footsore

and famished. Having eaten nothing all day during their urban adventures—acute awareness for the need to save every *pfennig* for America had become a family habit by now—and stopping only briefly to admire the monumental architecture of buildings and the landscape, they devoured the evening meal before falling exhausted into bed immediately afterwards. Like the curious cat which must have a look into each room, snoop in every corner and know every entry and exit before settling down and relaxing in a new home, the thirst to become familiar with their new surroundings had been well-slaked in a single day's wandering about. Sleep came soundly until the vibrant city sounds of morning penetrating through the window panes woke them from their dreams.

BALLINSTADT

Veddel, State of Hamburg, Germany, Summer 2008

After visiting tranquil villages and towns of Holstein where ancestors had lived, and then as far north as the city of Schleswig itself, we drove south towards the Free and Hanseatic City of Hamburg. It was big, sprawling and bustling in beautiful summer weather, the kind of temporal weather that beckoned so strongly it seemed impossible for anyone to stay indoors. The second largest city in Germany after the capital Berlin, Hamburg's importance reached back to the Early and High Middle Ages, to the period when it participated in a loose trade alliance with other northerly cities. It had even gained significance before the formalized trade agreement had been negotiated between the Holstein city of Lübeck and England, which culminated in the formation of the Hanseatic League in 1356.

At its height, the League comprised over three hundred coastal and inland city members whose locations enabled them to take advantage of ports on the Baltic and North Seas. Many of these cities to this day still reflect past affluence in the opulent architecture of the historic buildings made possible by the wealth gained from belonging to the League. Despite its demise in the mid-seventeenth century, the red and white colors of the League's symbols still play a role in signifying former trade alliance cities such as Hamburg.

By foot, as customary, we were once again reminded of German attachment to two-wheeled, self-powered transport on the city-wide network, combining sidewalks with bike lanes separated at a distance from the road itself. The side of the path designated for bikes only ranged in color from a pinkish hue to terra cotta, while the other side for pedestrians only was of a gray to dark greenish tone. Local cyclists appeared to be unfazed by tourists whose inattention at times took their wandering feet into the bike lane without looking to see if it was safe first. Strength in numbers had given cyclists a sense of entitlement power, a boldness to assert right of way no matter what the circumstances; they were not about to yield or stop for interlopers. So the season-fueled enthusiasm for feeling the wind in their faces and speed presented a constant risk of mishap, particularly in the more congested areas of the city such as around the central lake. Nevertheless, we managed to somehow stroll around without incident, but sometimes only narrowly avoiding accidents by the skin of our teeth.

As alluring as parts of the city were to visitors, central Hamburg was not the main attraction for us, but the harbor area was. A recently established museum had risen out of dilapidated old docks with the intention of capturing the story of millions of passengers who had sailed to the new world from its nearby piers. *Ballinstadt: Port of Dreams* had first opened its doors in 2007, just a year before our arrival in the city. First impressions were of a fairly small scale museum, which turned out to be the case. Exhibits were still in their infancy we would later learn. Much expanded and developed since our visit into a full-fledged graphic experience of what life in the so-called "emigrant city" was like during the height of outbound activity, it was better described in German as *Das Auswanderermuseum Ballinstadt Hamburg*. The inclusion of Hamburg in the title clarified its distinction from a rival emigrant museum; the *Deutsches Auswandererhaus* located in Germany's second major harbor city of Bremerhaven. Like most museums, it continues to be a work in progress, developing in size and depth as objects and displays are added or enhanced as the years roll by.

The trickle of emigrants leaving Germany beginning in the 1820s remained relatively small in number until the following decade. By the mid-1830s, the annual figure had more than doubled, from well-below ten thousand per year to over twenty thousand, departing mainly from Hamburg and Bremerhaven. But it was during the succeeding decades, from 1846 until 1890, that the rush towards exodus soared from an annual fifty thousand to more than two hundred thousand. Emigrants were not only of German ethnicity but made up of other nationalities as well, especially from countries in Eastern and Central Europe, like Russia and Austria-Hungary.

One of the most dramatic increases in emigration developed in the lead-up to and aftermath of the Pan-European revolutions of 1848. Dissimilar governing among the independent states of the German Confederation in terms of human and civil rights, living and working conditions of the working class, and other fundamental democratic freedoms were major factors leading to liberal-led uprisings. Eventual quelling of rebellions spurred swelling numbers of political refugees, some of whom marked for retaliation, to escape overseas to America and other countries. Cities in Wisconsin, Ohio and Texas were places where many *Forty-Eighters* chose to make new homes. But not all of them.

Concurrently, Schleswig-Holstein saw a group of its people voyage overseas in 1848 to rural Scott County in Iowa where support for home country causes continued *in absentia*. Unlike many other newcomers who sought work and fortune in a newly adopted nation's cities, émigrés from Holstein intended to emulate the farming life they had left behind. From the rich soils of Iowan farmland, American-based dissenters hoped the duchies of Schleswig and Holstein would become part of the German Confederation, as a unit as they had been historically, and there would be an end to Danish government involvement altogether.

However, even in German-oriented Holstein, neighbors with Scandinavian heritage lived side-by-side those with Germanic surnames. As evidenced by censuses, families with surnames ending in the typical Danish "sen", Claussen, Dressen, Hansen, Jacobsen, Jansen and Johannssen, for instance, were next door to those with distinctly ethnic German origins such as Altenburg, Behrens, Böhnke, Friedrich, Haselbusch and Lohmann. Intermarriage between the two ethnicities in generations past meant many individuals shared a genetic background with both identities, which would continue to be passed down to present day.

In 1866, when the Reither family pulled up stakes and left their village near Marne for good, Hamburg port facilities for processing departing emigrants were rudimentary compared to what was to come later, towards the end of the century. Readying passengers for the voyage was minimal during early years, medical and personal hygiene concerns only gradually inducing more stringent requirements to prevent outbreaks of rampant disease. One of the major turning points was the great cholera epidemic that spread throughout the city of Hamburg for ten weeks in 1892. Those housed in the sleeping halls and other lodging in and around the harbor piers of Veddel Island were particularly vulnerable to infection by the disease.

Some ten thousand deaths resulting from contamination of drinking water propelled a greater awareness of public health issues and a call for action needed to address them. Poor emigrants, including many Jews from the Pale of Settlement situated in the western region of Imperial Russia—today's Poland, Lithuania, Latvia, Ukraine and Belarus—and heading for Hamburg bore much of the burden of blame. Repercussions from the epidemic and other factors led to a drastic drop in registered emigrants, from over 140,000 in 1891 to a figure of around 40,000 in 1894.

New screening control regulations at German frontiers put into place in 1895 were maintained by the steamship companies themselves to deter another contagion from breaking out. Henceforth, inspection of emigrants was to take place at German-Austrian and German-Russian borders at one of thirteen stations placed at railway stops. Medical examinations along with sums of money in hand in proportion to destination country requirements became the basis for granting or prohibiting entrance to German territory. Thousands failing the physical and financial tests were sent back to their country of origin.

Despite these and other measures to control health and improve living conditions of emigrants waiting for embarkation, their initial impact found the number of low-priced steerage passengers booking on the Hamburg-American

Line, perhaps unanticipated, continuing to dwindle. For a short period Russian émigrés were banned altogether. The *Hamburg-Amerika Linie* had been a leading German shipping company for years until then. Slowing of emigrant passengers during the 1890s, partially based on the earlier reputation of undesirable housing conditions in Hamburg as well as inadequate and filthy sleeping halls situated on the American Pier itself, required new thinking if there was to be any hope of reversing the trend.

Albert Ballin, the shipping company's president, in conjunction with the city of Hamburg, imagined a grander solution to ease the situation; it was predicated on a set of controls to methodically shepherd emigrants through pre-departure stages of the journey. Buildings composing a new complex on Veddel Island and specifically designed for housing, feeding and medical provision were constructed in 1901 with Ballin leading the way. The new emigrant village on the outskirts of the city, expanded and completed in 1907, was successful in alleviating most of the health concerns and inadequate lodgings pressures attributed to the city of Hamburg.

Orderliness and cleanliness were paramount to the facility, which included provision of housing and meals, quarantine quarters, disinfectant baths, medical examination and hospital treatment. Even disinfection of baggage to protect against disease transmission and ensure a healthy passenger, at least at the outset, was viewed positively by many newcomers. Nevertheless, brick wall confinement, regimentation and authoritarian style of organization made it seem more like a military base and prison-like to some whose motivation for immigrating to a new country in the first place was for reasons of conscription avoidance. The advent of *Ausswandererhallen* emigration halls made likelihood of acceptance by immigration authorities at destination countries more certain. Departure country government inspection and police participation provided an added measure of control. Only the practice of vaccinating steerage passengers during the voyage instead of prior to it, and the exemption of first and second class passengers from leaving-day medical examination, remained as holdovers from the past. Fines levied against shipping companies by U.S Immigration for passengers refused admission at entry ports were much reduced as a consequence.

There were several choices for making our way from our hotel in Hamburg to the Ballinstadt museum, but since we were starting early in the morning of yet another beautiful sunny day and had a good hotel map in hand, we decided a walking approach was preferable to taking a bus or train. We could take in the sights along the way in exploring a route crisscrossed with waterways before heading into the Hamburg borough of Veddel on the island of the same name. It was clear from the outset there would be no easy, straight shot that would lead us to the objective.

After many direction changes to avoid obstacles, such as major highways and industrial estates, bridge crossings and docks, and after making a number of wrong turns, we eventually managed to navigate the bifurcation of the *Norderelbe* river and canals. Finally, the welcoming sight of the first street sign indicating Ballinstadt was not far ahead came into view. A second sign, even closer, displayed a historical photograph of a woman with two children labeled *Hoffnung und Vertrauen*—Hope and Trust—which we took as an omen of both of what to expect at the museum and that we would soon be there! When we reached the line of brick halls housing the museum's displays, there could be no uncertainty from their pristine appearance they were not of vintage build. In fact, the original buildings, numbering more than the current six and long in a state of dilapidation, had been pulled down many years before these new replicas had been erected to reclaim a visual sense of the past.

The original emigrant halls did not exist at the time the Reithers left for America in 1866, all the same the recently built structures and their contents managed to evoke a credible atmosphere of a time and place in which they must have gathered to set sail at the nearby harbor. Perhaps the most memorable but deceptively simple display was of a large map of the Midwestern American states with dots placed on towns named after their German counterparts. In Iowa alone place names like Hanover, Königsmark, Coburg, Minden and, naturally, Schleswig and Holstein were among others highlighted. By the beginning of the 20th century there were over one hundred thousand German immigrants living in Iowa, exceeding by far ethnic groups from other European countries. Reproductions of ship plans and living quarters, garments worn at the time, travel trunks, posters, photographs, Albert Ballin's office desk, and other memorabilia rounded out our visit to what was a small scale start spread out over three of the six halls in a now much-expanded reenactment of bygone times.

Veddel train station was easy to find after leaving Ballinstadt. With the heat of a scorching day at its pinnacle, returning by foot was immediately ruled out as an option. A smooth ride of only ten minutes on the S-Bahn took us back to the city center where a light meal was complemented by quantities of water to quench a serious thirst. Germany continued to amaze day-after-day with its torrid summer weather that we never expected to see!

SHIPBOARD

Atlantic Ocean, March 1866

By the time they had slept three nights at the hotel, shopped for last minute provisions and viewed some of Hamburg's well-known sites during daylight hours, the Reithers were anxious to start the next stage of the journey. They were more than ready to make their way to the harbor and board the ship, casting off their previous lives to start afresh in the land they would soon call home. It seemed a bit bizarre to them that only three days away from the place they had known for generations and they had already mentally moved on. It was partially due to having to adjust rural-oriented thinking to the attention-grabbing cultural experience that was Hamburg; it had demanded their complete focus so there was little room left for nostalgic feelings of regret to trouble them.

But enthusiasm to depart had also as much to do with dissatisfaction with political changes and constant threats to normal life routines in Dithmarschen. Nothing could be depended upon to stay the same for long there, and the time to take a chance on making a radical change in their lives had come, as it had for many others; there was no longer an ounce of fear left to plague them in risking everything for the road ahead. Optimism for a better future had conquered all of their misgivings and earlier vacillation on the question of should I or shouldn't I go. So there was nothing left to tear at them in the last minutes before there would be no turning back. What remained was only an unbending determination to take the next step forward as soon as they could. And now the hour to leave the hotel for the port had come and the carriage waited for them in front of the hotel.

Next to go out the door after Christina, the two brothers paused and stood ram-rod straight to give a sharp hand salute first in the direction of the lodging then, wheeling around, towards the city in general before climbing into the wagon.

"What did you do that for? Who were you saluting?" Christina quizzed, as they squeezed themselves in beside her. "You're not in the military, and anyway I don't see anyone around to be saluting."

Glancing at his brother in complicity, Johann answered: "For many reasons, little sister. Without you trailing us around, we were able to see a lot here in Hamburg and have come to understand a bit of what this city's all about. So we wanted to give it the proper goodbye it deserves. Much more than that, though. We were saying goodbye to everything else we've known here too—not good riddance because the land of our forefathers will stay in our blood forever and be part of us wherever we go. We are champing at the bit to take the next step."

"And some of it had to with you as well, Christina. We just wanted to see what you would do. We knew our little Rapunzel wouldn't be able to keep quiet and let it pass," Peter teased, using the nickname for Christina's fondness in running her hands through and tossing her very long shiny brown locks about many times a day. It was a habit not so uncommon for a young woman of eighteen, one that might be linked to having had the Grimm's fairy tale read to her many times over when she was a child.

Lastly joined by their father with luggage already placed in the wagon by his two strapping sons, they set off for the harbor at the base of St. Pauli, reaching it in less than a forty minutes ride. Excitement rising in thinking the first ship coming into view was the one they would be boarding, it turned out to be a different ship anchored at another wharf altogether.

Tickets, medical and other papers found to be in order, and after passing a visual health inspection to detect any signs of present illness, they were allowed to pass onto the pontoons serving as floating docks for the steamers. Soon they were on board and shown the way to their quarters to stow belongings and to get acquainted with some of the ship's amenities. Once settled, the young people returned to the deck, scattering in different directions to take last looks of the land they were leaving behind. Eyes scouring the shoreline and elbows leaning on the railing, Johann's attention was broken by a tap on the shoulder.

"Leave me alone, Christina, can't you see I'm busy," he snapped in turning his head half-way around, fully expecting it was his sister pestering him again with more questions.

"Surprised to see me, are you? You didn't think you'd get away that easily, sir."

"Maria…Maria Peers! Is it really you? I can't believe my eyes. You're really here!"

"I promise you it's me, alive and in the flesh. I'm not an

161

apparition, you know. Not this time, anyway. Here, feel my hand then tell me that it's not real." In the mere touch of hands, no further words were necessary. Instantly he was transported back to the past, to when they had shaken hands for the first time outside the church in Marne. In that moment a bond between them had been made. The same magical feeling was repeated now.

"When I didn't see you at the train station, I thought something unexpected had happened. But I was still praying that your family hadn't changed their mind about going on the same train right up to the last moment. Then it pulled away from the station and I still thought you might be on board so I looked in every carriage."

"I tried to get word to you that we weren't going to be able to make the same train after all, but you had already left for St. Michaelisdonn. We took a later one to Hamburg on the same day instead. When we arrived at the station there was no way of knowing where you were, but I kept looking up and down the streets and around every corner everywhere we went anyway, even though the city is so immense. The streets seemed endless in every direction and broader than whole villages in places. There were so many people I didn't believe there was much chance of finding you."

"So that's it. Of course I had no idea of what happened to you. I was hoping whatever it was we would still be able to meet somewhere. If for some reason you weren't on board the Germania, then we'd just have had to wait until we were in America. Maybe not even until after we all arrived in Iowa, since we had purchased tickets all the way to Davenport from New York before leaving Marne."

"I'm sorry this happened, but there was nothing we could

do about it, really," she started to explain. "We broke a wheel on the way to the station and either had to wait for the driver to find a replacement or get another wagon. By the time we were ready to go again your train had already left long before. We had to wait for hours until the next one came. It was so upsetting to have missed you and I know you must have been worried even more. At least we knew what went wrong. Looking back, I know we should have stayed with our cousins in St. Michaelisdonn instead of at the Möller's in Diekhusen the day before leaving. If we'd done that we could have walked to the station in a few minutes."

With her arm resting on his, they circled the deck on a cloud of euphoria, almost strolling right past Christina and Peter near the front of the ship as they chatted.

"Ahem, you two passengers; have you already forgotten about your brother and sister now that we see you've found each other again?"

"Oh my gosh! We're so sorry Peter. I don't know how we could have been so rude. We didn't mean to ignore you, not in the least," Maria instantly apologizing for the both of them.

"Don't feel too badly. We understand you both have good reason to be distracted. But it's so good to see you here, Maria. You had us all concerned about what was going on." From Christina's friendly look and words, it was clear she sincerely meant what she said. The minutes they had just spent alone together had been short, but that didn't prevent them from willingly joining the other two in promenading the deck until they bumped into the rest of Maria's family. Then Johann's own father came upon the group and friendly greetings, at least on the surface, were shared all around. Johann, notwithstanding the semblance of cordiality, was on the lookout for trouble between them from the outset. Almost immediately he sensed a subtle difference in his father's quick sidelong look at Maria still standing by his side. And when his father did speak a few words without looking at them directly and with a body that had become rigid as if to say a distance should be kept between them, Johann's own body stiffened as well. It all happened in the blink of an eye, but he was sure he wasn't imagining it. But he was probably the only one, besides Maria, who could detect the signs of disapproval from his father veiled as they were. But he would have to let it pass for the moment.

In less than two hours the gangplank was withdrawn, the rumble of the steam engine sending vibrations through feet, up legs and into their heads as the vessel shuttered into motion. It would be more than three hours before they reached the North Sea after slowly navigating the winding and island-strewn Elbe River at high tide. When they reached the river's mouth, they were not far from their old home again. It was a strange feeling seeing the profile of Brunsbüttel, a coastal town only seven miles from Marne, from a totally different vantage point. Soon after last nostalgic looks homeward were over, the Germania rounded the port of Cuxhaven on the left shoreline—the northernmost point of Lower Saxony clinging to the continent's edge—and turned southwards towards the English Channel.

Met immediately after passing the promontory by strong northwesterly crosswinds, the ship rolled and pitched through the white-crested waves, leaving passengers with heads spinning and stomachs churning like the sea itself. If this was what it was like at the start of their voyage on a relatively small body of water, what could they expect once upon the even rougher open seas of the Atlantic? Before finding out, they passed through the Strait of Dover with the French town of Calais on one side and the British town of Dover on the other side of the Channel. The ship docked at the port of Southampton before long where new passengers would be welcomed aboard and more cargo would be loaded into the hold. Hamburg passengers were encouraged to go ashore on what was to be a stay of more than three full days in port.

This time it was Christina who was first to jump at the chance to get a look at the ruins of the famed medieval defensive walls of the city they had heard about before. Peter was almost as quick to seize the occasion to sample a small taste of English culture in letting their father know the three of them would be going ashore together. Johann warned his siblings not to mention to him that Maria would also be joining them. Since seeing her again, his father's moodiness had become even more noticeable; he had not uttered a word to any of them after going to lie down after the encounter on the deck. They were all used to being in small fishing boats on the North Sea when waves were heavily rolling so they knew it wasn't seasickness that caused his silence. But it was better for everyone's sake just to let him be until he hopefully came around. In any event, Johann was not of a mind to let his father's feelings interfere with his own plans. If he was unable to accept his son's affection for Maria, then so be it.

Away from Hamburg and their Dithmarschen ancestral home for only a few days, the siblings were experiencing the first taste of a newly found freedom. It was like shedding trappings of the past when they left the bustling harbor and shipyards and headed towards the heart of Southampton. Shadowing the first segment of wall ruins closest to the port itself and overlooking the quays, they proceeded to the Arundel Tower and continued on from there to remnants of ramparts near the town center. With the sure-footed giddiness of youth left to explore by themselves, they were able to cover many of the town's cobblestoned streets while still finding their way back to the ship on time, thus avoiding ruffling parental feathers or causing alarm to the ship's crew. Besides, they needed to show trustworthiness if they wanted to be allowed to go ashore again during the next two days before the ship would continue onwards to New York on the 7th of March.

When it did set sail again, it wasn't long before the tedium of nothing but vast expanses of water day-after-day—except for the occasional sighting of an albatross soaring overhead—took over.

"If it wasn't for there being so many of us crowded together in steerage and the lack of daylight when you are below deck, this trip wouldn't be half bad." Johann was doing his best to shake his brother and sister out of the throes of boredom that had set in like a well-compacted dike, affecting not only them but apparently pervasive throughout the ship as well. Now on their fifth day out from Southampton, the ship had steadily plodded ahead on a course of mostly calm seas.

"Crowded is too lenient of a word," Christina, never at a loss for words herself, immediately rejoined, "for describing these conditions where you are always in the midst of noisy, sick or anxious passengers. There's no chance of any privacy in the sleeping cabins and you have to fight for a place to sit down on the benches at mealtimes. If you do find a place, it's always elbow-to-elbow. I know it can't be helped and everyone feels the same way but it's growing more and more tiresome every day. Sometimes it seems too much and I just want off now, even though there's nowhere to go!"

Not to be left out of the conversation, Peter quipped, "You can try swimming fin-to-fin with the pack of killer whales spotted this morning trailing the ship. I'm sure they would make room for you at the dinner hour. Just kidding, Princess Christina," he hastily added.

"You know I'm not the only one who sees the need for some improvements around here, like separate quarters for men and women, for instance, or at least sub-divided space for families. Remember in Hamburg, you were the one who wanted to buy extra bedding to make hard wooden berths a little more comfortable to lie in. And it was you who wanted to be sure we had enough knives, forks, spoons and plates just in case something happened and there were a shortage of them on board. So don't be so high and mighty with me. Have you taken a peak at the wood paneled saloon covered with beautiful paintings where the first class passengers dine? There's a piano and even the use of a library to keep them occupied. Our quarters are all right but nothing like that!"

"Don't take it too seriously, sister. I agree, with a few changes, they could make things better. I just don't want to let monotony get us down for long. We've heard all of the stories, seen enough waves, walked on every plank where we're allowed to go a dozen times by now. So we need to think of something else to keep us occupied besides drinking lukewarm tea or coffee with dry biscuits and the so-called butter—not to mention soups of all the unidentifiable varieties imaginable and potatoes tasting nothing like the ones at home."

"It's easy for you to say, Johann. You have Maria to keep

you interested when you're not with us. Her parents seem to have changed their opinion about you for some reason and are now almost as smitten with you as she is. From what you told us about her father's attitude towards you before we left home, it's a turn of a hundred and eighty degrees and you've practically become one of their sons now!"

A half blush slowly formed below his cheekbone while the effect of her comments creased the corners of his mouth at the same time. It was true. He really couldn't account for why Maria's father had changed his opinion about him. It did seem he had actually begun to like him. Maybe it was the fact they were all starting out afresh on a new venture, or it could be the positive portrait Maria had painted and repainted of him to her parents. Even his own father's disrespectful attitude towards Maria may have served as a lesson to banish the same feelings towards him. Something had changed for the better and Johann was glad no matter how it had come about.

Now if only his father could be persuaded somehow to feel the same way about her. It seemed like a hopeless task since his stance only seemed to harden as days passed. His barely disguised distaste for their relationship had evolved into avoidance of the Peer family altogether, something not so easily accomplished sequestered as they were to the confines of a shipboard home. Indeed, complete avoidance was impossible, and when paths did eventually cross, they met with only minimal acknowledgement.

During that night the outdoor temperature dropped substantially. And the normal tunnel of wind generated by the ship's forward progress was negated by an equally strong, countervailing one blowing down the deck from the stern. The few passengers who took a last stroll before going below enjoyed calmness hitherto inexperienced on deck. It was like the ship was at a standstill—just as when they had been occasionally bereft of summer breezes and in the doldrums while out fishing on the Wadden Sea. For the first time since the voyage began the flag barely moved, either hanging limply or with just a whisper of a flutter. It was a welcome gift for once not to have to tightly grip hats and neck scarves while struggling to hear the words of companions by aiming ears towards mouths. When they returned to their cabin the thought of others who had retired earlier crossed their minds; it was a unique and unforgettable kind of night, one that should not have been missed.

Johann and Maria were two of the fortunate ones. Slowly meandering up and down the various walkways, pausing at times at the railing to peer into the waters then into each other's eyes, they were free from formalities and family constraints. And when the hour grew so late that the evening must come to an end, it was with great reluctance that goodnights were finally said.

Even passengers most susceptible to feeling uneasy with the motion of the sea were able to fall into a sound sleep that night. And even from Emily, the sickly infant girl belonging to the family not far from where the Reithers slept who seemed to have been suffering since the beginning of the trip, not a whimper was heard. Johann soon joined his fellow passengers in undisturbed slumber.

In the early hours of the morning of the sixth day at sea, the abnormal atmosphere of windless serenity came to a sudden end—in spades. Tossed from side-to-side in their berths and sometimes from the berths themselves, the violent rocking of the ship shook them to the core.

"What on earth is happening—we need to find out," Peter sputtered while shaking Johann's shoulder with one hand and struggling to pull his pants on with the other all the while trying to maintain his balance in a badly listing craft. "Hurry up. Get dressed. Let's go upstairs," he urged with a body trembling in the morning chill and adding to his unsteadiness.

"Give me a moment. I'm coming."

Faces blasted by gale force gusts as soon as they stepped through the doorway, the two of them hugged walls and gripped handrails along the inner side of the deck's walkway. Life boats were swinging to-and-fro in their cradles and the main smoke stack itself appeared to be about to topple over under the pressure of the terrific force. Certainly it was no illusion that the three masts were straining to retain a vertical position. Crewmen who would rather have been hunkered down followed Captain Ehlers' orders to roam the decks for anything loose that needed tying down. When one of them sighted Peter and Johann, he emphatically motioned for them to return indoors, which they obeyed willingly.

Windblown and numbed to the bone by their brief sortie, it took a moment for them to regain composure after rejoining their family—a moment too long for Christina who glared at them with a posture demanding to know what was going on above. A lengthy explanation was unnecessary to provide the answers she wanted; disheveled appearances attended by the sound of the howling winds whistling down from the main deck and through the corridors into their steerage compartments nearly said it all. Equally unpleasant sounds— wailing, moans and groans—along with the murmuring of prayers greeted their ears as they crawled back into bunks.

Morning broke with most of the worst part of the storm

passed. A few patchy black clouds and sporadic wind blusters were all that remained to remind them of the nauseating and sleepless night they had just spent. Any rush to leave cabins to breathe fresh air again on the main deck was kept in check by seamen standing guard at the end of passageways. With over seven hundred passengers on board, an unmonitored flood of bodies above deck would be a recipe for chaos. And as anxious as the Reithers were to make their way outdoors to breathe fresh air again, they felt compelled to stay with their families and comrades, and especially with the family of little Emily, for her will to survive had given out sometime during the night.

Deaths at sea occurring on steam ships made of iron hulls and travelling faster by virtue of screw propellers had become much less common when compared to the much higher death rate of the nearly bygone days of the wooden sailing ship era. This was especially true with the more spacious and sanitary living conditions of the newer craft. But for Emily's family that would be of no solace. She was gone and no modern-day convenience could undo that. A Lutheran minister travelling in second class had already been summoned and a service would be held for her later that morning, after which her body would be given over to the sea.

ALMA

Central Coast, California, March 2009

Supplied with a wealth of information about my father's paternal ancestors in America from aunts and other relatives, the task of identifying the precise origins of the Reither family in Holstein had been given a huge boost. Using the names and dates provided for each of the individuals included— information which turned out to be more accurate than not when later verified by other sources—it was possible to focus on a narrow range of dates for when they most likely came to America. And before long, in searching online passenger lists, it was confidently documented that they had left the old country in 1866, two years after it had been invaded again and fallen under foreign jurisdiction. Hamburg ship departure manifests—a testament to the German gift for detail—had noted the exact village they called home when it was still in the Duchy of Holstein but not for long. It remained so only until later that same year, a few months after the Reithers had emigrated from Europe, when its short-term Austrian rulers were forced to cede Holstein to the more powerful Prussia.

To avoid the often time-consuming and futile effort of understanding microfilmed copies of German handwriting of birth, marriage and death records, a researcher had been hired to consult the archives in Schleswig as noted earlier. From his expertise, especially in relying on indispensable godparent connections, he had been able to push parish paternal family history back in time, tracking direct line Reither generations to the last decades of the 17th century. Danish 19th century census records had then been used to supplement parish records in filling in associated family members.

Discovering the truth about Alma Gerhard's European ancestry would be a more troublesome challenge to tackle. Only the sketchiest of facts about my grandmother were included in the black binder, along with a photo and article from a local newspaper; nothing had been mentioned about the names of her parents or where they came from before arriving in America. Clearly, she was not the primary focus of that family history project. Given all of the details presented on paternal Reither ancestry, it was an understandable omission. Since her maiden name of Alma Gerhard and birth in Illinois were the only clues to go on in starting an investigation into her history, working from recent generations backwards would be the only course to follow for her in researching her origins.

While my grandfather's parents had lived for ages in the same small locale in Dithmarschen before going to America, it was beginning to look like this might not be the same situation in her case. Federal censuses and several other sources were in agreement that she had been born and raised in Illinois. The censuses, as well as unauthenticated pedigree information often posted indiscriminately with errors to the *International Genealogical Index* website, pointed to only one of her parents of European birth: her father, Friedrich, was said to be from Prussia and her mother, Louisa, from Illinois. Back one generation further, the reported place of birth for one of her mother's parents, Alma's grandparents, was startling. Her grandfather's was noted as Germany, as expected, but totally off the charts was the birth place of his wife: **France**! Could this be simply an error in reporting or recording? Because it was the one and only written or oral mention of any relative with French nationality up until this point, it seemed definitely suspect.

From census record data on ages and places of birth of Alma and her siblings, it could be calculated that her family had migrated from Illinois to Iowa sometime in 1895 or 1896. A definitive answer as to why they decided to leave may never be known for certain, but one plausible scenario could be the timing of when Alma's father, Friedrich, arrived in Stephenson County. This was the county in which he established residence in 1882, when much of the choicest farmland surrounding village centers had already been sold to earlier immigrants. Five years after his arrival in 1887, Fred married Louisa, a descendant of earlier local settlers in the northwestern corner of Illinois.

Original German settlers had acquired a good deal of land from even earlier Anglo-Saxon pioneers. They were certainly among the most well-to-do of the inhabitants in the community. *Illinois Public Domain Land Track Sales* records show Louisa's father, Henry Meier, had purchased forty acres of public domain land for fifty dollars at a price of one dollar twenty-five cents per acre in 1846. According to a biographical sketch in the *History of Stephenson County, Illinois*, Henry eventually added to his earlier purchase, owning one hundred and eighty acres of farmland as well as thirty acres of timber by the time the volume was published in

1880. Alma's maternal grandfather, Jacob, also a significant land owner, purchased one hundred sixty acres for two hundred dollars in 1845.

Louisa, one of ten children, would not be so fortunate regarding land acquisition. Even though her father had married the daughter and granddaughter of two different patriarchs, there was no evidence to suggest that she benefitted from these relationships by coming into possession of land when she married. A minimum amount of acreage was necessary to support a decent living; dividing the land and parceling it out in smaller plots among ten children would not have been feasible for living sustainability. And it is likely female children would not have been recipients of land passed down even if it had been sustainable, expected as they were to marry a man of means. Alma, another generation removed as granddaughter and great-granddaughter of original land purchasers, would have been even less likely to see land transfer derived from marriage.

The rural area in northern Illinois in which they had lived comprised a group of four small villages. Local history chronicled the influx of early German settlers, a group of fifteen families arriving around the same time in 1845 and 1846 then founding a church of their native faith soon afterwards, in 1847. Although these German families were not the earliest to acquire land in the area, they still ranked as pioneers in creating a cohesive and enduring community, retaining farms and developing the villages for generations to come. During the next few years reasonably priced land located further afield became available on the property market in order to attract more immigrants—especially those from the area of North Rhine-Westphalia in northwestern Germany, the same place where many of the first German settlers had come from. A few years later, the completion of the Western Union Railroad in 1859 would create another growth spurt in the village nearest to which it ran to the detriment of the other three. Other events would impact the group of villages, but all would manage to survive through good times and bad.

That Alma Gerhard's parents might have heard of better prospects for acquiring a farm of their own in a town some three hundred and seventy-five miles away in Iowa remains speculative, but there they went with children in tow, according to census and other documents. Farm work was stated as her father's occupation from 1910 to 1930, and the letter "O" placed in the Occupation and Industry column of the 1930 form indicated a person working his own farm.

***

Setting aside life in Illinois and Iowa for the moment, new leads were sought to ferret out Alma's ancestral roots in Germany, and possibly in France as well. Her father, Friedrich, going by Fred in Illinois, was selected to be the first to focus on because he and his parents had been born somewhere in Germany. As an initial step the massive sixty-seven volume set of passenger data entitled *Germans to America* held at the local family history center was consulted to see if any of the Gerhard families in question appeared among the over four million names listed. An online equivalent data file, non-existent at the time of research, can now be accessed from anywhere. Using immigration dates gleaned from federal censuses, the search for passengers with similar names could be narrowed. Both Friedrich, under the forename of Fritz, and his brother Carl were located on the vessel Wieland in 1882; their parents and three younger siblings were also spotted but in another volume, arriving in 1883, more than a year after the two brothers. Both family contingents had left from the port of Hamburg, which had been auspicious for tracing them later because they just as easily could have gone from Bremerhaven. If they had, their home before coming to America might never have been discovered since those ship manifests were intentionally destroyed years ago.

With arrival dates in New York verified, and the name of the ship known upon which they travelled to America, the next step in searching online for their names and home residence, hopefully noted on the German passenger lists, would be much easier to undertake. And this time corresponding entries for 1882 were found with both satisfactory page image quality and legible penmanship. Alongside the names of Fritz and Carl Gerhard in the *Bisheriger Wohnort* column, their previous residence of **Bernstein Brdbg** had been penned. But a search for Bernstein, seeming to be as much a person's surname as a place name, did not reveal a town by that name when it was looked for in conjunction with Germany. Perhaps the spelling was incorrect, just imprecise enough that close approximates were not even offered as alternatives? Or possibly it wasn't the name of a true village or town after all? But that would be unusual for German care with details. Checking the 1883 manifest for any indication of former residence for the parents and siblings of Fritz and Carl became the next objective. In 1884, over a year later, in identical handwriting, the words **Bernstein Brdbg** appeared again. The evidence needed to confirm this place as their home residence was now almost certain. But where was it?

In coupling Bernstein with Prussia instead of Germany—ignoring the **Brdbg** part for the moment—a second attempt at searching produced a slightly different result and two of the hits looked like they could be solid leads. In former times, there were at least two places named Bernstein, both located in present-day Poland: the historical province of the first listing was Pomerania, the second Brandenburg. Now it was the time for those five little letters of **B-r-d-b-g** to play a crucial role in establishing which of the two provinces the Gerhard family belonged: clearly they were the five letter abbreviation of **Brandenburg**! Further investigation disclosed there actually was a small town named Bernstein that had existed in the administrative district of Kreis Soldin, a county in the Prussian province of Ostbrandenburg, part of the East Brandenburg region of Neumark prior to World War II.

Over the centuries before the war, the same area had also been part of the province of Pomerania at various times. Following cession of German lands east of the Oder River to the Soviets after the war, new Polish names were created to replace their German predecessors: the town of Bernstein became **Pełczyce**; Soldin changed to Choszczno; and Brandenburg elongated to Zachodniopomorskie, the Western Pomeranian Voivodeship. Bernstein, the very town in which the Gerhard family had dwelled before they immigrated to America had now been nailed down and one mystery had been laid to rest. Or had it? At least the 1920 U.S. census was supportive in uncharacteristically citing Brandenburg instead of the more typically found country of Germany for the birth place of Alma's father.

The story did not end there.

Around the same time the volumes listing passengers had divulged the names of the Gerhard family members leaving from ports in Prussia in 1883, the marriage license for Alma's parents had been requested from the *Illinois Regional Archives*, part of the *Illinois State Archives*. The *Illinois Statewide Marriage Index* had been used first to establish their date of marriage in Stephenson County. The document's contents were a windfall; there were loads of data scattered about on one of the longer, more detail-oriented marriage forms yet witnessed. Normal information, such as ages, places of residence and, of course, full names were included.

Neither Fred nor Fritz nor Frederick was written down for the groom's given name, as had been found in other records; for this important occasion his actual German birth name of Friedrich had been used instead. But atypically, the inclusion of occupations, farmer in his case, nativity and names of the parents of both Friedrich and his bride Louisa made it one of the most informative documents tracked down to date. The final piece of information about Friedrich, falling under the heading "Place of Birth", was boggling: it was not Bernstein that was listed but Barfelde instead!

The rest of the information on the document exactly matched what others had previously disclosed. But a birth place differing from what had been noted before was both disturbing and puzzling. It didn't seem plausible that the effects of time gone by from a marriage taking place only five years after Friedrich had left Prussia could be an explanation for a memory lapse. So what could be behind two different birth places beginning with the same letter of the alphabet? Could these words simply be variant spellings of the same town or village, or possibly even a conflation of neighboring

179

places? Sounding out how different pronunciations of Bernstein and Barfelde might be spoken made the first seem unlikely. And the spelling was different enough to suggest that they were probably not the same place at all. Then could it be, perhaps, because Friedrich Gerhard had lived in a different place at the time he left Prussia than where he was born?

Old paper maps drawn prior to World War II had already been used to place the small town of Bernstein less than five and a half miles from the larger city of Berlinchen. They were now consulted again, as were online maps, without success. Newer maps were useless because of names changing from German to Polish after the war. Finally, in searching a historic map database, on a sheet from *Germany, Topographical Maps, 1860-1965*, a likely candidate for Barfelde was sighted. Sticking out beyond the edge of the main map itself and barely visible in the margin reserved for latitude coordinates, **Bärfelde**, with an umlaut accent over the letter "a", was marked in tiny light gray print.

The old German map was highly-detailed, a spider's web of lines depicting small roads crossing one another as if a road engineer had gone network mad. Names of locales, no matter how small, all in gradients of gray and black for distinction denoted speckled forests, streams, lakes and railroads. Starting from Bärfelde on the sheet's edge and scanning across to the nearest towns among the morass of lines, the closest one in larger print was Bernstein! A clearer picture now emerged. For official purposes, such as boarding ship, the Gerhard family had probably decided the neighboring "big town" was a better choice for recording of last residence purposes. A town of around two thousand people a mile and a half down the road from Bärfelde, Bernstein must have served as the marketplace to a village of some three hundred and seventy inhabitants working ten to fifteen farmsteads in 1870. Bernstein would have been a place of more importance, perhaps even significant enough to be recognized by someone entering passenger information before a voyage commenced.

Because there was more than one place called Bärfelde in Prussia at the time, with and without the umlaut, using the online version of the standard geographical resource *Meyer's Gazeeteer of the German Empire* or *Meyers Orts- und Verkehrs-Lexikon des Deutschen Reichs* required caution to avoid confusion when dealing with German script. There were even two instances of Bärfelde in the same region of Neumark in the Meyers Orts. But since the nearby town of Bernstein could be used to zero in on the right area and the little village, it was easy to tell the more concise entry in the volume was the right one. It was disconcerting, however, to find the associated Meyer's Orts map incorrectly labeled Bärfelde as Beerfelde, slightly tarnishing its reputation as an authoritative source and the perception of peerless German precision!

A single instance citing this small village on a marriage license was not enough; it called for additional support. If the Gerhard surname appeared on other historical vital records naming Bärfelde as place of birth, the odds were high that these people might be relations. Also, in the event that Gerhards were found still living in the village, there might be a possibility of fitting them somewhere in the ancestral line. This was extremely improbable, though, because under Polish governance expulsion of ethnic Germans quickly followed the conclusion of the Second World War and the village of Bärfelde had then been renamed **Bolewice**.

The question was to whom such an inquiry should be

directed. Were old East Brandenburg records kept in Germany or in Poland? Or had they disappeared altogether during the course of multiple wars? Online resources indicated these old German records never made it to archives in Berlin but had fallen into the hands of their Polish inheritors. A first attempt in contacting the archives at one of the most likely Polish states turned out to be misdirected, but the response received contained both bad and good news: the current whereabouts of the church books for Bernstein was unknown, however civil records for certain dates were located in the Polish state's Civil Registry Office. Provision of referral contact information inspired a second email effort:

> Archive research request
> Monday, August 31, 2009
> To: State Archives in Gorzow Wielkopolski, Poland

> Please accept my apologies for writing in English rather than Polish. I hope you will be able to forward this request to a staff member who will understand.
> I have recently learned from the Archiwum Państwowe w Szczecinie that the State Archives for birth, marriage and death records for the parish of Bernstein (now Pełczyce), including the hamlet of Bärfelde (now Bolewice) in Standesamt Gross Mandelkow (now Będargowo) are located at the Archiwum Państwowym w Gorzowie Wielkopolskim.
> I am interested in locating any Civil Registration Office records for my ancestors. The ancestor surname I am looking for is Gerhard (sometimes spelled Gerhardt). Any birth, marriage or death records from Bärfelde or Bernstein (Bolewice or Pełczyce) would be of interest.

My great-great grandparents and their children immigrated to the U.S.A. in 1882 and 1883. Before that they were farmers in the small village of Bolewice (formerly Bärfelde near the town of Pełczyce (formerly Bernstein located in the present day Choszczno district and province of Zachodniopomorskie.

I understand your records probably do not start before 1874, but I am hoping you will be able to find vital records after that date.

Thank you/Dziekuje.

Almost on the verge of giving up after three weeks went by without a reply, a message appeared making it worth the wait:

Tuesday, September 22, 2009 11:22 PM
From: State Archives in Gorzow Wielkopolski

The State Archive in Gorzow Wielkopolski informs that in its resources we do not have a directory for the Book of Civil Status Będargowo (Gross Mandelkow). Desired marriage books from 1874 to 1900 and the name of Gerhard were not found. Birth and death records from the above mentioned books from 1874 to 1905 were found as follows:

1. Death certificate: Emma Augusta Elise Gerhard - death in 1887 (father Martin Gerhard, mother Ernestine from Gerhard's house).

2. Birth certificate: Emma Augusta Elisa Gerhard - born in 1887 (parents as above).

3. Death certificate: Luise Zimmermann from Gerhard's house – born Luise Gerhard, died in 1896.

If you are interested in receiving the above mentioned metrics then please contact us and a quotation will be sent.

Best regards,

Danuta Z.

There were a series of subsequent emails about payment methods, bank transfers and incomplete transactions, all made more complicated by the language barrier until the initial request for records was nearly lost in the haze of governmental bureaucracy. Months later, in April of 2010, a zip file arrived attached to an email; three full birth and death documents, scans of the originals, had finally arrived! And Bärfelde as proper residence along with the Gerhard family surname were marked in recognizable handwriting for each of the concerned parties.

Related as all three items were to a single farm household, and seeming to be the only documents in the post-1882/1883 archive—the years when Alma's father, his parents and siblings had immigrated—a tentative conclusion could be drawn that during the last decade of the 19th century there was only one household occupied by individuals bearing the surname of Gerhard among the handful of farms in Bärfelde. How long they continued to live there after the close of that century and nearly the first half of next one, between 1900 and 1945, is unknown. Indisputable, though, was that they would have been summarily expelled along with the rest of ethnic Germans living in East Brandenburg and removed to the other side of the Oder River when Poland took over at the end of the war.

***

Establishing the home village of Alma's father had now been accomplished. Turning to her mother's heritage, the challenge of going back one generation further lay ahead. For while her mother Louisa's birth place was known to be a small town in the state of Illinois, the parents of Louisa, Alma's maternal grandparents, had been born in Europe. Henry, her maternal grandfather, according to census schedules, was consistently reported to have been born in Germany while her maternal grandmother's birth place vacillated between France and Alsace-Lorraine, depending on the year of the census. Was she really of French ancestry then? And what was her actual birth name? A potential French connection sparked an interest in pursuing the origins of Alma's maternal grandmother first.

Alsace-Lorraine obtained its name as a territory when it was acquired as spoils of war from France by the German Empire in 1871. As a region, it had bounced back and forth between Germanic and French possession over the millennia. When Louisa's parents immigrated to America in 1849 it was still part of France, but because of its long contested history it was comprised of peoples of both French and German ethnicities. In the larger area of Alsace, the majority of the population was ethnic German speaking several different German dialects among themselves while reserving the official language of French for all other occasions. At times there were even penalties for not speaking in French in public, such was the political sensitivity. Nativity and mother tongue data collected in the 1920 U.S. federal census for each person born outside the United States, as well as the same for their unlisted father and mother if they were foreign born, provided a clue to which side Alma's grandmother fell on the ethnicity fence: while nativity was noted as France, her mother tongue was German!

Alsace-Lorraine, presently part of France, encompasses a large area. To continue the hunt for the actual birth place for Alma's maternal grandmother would require deeper research; her maiden name, or the surname of her father would be necessary. Happily, the unusually informative Illinois marriage record for Alma's parents that had exposed her father's specific birth place in Germany also provided the same critical information for the names of the bride's parents, including the birth name of Louisa's mother. Another visit to the online Illinois marriage index determined Louisa's mother, Barbara Wendt, had married her husband in 1848, a date later confirmed after obtaining a copy of the actual marriage record. But that's all it managed to do, because this record for Alma's maternal grandparents was bare bones.

Entering all of this information into an online database search resulted in a possible lead on Barbara's birth place. In several questionable genealogical databases the birth place name of Medesheim was given for her in multiple entries. It appeared, due to identical details for both Barbara and her husband in each of the different databases, that there was likely only one source from which the same data had been shared and copied into several family histories citing her as an ancestor. Without supporting documents, this practice is sometimes the origin of erroneous information becoming widely spread.

Fearing this was the case, the place name of Medesheim would need to be located as a real place somewhere in Alsace-Lorraine before it could be believed as really existing. It was not. Next, an online list of town and village names in the region was scanned for all those starting with the letter "M" and resembling Medesheim. The one entry that stood out was **Mietesheim**. Distinctively Germanic sounding, the commune of Mietesheim was spotted on a map of the Bas-Rhin department of Alsace, France. Scattered to the south on the same map were many other small farming communes with names containing the suffix "heim", meaning home in German. The influence and legacy of ethnic German occupation of these lands was indisputable, inscribed in the very place names themselves, even though they were now in France. Current borders with Germany lay sixteen miles away at their nearest and only twenty-seven miles separated the major French city of Strasbourg from the little village of Mietesheim.

France has done a remarkable job in digitizing many civil vital records and making them openly accessible; the records for the Bas-Rhin constitute part of them. Although still time-consuming to use because of needing to search year-by-year for vital records, pay dirt was eventually achieved with the discovery of not only the 1830 birth of Alma's grandmother but the birth of Alma's great-grandmother and her parents as well. Any questions about Alma's maternal European origins had now been eliminated by two generations of proof. Particular to the times, official forms were in French with German names converted to French equivalents: Jacob to Jacques, Barbara to Barbe, Johann to Jean and Margaretha to Marguerite. Within Germanic households, German language still remained the preferred means of communication, testified to by names later found in documents for the same individuals who had immigrated and become American citizens.

187

***

Henry Meier, Alma's maternal grandfather, reputed to have been born somewhere in Germany on census surveys, was the last of her ancestors to be tackled. The first nugget of gold found was in the 1870 federal census form for Stephenson County, Illinois. Instead of Prussia or Germany, the more specific Lippe Detmolt was entered for his place of birth. Two facts were gleaned from basic background research: although pronounced as if it there was an ending "t" in the second half of the name, the true spelling was Detmold and the correct name should have been **Lippe Detmold**; secondly, Lippe had never been formally incorporated into Prussia. It had become part of the North German Confederation in 1867 and, in 1871—only a year after the 1870 U.S. census and long after the Meier family had immigrated to Illinois in the mid-1840s—a state within the German Empire. At the time of their departure, Lippe had been an independent principality equivalent to country status, just as the 1870 census had accurately recorded and similar to present-day Monaco. Currently, the district of Lippe and its capital city of Detmold reside within the German state of North Rhine-Westphalia.

But where had the Meier family actually resided within the Lippe district? Another search of the *Illinois Statewide Death Index* for a possible death record for Henry Meier became the next objective in drawing nearer to the answer. There were two possible hits in the Pre-1916 death records for decedents with the same name: the first person had passed away in 1901 at the age of seventy-six; the second, a man of eighty-two, died a year later in 1902. Both deaths had occurred in the county in which the family was known to have lived. Henry's date of birth, unlike many other relatives whose dates widely fluctuated, had remained stable in U.S. federal censuses surveyed over the decades from 1850 through 1900. His name did not appear in the 1910 census, giving rise to the assumption he no longer lived by that date. Regardless, if he was born about 1820 according to the censuses, he would have been eighty-two in 1902. So it was the second Henry Meier for which a request for a death certificate was made to the *Illinois Regional Archives Depository System*, the centralized place which holds older records should they exist.

When the letter containing the Physician's Certificate of Death came in the mail, eyes immediately roved down to line four, the "nationality and place where born" section of the document. Plainly written was **Brakelsiek**, Germany. The informant, whose name was not given on the form, must have been familiar with Henry's background and had a very good memory to boot. It was the breakthrough necessary to solving the whereabouts of the former home of someone who had left Lippe so long ago to come to America. And after plugging Brakelsiek into an online map search, it popped up instantly on the fringe of a large forest called Schwalenberger-Wald. The next question to be certain was whether or not Brakelsiek fit within the boundaries of North Rhine-Westphalia. Another search yielded the desired answer: Brakelsiek, Lippe, Detmold, Nordrhein-Westfalen, Germany.

The heritage of Alma Gerhard's maternal, foreign-born grandparents had now been traced to two villages: Mietesheim in France's Alsace-Loraine region for her grandmother and Brakelsiek in the Lippe-Detmold region of Germany for her grandfather. Save from knowing their specific residences, if they still existed, and visiting the villages in person, the research mission had come to a successful conclusion this time.

CASTLE GARDEN

New York City, New York, March 1866

The hazy glow from thousands of gas streetlights could be seen from the deck of the Germania as she slowly pulled ever closer to the docks at the southern tip of Manhattan Island. The faint outline of The Battery, the port where the ship would soon arrive, told them they were almost there. The Reither family huddled shoulder-to-shoulder to stave off the chill of a cold predawn March 17th morning and to share together their arrival. Without the artificial luminescence in the distance it would still have been pitch black. By the time the ship was anchored and the gang plank lowered in an hour or so, dawn would be upon them and the ghostly night's glow from the misty gas-lit streets would be extinguished.

At daylight the shuttling of passengers from the ship would begin, crowded into a flotilla of small boats ferrying them to the immigrant processing building. Looking more like a round fort than a welcoming center, its appearance was well-deserved. With thick walls made from light pinkish-tan stone, its initial purpose in 1811 when it was completed had been exactly that—a fortress. Even with modifications and additions over the years it had not changed much from its original design.

Well away from the Reither group at the other end of the ship, the Peers' family members had also gathered to watch the culmination of the voyage. After passing the halfway mark Maria's father had conceded that the two families should keep their distance from each another. Having observed firsthand how a casual mention of Maria and Johann in a brief conversation had set Johann's father off at the end of the first week—falling silent immediately then abruptly stalking off—mutual avoidance would be the best policy. He should not be given a reason for any further provocation, as unintentional as it might be.

The one other time he had tried to talk to him alone about the young people at the outset of the crossing he had been left swallowing his pride when reproached for permitting his daughter to engage in an inappropriate relationship. Trying to explain why he had changed his own mind to acceptance of their relationship instead had gotten nowhere, bringing the conversation to a swift end. Even after that exchange he had already thought it would be best if they were to steer clear of the Reither family for the remainder of the time. But that was easier said than done.

***

"Christina, stop for a moment. Wait for me." On the day before their arrival in New York Maria had run into Christina while pacing the deck for a breath of fresh air. She had not really expected to hear Maria's voice again since it had been some days since the incident that kept the two families apart; and her first impulse to keep on walking. It just wasn't worth risking any further stirring of bad blood between fathers even with Maria's father change of heart about Johann. However, against her better judgment, she did stop.

"Do you think we ought to be talking together like this, Maria? What if one of our fathers was to see us together and talking?

"We can't let them create problems between us, Christina. If they want to build walls, let them do it with each other. But not between us!" Just in case anyone might be nearby Maria took her by the arm and guided her over to an alcove behind one of the cabins running down the center of the deck.

"Listen," she began again, "tomorrow we arrive in New York and then we'll all be off to Iowa shortly afterwards. Let's make sure you and I, Johann and any of our brothers and sisters who would like to join us start off on the right foot. It's going to be so new and different when we get there that we'll all need to stick together."

"What can we do, Maria? We can't disobey our parents."

"No. You're right. We can't let them feel like we're doing that at the moment here on the ship, anyway. But I've been thinking the last few days about what we could do for later. I think we should get the young people together one last time before we land tomorrow. And I propose we choose a place and time tonight to meet. It's a bit risky, but if we're careful to keep a sharp lookout in each direction, we should be safe from unwanted eyes. We need only stay for a few minutes which should be enough time for all of us to agree on a plan in spite of our parents' attitudes." Maria had not held back in expressing her thoughts—outspoken as always in what she believed to be right just as she had been even as a child. It was part of her makeup, but sometimes she paid a price for it.

"Let me ask Johann. He's the oldest and if he agrees, then I think it's a good idea too and we should go ahead. We will need to be able to count on each other when we finally reach our new home. But let's figure out a secluded place to meet now; why waste time because I'm almost sure he will go along with it."

"Right where we are standing now seems as good a place as any to me. It's a big enough space for us all and about as out of the way as we can get. Let's say nine o'clock for now? We can change the time or the place if Johann has an idea for something better. I'll walk the deck a bit now and be back here in fifteen minutes to meet you again and hear what he thinks."

When Christina found Johann and told him about the idea, his first reaction was positive, followed almost immediately by the same worry of being seen by a parent and causing further problems between them. However, it lasted only a few seconds, the thought of seeing Maria once more before they all went separate ways in the morning overriding everything else. Christina, scampering back to Maria stopped in front of her, and without saying a word vigorously shook her head up and down to signal all was okay. Then backing up a step or two she swiveled on her feet and slipped away to rejoin her family before meeting again later that evening.

The Reither youth were all there under cover of darkness at the designated hour. Peter, Christina and Johann had left their father after he had taken to his berth to rest earlier than usual. It was not by chance that he had retired early; they had counted on it since it was their last evening before arrival in the morning. After the evening meal the conversation had focused on the need to be packed and well-rested in order to be ready to be on deck before dawn to watch the ship's docking.

What they were doing was a bit sneaky. But in their minds it could be justified in order to avoid the chance of long-lasting family feuds. Much larger now, counting eight in all with Maria Peers and her siblings, they were ready to begin. Given their number, it was impossible to go completely unnoticed. But they had all paraded around the deck in smaller numbers many times before so it wasn't likely much notice would be taken of a group of passengers sheltering out of the wind together. Then Maria stepped forward while sliding a sheet of paper out from beneath her coat. Rather than pass it around for all to read and take too much time, and after making sure she had everyone's attention, she began to slowly read a short paragraph:

> We the undersigned promise to remain as friends in our new home in America. We promise to work together when we can despite any obstacles that we may face. And we promise to come to each other's aid in times of trouble and to share in the joy of each other's successes. We stand united together.

It was simplistic in some respects, but Maria had managed to convey the essence of what were almost marriage-like vows in the pact. And positive responses were heard from all around. Signatures were then collected at the bottom of the sheet, Herman, who at four the youngest of the Peers, made his mark instead. In a few strokes of the pen an enduring commitment had been made. Dispersing into smaller groups after handshakes, the conspirators returned to their cabins for a short night's repose. But not before Johann's grip of Maria's hand had lingered a little longer.

***

Frosty winds whipped about as the two families looked down upon the first tender transporting passengers eased away from the side of the ship towards the shore. Soon after, the Peers family had taken another barge for the short trip to the immigrant depot at the Port of New York. They had all, thankfully, passed a cursory health examination conducted by officials from the Emigration Commission who had boarded the ship at first light and had already gone back ashore. The Reither family of four followed suit within a half hour, gliding across the last few yards of sparkling seawater to set foot once again on solid ground. The landing-stage was abuzz with customs officials directing passengers towards the rotunda where they would be ushered into the immigration center. As much as its mandate was to inspect documents and bodies, the center's purpose was also to protect and facilitate potential new citizens.

Long past were the chaotic days when it had first opened in 1855. That was the time when The Battery wharves were laden with schemers striving to relieve gullible immigrants of what little wealth they possessed. The reception they had experienced just a couple of weeks ago at the train station in Hamburg on the other side of the Atlantic would not be relived here. Control of nefarious activities inside the arrival center had been made a priority at the Emigrant Landing Depot of Castle Garden. Even the officially sanctioned military recruiters were no longer there to pester them with an offer of an immediate "employment opportunity" as a soldier.

Enlistment tents that had been outside the building itself but nearly unavoidable when exiting since the first years of the war had disappeared entirely by May of 1865, about ten months prior to the Germania's arrival.

Now men and women of all ages, some standing tall, some bent over from years of labor, some with a wriggling baby or toddler in their arms but everyone dressed in the fashion of the country they had just left, slowly advanced in the long line that led to the examiners tables. Questions were posed and health conditions assessed under a critical eye with the aid of staff speaking all manner of non-English languages before admission was granted—or not. Immigrants who were taken aside to undergo further interrogation did not escape notice by those still nervously waiting their turn and wondering what their own fate would be.

Only the Reither family had purchased American train tickets in advance before leaving Marne. But rather than leaving New York immediately after arriving, they had decided to spend the night in lower Manhattan. With the cost of accommodating a large family in an expensive city a concern, the Peers family had gone directly to the kiosk where railroad tickets were sold as soon as they had cleared immigration authorities. The first train would be departing in three hours so they had enough time to exchange money and visit the lunch counter. Davenport itself lay at a distance of almost one thousand miles due east of New York City. It would be another long trip and they would have to make several transfers en route before reaching Chicago. From the shores of Lake Michigan, sharing a southeastern border with the state of Indiana, the train would carry them from Chicago to Rock Island, the Illinois town directly across the

Mississippi River from their final destination of Davenport.

"I'll be back in a minute," Johann whispered in Peter's ear before leaving his brother to zip off towards the exit door. He had kept his eye on the Peers group as soon as he had spotted them ahead in the processing lane. When they left the building, Maria turned to look backwards. He knew for whom it was meant because she had seen where he was as well.

While harassment from often unscrupulous vendors had been banished inside the emigration center, there was no one to intercede once they had gone out the door, but Johann was by now adept at waving off with authority unwanted advances. He rushed through the crowd and caught up with them a hundred yards down a curving pathway, tapped Maria on the shoulder then took her by the hand pulling her back from the rest of her family. Before the others realized what had happened her cheek had been brushed with the palm of his hand and her shoulders squeezed then he wheeled around and went back the way he had come just as quickly. In a few more seconds her wide smile dissolved into tear tracks down the cheek so recently grazed, her parents only catching a glimpse of Johann's back as he receded. But they knew and were ready to comfort her.

"Don't worry about us, Maria. We don't mind. We've come to know he's a good man" her father began as soon as she turned around.

"Not now, father. I need just a minute. But thank you—and mother too. I do know what you think about him, about us, and it makes me very happy. But it's so hard not to be allowed to be seen together. We've been forced to tippy-toe around because...well because of one person. It's just not right. But I don't know of any way out of it."

They walked the short distance to a smaller dock with luggage swinging in rhythm to the cadence of their footsteps then onto the ferry that would take them across New York Harbor. From there it would only be a few more steps to the grand New Jersey train station where they would begin their travel westward. Still in a semi-daze from the two hours it took to clear immigration, they had started to find their land legs again. After the brief journey and now at the station, it wasn't but a few minutes before they found the right train to board. By the time they were seated and ready to start the last leg of the journey to the Midwest, Maria had recovered enough to sit back and reflect; the first thought that came to mind was the pledge the young folks had taken, and it made her feel good.

By now Johann had rejoined his family, the soul of a happier man reflected in his chameleon-like eyes; sometimes seeming deep blue, sometimes sky blue. Today, however, to an observer eye tint was unimportant, what mattered was that they were remarkably brilliant and alive. He had done what he could to give Maria a positive send-off. Now his family was off to one of the emigrant boarding houses in The Battery, not one they'd taken a chance on by choosing it themselves but one recommended by the Castle Garden staff. They had learned well from their experience in Hamburg!

Still, caution was needed. Forewarned of pickpockets around the dock areas and elsewhere, Johann's father decided before going down to breakfast the next morning to hide most of the cash converted into dollars at the emigrant center between layers of clothes in his suitcase. It would be safer kept in a locked room than carrying it around during the day with thieves in their midst.

"Does anyone need to go back upstairs, or can we get started right from here?" Peter, always eager to be the first one had stood up, dropped his napkin on the table and pushed his chair in.

"I think I'll change sweaters—by the looks of it out the window, the heavier one would be better today. It won't take me but a minute." Christina was joined by her father who had the room key and who also felt he might be underdressed for swirling March winds shooting down avenues and streets. Johann and Peter moved from the table to the lobby to wait for them. In literally less than a minute, Christina raced back down the stairs.

"You both need to go with me. Now! Father wanted to check to see that everything was okay with the money he hid. He can't find it and he's sure he's looking exactly where it should be," she sputtered breathlessly. The three of them were off in a jiffy, taking the stairs two at a time, faster even than Christina had descended. The door to the room was wide open and inside their father sat slumped in a chair obviously stunned. He barely looked up but when he did it was with a non-seeing stare. But inside his mind was churning double-time with thoughts vying for priority in trying to recall every move he had made before going downstairs to the breakfast room. Did he really place the money in the luggage or had he just imagined that he did? If he hadn't, could it still be somewhere in the pockets of his clothes?

He had changed to a second pair of pants in the morning because the other pair needed cleaning. But after rifling through the pockets again, he went back to the suitcase, this time practically ripping the contents apart in frustration. He refolded and unfolded again every item spread out on the bed, checked for the fourth time under the bed, between the bedclothes and everywhere else he could think of. It just wasn't there. Finally he collapsed into the chair once more, continuing to play out over and over again the movements he had made.

The brothers and sister began their own search, starting again with the clothes still laying on the bed, shaking each piece to be sure nothing was clinging inside a fold.

"Everything seems to be in order except for the things that father has rummaged through. Even the books I always carry with me are in the same place I left them. And the one I was reading last night hasn't been touched either." Storm's *Drei Novellen* lay open to *Veronika* face down on the small bedside table. Johann's words brought the searching to a halt. What he had just said had been true for rest of them as well for some time now. There was no evidence of a robber having ransacked the room in hunting for anything of value.

Their father was the only one who had come with a more-or-less proper travelling valise. The others had packed their meager possessions into modest-sized bags made of cloth, and all of them seemed to be where they had left them. And even his suitcase had given no appearance of having been moved or opened when he first had reentered the room. It was pointless to continue looking when every corner had been thoroughly searched and when their father could think of no other possible place where the money could be. Reality began to sink in: the bulk of their savings had disappeared in the hour between breakfast and returning to their room. It could only have been done by a person experienced in where money would likely be tucked away for safekeeping, someone who had known what they were doing and just when to do it.

"It must have been someone inside the hotel who had a key. We locked the door before going down to breakfast and it was still locked when Christina and Father went back. There are several workers here that we've seen in the halls and cleaning rooms. It could have been anyone of them," Johann said to himself while pacing from wall to wall. "What could be done now?" he pondered. "What we had to lose wasn't a whole lot for most people, but it was nearly everything we had. It puts us on the edge or maybe over the edge. We had nothing else of value to steal or that probably would be gone too. Luckily we kept our train tickets with us. We'll have to watch every penny we have left until we reach Davenport". His mind began spinning, like his father's but looking forwards instead of backwards.

"When we arrive in Davenport, Uncle Hinrich and Aunt Mathilde should be there to meet us," Christina chimed in. "Father, are you listening to me? Do you think there's any chance they would be able to help us—at least for a short time, just until we get our feet on the ground?" she asked in placing a hand on his arm holding a head in misery.

He slowly looked up: "My brother will always do what he can for us. But he has five mouths to feed and he's no longer as young as he once was to be breaking his back on a farm. It's a lot to expect of him. Besides, it's been over nine years since we last saw each other. Mathilde must still have her hands full with all of the children, although from the last letter they sent to us at home, she was still doing some seamstress work too when she was able to fit it in." More animated now, he added: "We must get started working as soon as we can when we get there of course, but I think they will help us with whatever they can."

The two brothers looked at each for reaction but saw only worried frowns. The words were encouraging, but after they were said he seemed to shrink in stature again, sliding further down into the chair in which he still sat. It was clear the theft was one more blow too many and it was eating away at his own worth. But on a positive note at least his words had been rational.

To escape the cloud of depression hanging over them they decided to spend the remainder of the day together taking in a few of the city's wonders. It was a needed diversion from an inauspicious start in a new land. They were aghast when they peered in shop windows—sometimes taking the time to wander into a few them—to see the high prices marked on common items such as a loaf of bread or a chunk of cheese, not to mention the scandalous out-of-reach cost of basic clothing. Even if their small resources had not been stolen, inflated post-war prices, which had already been higher relative to their home country before the end of the Civil War, would have prevented them from making any but the most essential of purchases. It seemed to them like every Tom, Dick and Harry shopkeeper was making a concerted effort to pave his own private street with gold!

WEST POMERANIA

West Pomeranian Voivodeship, Poland, July 2009

Just as had been done earlier in exploring small villages and surrounding towns for grandfather Johann Reither's roots in Holstein, a road trip was planned to experience firsthand the native homes of grandmother Alma Gerhard's ancestors. They had immigrated to America in two groups, a pair of sons arriving first in 1882, followed by the rest of the family in 1883. Even with all of the intervening years, everyday images of the lay of the land—the spectrum of colors defining the local sky, the contours of fields and forests, the qualities of the very air itself—all the attributes that make each area of the world different from anywhere else—would become ours to absorb. Taken together, they would become the unique impressions the Gerhard family would have carried with them to Illinois; and now the same images we hoped would soon become recorded in our brains. So a trip to what is now northwestern Poland was planned to acquire a basis for commonality by stepping into shoes of those who had left for new horizons so long ago.

When the Gerhard family departed the Neumark region of Prussia, it was part of East Brandenburg. Berlin was the largest city in the province at the time, roughly one hundred miles from the medium-sized town of Berlinchen, which was, in turn, less than eight miles from the tiny village in which they had lived. From Switzerland tickets were purchased for a flight from Geneva to Schönefeld Airport, Berlin's second largest, and a car booked for pick-up upon arrival.

Although we would be eventually staying in Berlinchen, now retitled Barlinek and to the northeast of Berlin, there were no sizable west-east roads leading directly to the town. The choice became either going further north or south to avoid multiple changes on a tangled mass of secondary and even smaller back roads. North was chosen as the better option for finding accommodation for the night in Poland so we struck out immediately from the airport for the large crossroads city of Szczecin. Formerly known as Stettin when it was part of Prussia then afterwards Germany, its position on the banks of the Oder River not far from the Baltic Sea itself was ideal for sightseeing on foot.

The central location of our hotel was also a good choice for learning about Szczecin's historical importance as a major seaport serving Berlin and other parts of Germany, and then Poland after the close of the Second World War. Parts of the medieval old town and many of the factories and other buildings were destroyed during the war. But Stettin's industrial interests were gradually revived, even expanded, when it transformed into Polish Szczecin afterwards. A variety of architectural styles coexisted: Classically-styled buildings from the Stettin period as well as Gothic and Renaissance structures from the more recent Szczecin conversion were melded with modern styles of the 19th and 20th centuries. Most of the older buildings were topped with the characteristic red-tiled roofs that were also often found on the minimalist modern ones next door. From the edge of the old town the port on the impressively wide Oder River was easily accessible for riverside walking. Ship loading and other commercial activities took place down river—far enough away to make the pristine appearing water and litter-free quays a noise-free sanctuary. Overall, the riverside ambience was relaxed and slow-paced in spite of being an integral part of the city where tourists are drawn.

The distance to Barlinek in Poland where we had pre-booked a room for two nights was about forty miles as the crow flies from Szczecin. Again, using a combination of larger and secondary roads, the actual mileage would have ranged between fifty and sixty-five miles, with the longest route actually the shortest in time because of the size of the highway. Not in a rush, the slower and less travelled rural route was taken to get a feel of what the smaller villages were like and to observe the countryside up-close.

A tidy small town with our residence facing the main square, perhaps the greatest attraction of Barlinek was its idyllic situation on the shores of a lake. Sail boats glided all-about on summer breezes while pedalos and rowboats plied the waters closer to shore as we meandered along on a sun-drenched afternoon. In past and present times as well, an attractive stretch of curving beach—called *Am Strand* on old tourist postcards from the pre-war German era—bordered the edge of town itself. Popular for lakeside promenades, or simply sitting on a bench looking out on placid summertime waters, views from the beach were enhanced by a v-shaped plume of water spouting from a large fountain offshore. When the distant forested background was combined with a smaller strand of green conifers nearby, the charm of the setting was undeniable. Traditional wooden buildings substantially sized along other sections of the lakefront completed an image of a peaceful place to visit for a number of reasons: natural beauty, fishing, walking, water sports, and simply unwinding in a healthy, uncrowded environment.

A visit to the Barlinek cemetery, the largest of the three burial places on our agenda, was made in the late afternoon to check for any gravestones with recognizable family surnames. Only large granite and marble slabs—around six by three feet placed flat on the ground or slightly tilted a few inches—were to be found, none with dates earlier than post-war 1940s. These lavish markers were typical for a contemporary Catholic Polish population obviously devoting a good deal of importance and expenditure to memorialize their dead. All traces of German Lutheran graves and markers from former times had been removed, repurposed for construction purposes. Conversely, German Jewish tombstones had been retained but removed from their original locations. They were now stacked in upright piles leaning against the interior of the walls encircling the cemetery.

According to the *JewishGen* website, there was a Jewish population of about one hundred thirty in 1880 out of total population of around five thousand in Berlinchen. By 1933, the number was down to thirty-three. This same ratio held true for Bernstein, the small town next to the Gerhard home village where a Jewish population of seventy out of twenty-five hundred total inhabitants in 1871 had dropped to twenty by1932. Small in number to begin with, the percentage had gone from around two and a half percent to less than one percent for both places in the fifty year span leading up to the

Second World War.

Next morning, the first stop was the smaller town of Bernstein, first noted on the 1866 passenger lists for the Reither family and at that time part of Prussia. Now known as Pełczyce and within Polish borders, Bernstein/ Pełczyce was smaller than Berlinchen/Barlinek, but it was still much larger than the pint-sized village just down the road; Bärfelde/Bolewice was the actual place in which the Gerhard family had lived before leaving for America. Although Bärfelde was disposed of a small chapel sufficient in size for its small number of inhabitants on most days of worship and especially convenient when winter storms were at their fiercest, the main church for official passage rites was the much larger one in Bernstein. Like many hitherto unheard of places, Bernstein was steeped in its own historical significance.

Before the town was turned over to Poland by Germany after the war, past centuries had seen Bernstein in the possession of Polish Pomerania at times and under Prussian Brandenburger control at others. Changing several more times, it passed into the hands of the Teutonic Knights then belonged to a Cistercian Order between the 13th and 15th. It was taken over eventually by a noble family by the name of Waldow, or von Waldow, in 1571. Under this family which had ancient associations to the Knights as well, both the town and its related lands were held in fiefdom.

Ultimately, Bernstein was restored to Brandenburg, thus putting an end to the longstanding rivalry among knights, religious orders and the bourgeoisie. Feudalism played a large role over these centuries during which time a major castle was built and later destroyed. Under Templar Knights, succeeded by the Knights of Saint John and Cistercian nuns, the surrounding villages, including Bärfelde, were also feudal estates where peasants were serfs, just as was Bernstein.

While walking the sites, photos were taken of three well-placed signs describing local churches and ruins written in both German and Polish. When we returned from the trip, these images were sent to longtime friends who meticulously translated the German texts into English. Valuable as primary sources providing historical background and details about the relatively obscure area in which the Gerhards had lived, the first sign told the story of Bernstein as a place of pilgrimage and miracles:

Church of the Birth of the Blessed Virgin Mary in Bernstein (13th century)

Pilgrim traditions

The village of Bernstein (Polish: Pełczyce) was known for various 'miracles' and soon became a place of pilgrimage for the faithful from Pomerania, the Mark and Prussia. The local worship of the Host (consecrated wafer) probably can be traced back to the visit of Bishop Otto von Bamberg in Bernstein and the surrounding area (1124), who at that time Christianized Pomerania. The church owned holy relics, among these probably an image of the Holy Mary that was said to effect miracles, that has been recorded in a document dated 1290.

In 1314, an edict of the Bishop of Cammin gave the nuns of Bernstein the rights of patronage over the chapel of Corpus Christi, which since the end of the 13th century had been the center of the pilgrimage.

209

In 2004, relics of St. Francis of Assisi (1162-1226) were brought from Italy to Bernstein. The founder (canonized in 1228) and patron of the Franciscan order (Minorite) had been worshipped in Pomerania since the 13th century. Several abbeys in Stralsund, Greifswald, Stettin, Pyritz, Greifenberg and Arnswalde are testimony to the worship of St. Francis.

A second sign specifically mentioned the little village where the Gerhard family had resided in the context of its larger neighbor of Bernstein/ Pełczyce:

The abbey of the Cistercian nuns in Bernstein

The abbey of the Cistercian nuns in Bernstein was founded around 1280 by the Margraves of Brandenburg. The property of the nun order included the Jungfrauensee (the Virgins' lake, polish: Jezioro Panienskie) and the castle with the peasants. During the following years, the estates of the neighboring villages and mills, the land for the construction of the abbey, as well as more lakes were added.

After the secularization of 1537, the estates of the order comprised in total eight lakes (current names: Male Połcko, Wielke Połckon, Panieńskie, Grodzkie, Kromieszńskie, Łakie, Trzebień and Diabelskie), the mills in **Pełczyce**, Sitnik, Rakoniew and Kukadio, each with several hides of land, as well as the villages Side, Ruwen, Niepöelzig, **Bärfelde** and Klausdorf; the estates also included four hides of land in Blankensee, two in Gottberg, three in Hohengrape, five in Jagow and the forest Buchholz (today Bukwica). In 1537, the estates of the abbey were turned over to the government administration.

And a third sign described the religious significance of the village of Bärfelde itself:

Bärfelde – a knights' village (1337)

The daughter Church of Our Lady of Czestochowa dates back to the 14th century; founded by the local knights, but probably under the patronage of the Bernstein Cistercian nuns since the 15th century. Alterations (windows and roof) were made in the 19th and 20th centuries. And a tower made of brick was built. The church, consisting of a single nave, built with stones taken from the fields, dates back to the 13th/14th century; it contains a statue of the Evangelist from the 15th century and a bell from 1691 (newly cast in 1900). The tower is on the west front. The western portal is made of stone. Two gates dating back to the 15th century have been preserved. The church was consecrated in 1946.

Bolewice was like taking a step back in time—to when the village was called Bärfelde, and maybe even way before that. It seemed to have been spared so far from the heavy hand of the developer. If there were a small shop or two, they were well hidden from the passerby, perhaps operating out of the back of someone's house or barn and selling local produce. A paved road bisected the village, with dwellings scattered here and there along either side. Although there were a handful of houses appearing to have been built during the 20th century, the bulk of the buildings showed the wear and tear of a much older vintage, many low-slung under typical red roofs with living area and barn combined into a single edifice.

There could have been some more modern structures somewhere in this small farming conglomeration too.

211

However, the lack of traffic—seldom a vehicle passed by as we walked down the side of the main road and only one parked car was seen on the chapel grounds—and the sighting of only one piece of shabby farm equipment near a decrepit and apparently abandoned farmhouse suggested differently.

The only living soul in sight stood in front of an ancient tan brick and stone housebarn. An elderly lady dressed in a long sweeping skirt, black blouse and pink peasant kerchief on her head held in one hand a bowl from which she tossed feed to hungry chickens and in the other a simple wooden staff. Above her, on the corner ridge of a steeply pitched roof, a scraggly stork's nest could be seen shaped like a massive round cauldron but of sticks instead of iron. Two storks perched on its top, one sitting and the other standing like a sentry.

Golden fields, some already cut down to stubble, some with tall barley stalks still upright in the heat of a windless summer sun, and some with a few trees mixed in to break the sameness completed a picture of rural tranquility. In the far distance several very large fields sprinkled with delicate blue flowers were bordered on one side by a solid green row of trees to mark off property lines.

Documents that could identify a specific residence for the Gerhard family had not yet been discovered. If old German census records had still existed for the area, they might have been helpful in narrowing down the location. Nevertheless, a true sense of their home territory had been gathered. With the objective of widening our coverage and forming a more comprehensive vision of the region, a driving tour through a nearby national park was made after leaving Bolewice.

Taking back roads once again, the views out the windows

of the car were striking; endless fields of enormous size and open countryside without any sight of human activity or agricultural machinery. The isolation and unusual depths of browns and golds on undulating terrain lent a feeling of being on some part of the planet that was alien-like. Then the small road suddenly changed from paved to cobblestones, becoming a bumpy, teeth-rattling ride for so long we wondered if it would ever end. How could there have been enough labor to have placed an infinite quantity of stones like grains of sand for mile after mile? They must have been laid long, long ago at a time when large scale manual labor was economically feasible! When we finally emerged from the rocky ride, secondary roads were a welcome change for a smoother trip to Soldin, the German town which gave its name to the district before the war but was now the Polish town of Mysliborz.

***

Berlin was our final destination and where we would return the rental car at Tegel Airport. When we had first visited the city long ago, it was twenty years before the Berlin Wall dividing the city had been torn down in 1989; reunification of West and East Germany had occurred the following year. East Berlin, entered via the Checkpoint Charlie crossing post in 1969, was a grim and desolate place back in those days. Slate gray winter skies matched dull gray buildings, some in complete ruin, others left pockmarked with shell and bullet holes from the war years before. Few people could be seen walking the streets and even fewer driving cars. In visiting the spectacular Pergamon Museum, the entranceway and exhibitions were guarded by only a handful of stoic and drably uniformed staff most of whom were women. The unrepaired condition of the building's dismal exterior belied the magnificence of its interior collections. Totally alone, we walked the length of the reconstituted Nebuchadnezzar's Processional Way starting from the Ishtar Gate. Constructed in about 575 BC in Babylon and acquired by the *Pergamonmuseum* in the 1930s, Nebuchadnezzar's walk involved dismantling, shipping and reassembling piece-by-piece like a jigsaw puzzle in the huge space set aside in the museum.

East Berlin was a place that was a bit unworldly in the sixties, with a foreboding atmosphere that could easily create a sense of paranoia in the tourist. When a group of young men milling about were met around a corner, their cold stares made for moving on quickly. Regardless, there was an abiding curiosity to know more about what lay behind the bleakness so the wandering of streets continued with eyes wide open. At the end of the day, a visit to East Berlin made one feel very fortunate to be able to return through the checkpoint back to the opulence of West Berlin when so many were forcibly kept from doing so. In no-man's land the famous Brandenburger Tor stood alone as a symbolic gate closed to East-West freedoms. A strip of land off limits and unoccupied, this fenced off zone was taboo to inhabitants on either side of the Wall and tourists could only view it from a distance.

But now, as we drove into a reunified city—intending to take a periphery route around Berlin's edge to avoid getting embroiled in modern city center traffic congestion—to reach the airport on the other side, a wrong turn took us directly where we didn't want to go. Like a magnet from which there was no escaping the force of its pull, we were drawn from the outskirts of the former West Berlin down *Unter den Linden*, the great boulevard leading straight ahead to Brandenburg Gate.

Unable to find a road on which to turn-off and growing more and more nervous by the minute about coming soon to a dead stop in front the gate then having to negotiate turning around to head back the way we had come, we were totally taken by surprise. There was no longer a blockade of fencing so vividly remembered from our visit many years ago enclosing the monument. Instead there were throngs of tourists taking photographs directly in front of the monument while others leaned on its supporting columns. And not only was it unnecessary to reverse course, the road we were on ran directly under and through the two center columns. In a few seconds we were in what had been East Berlin. From the car window, the gloomy memories we had carefully stored away so many years ago were replaced by new ones of an unrecognizable part of the city. Navigation to the airport to drop off the rental car was easily accomplished by following directional signs strategically placed along the highways as our guide.

A train ride from the airport took us back from where we had just come from, to the center of Berlin and the *Hauptbahnhof*, a multistoried building of a dizzying grandeur. Built in 2006 in the modern architectural style indicative of the vibrant and creative art culture for which the city has gained renown, the central train station oozed a steely atmosphere akin to the contemporary art motif. It was a roll of the dice in selecting what floor and which of the many exits would lead to the *S-Bahn*, the city rail system; but once discovered it was a speedy trip to our hotel.

First priority on the next day was a return to the former East Berlin, this time to explore at a leisurely pace. The *Reichstag*, the singularly-styled building where the national parliament meets, was passed on the bank of the *River Spree*. A perfect example of melding past with contemporary, the historic restoration of the old German Empire structure housing the *Bundestag* had been joined together with an ultra-modern, glass-domed addition of a modernized Berlin. A short walk from there and we were again at Brandenburg Gate, this time to walk under the monument and onto the streets of the eastern part of a single Berlin.

Old buildings had been restored to their former glory and new ones were built where only rubble had existed before. It had been transformed into a place more architecturally attractive and culturally alive than some western parts of the city. A return to the Pergamonmuseum, one of five museums of the UNESCO World Heritage Site on Museum Island, was in order. Exterior cleansed of the ravages of time and war, fresh and light with mobs of visitors coming and going, it was hard to believe it could be the same place visited in the past. Not a trace of gray grimness remained. It was definitely on a par with other important Berlin sites in terms of popularity, such as Potsdamer Platz, the Tiergarten zoo, Alexanderplatz with street performers providing impromptu entertainment, and the Holocaust Memorial.

PETER

Saint Louis, Missouri, April 1866-May 1867

It had been difficult to get used to the hordes of people at the Hamburg train station, in the city itself and at its harbor facilities. The same had been true for endless lines at the Castle Garden immigration center upon arrival in New York and afterwards in walking the streets of Manhattan. But from their experiences the Reither family had learned how to keep their wits about them while negotiating a moving stream of people with very different agendas—some friendly and helpful, others friendly and deceitful. The level of commotion and noise from so many people and horse-drawn vehicles reminded them of the sounds of soldiers in battle on the marshland, sometimes moving forward sometimes in retreat across fields and over dikes. The howling and battering force of major storms and the problems they caused brought about a similar reaction.

But those were memories from the past and a world apart now. When they crossed into New Jersey to board the train going west, they anticipated contending with yet another swarm of noisy and often rude voyagers. They were pleasantly surprised to find the station to be relatively calm, and their

217

boarding was civilly done without incident. But they were certainly not unhappy to be on their way and leaving the chaos of the big city scene behind.

Their journey to Iowa would be long but hopefully not an arduous one. At least it was taking place during the springtime, before the heat of the sun had yet to rise to its extreme; they had heard about such conditions from others journeying during summer months. Even though they would not have to worry about wilting inside a stifling railcar in April, the canteens they had bought in Hamburg were kept handy as a precaution. Whenever the train made a stop at a station they would be refilled but only from water sources marked safe to drink. The risk of disease from contaminated water was always on their minds. They had received more than one letter from Uncle Hinrich in Davenport forewarning them of health conditions, especially the danger of contracting cholera, before they had left Holstein. By the time the train arrived at Elmira in New York, a turn had been taken by each of them at least once in replenishing the water.

"I'll go this time. It's my turn again, I think. Pass me all of the canteens, will you?"

"Let me go with you, Johann. I need to stretch my legs and I want to see what there is to eat that's different from what we brought with us." Peter hopped to his feet to join his brother. Once in the station and out of sight of the train, he grabbed Johann by the arm and in low voice said: "Stop for a moment, I want to tell you something."

"Why are you speaking so quietly? And let go of my arm."

"I guess I am. Sorry. Don't know why myself, since all the others are still on the train. I just wanted you to be the first to know what I plan on doing. We don't have much time at these stops, Johann, so just listen carefully to me for one moment. You're the person who realizes most that I'm not cut out for farming, or even halfway good at it for that matter. Working with my hands and head to make things is what I've wanted to do for a long time. And the place where the need for woodworking is the greatest is a big city.

"Carpentry is what I like to do and what I had some experience in doing at home before we left as you know. I've been thinking about this for a long time, long enough to have even put aside a little money from the odd jobs I had back home. So here's what I intend to do. When we get to Chicago I am going to get off and catch another train directly south to Saint Louis as soon as I can. You're the only one to know about this so far."

Johann's jaw dropped a notch as his brother spoke. He had long been aware of Peter's fascination for all things wood, and he definitely had a talent for shaping and constructing wood objects with his own two hands. But now it dawned upon him that his brother's passion was as tenacious as his own for working the land. So it should not be astonishing Peter would try to find a way to do what he wanted to as well.

"But why did you choose Saint Louis and not Davenport? Or just stop in Chicago, since we're passing through there anyway? It's closer to Davenport than Saint Louis and has all of a big city's benefits as well."

"For one thing, because the number of German-speaking people is supposed to be huge in Saint Louis and I'm sure it won't take long before I have a place to live and jobs lined up. It should be easy to fit right in quickly there. Do you remember, Johann, the letter we received from Uncle Hinrich and Aunt Mathilde, the one that told about their stay in Saint Louis on their way to Iowa? They had arrived by ship in New York, like us, but stopped over in Saint Louis for a few days for some reason before carrying on to Davenport. It stuck in my mind when they wrote about how much they liked that city, that business seemed to be flourishing there, and especially the many people who spoke in German to them."

"I sort of recollect the letter. But what about father? He believes we'll all be on a farm together as a family. I know he will take it hard."

"Look, I'm twenty-one and will be twenty-two soon," he pleadingly replied. "I could have already left the household anyway. Many have by my age. In any case, I'm won't be staying in Saint Louis forever—maybe six months or so at most then I'll be back in the family fold. But this is a golden opportunity to get the kind of craftsman experience I need in working in a real city. When I'm finished I think I will be prepared for anything Davenport has to throw at me—whether it's making cabinets—or even tilling soil, if I have to."

"Then, I guess, if your minds made up and it's what you really want to do, you shouldn't let anything stop you. I wouldn't either, Peter. I'll do what I can to help in explaining to father. He will be a bit shocked and upset at first for sure, but together I think we can lessen the impact by telling him it's only temporary and in the long run better to follow your dreams than regretting it later. Let me talk to him first when we get closer to Chicago. It's no use having him fret about it for too long before you get off to change trains for Saint Louis.

"You're right, let's wait a bit. I'm glad you understand even though it's different for you. You have a good reason not to dilly-dally in getting to Davenport. Maria will be there before you are and dying to see you. There's no one special waiting for me so it's a good time to try my hand at doing something different by trying to figure things out on my own, apart from the rest of the family entirely."

They were right about their father; he was not pleased at all; very far from it. He did his best to change Peter's mind, to show him there would be plenty of opportunity to develop his craftsman's skills around Davenport—or even later in Saint Louis, if he remained set on going there. Why not wait until after they were all established on a parcel of good farm land? Think of the family first then go off on a solitary adventure.

Johann used his position as the older son to support Peter the best he could, to convince their father that now was the right time for Peter to seize the opportunity to do something new, before the trappings of daily life routines pinned him down for what could be years. At first he was unmoved by Johann's attempts of persuasion, reacting strongly to any line of argument he put forth. To him it was just one more blow added to a string of misfortunes the family had already suffered. First it had been the loss of his wife then the decision of his oldest son staying behind to wed in Dithmarschen. Then there was the unacceptable ongoing association of Maria and Johann. Finally, the devastating theft in New York had compounded everything.

And now this nonsensical idea of Peter's to break the family strength. It scared him to think of what could be next. Sorrowfully, however, as the train drew closer to Chicago, he realized Peter's mind was made up and not going to be changed. All of his children seemed to have been born with a streak of stubbornness once they had made a decision. To his credit, he recognized the same family trait in himself and decided at the last minute that it was better to give his son his blessing than to part on bad terms. Maybe he was right to strike out now, anyway. Upsetting what was supposed to be a family enterprise might even have had greater negative consequences after it was underway.

Arms waving out windows and watery eyes he knew were meant for him and him only; it was like he was standing there alone on an empty platform. Both son and brother to those pulling away from the station, Peter grew smaller and smaller until he had vanished from sight but never from their thoughts. When he boarded the train for the journey to Saint Louis with his bag of possessions in hand, he felt a burden had been lifted from his shoulders. Passengers whose eyes met his own ever so briefly in the corridors of the car would have noticed a person with a renewed confidence in his step, if they had seen what he was like earlier. It came from a readiness to tackle whatever life had to offer. His family had made a life-altering decision and now he was experiencing the freedom to do the same. There were, and would be, no regrets.

Brown dirt fields, green forests and repetitive frontages of small towns fled before his gaze out an often rain-streaked window as the train jostled along endless silver tracks. It seemed like an eternity before he arrived on the doorstep of his destination. After stops in Joliet, McLean, Springfield and Alton, among the larger towns on the route, the Chicago and Alton Railroad had finally brought him to the East Saint Louis station in Illinois. Wasting no time, he made his way to the ferry taking him across the Mississippi River. Almost immediately he was struck by the difference in Missouri air. And it didn't take long to understand why. In the distance he could see a host of smokestacks poking their noses into the sky and belching black and gray smoke. They were an ugly sign of the city's post-Civil War return to large-scale manufacturing. When taken together with plumes from dwelling chimneys and steamboat stacks, besmirched skies could only be the result.

But this did not deflect him from the thrill of being in the place he had chosen on his own to go. He decided to ignore industrial blight and focus on the rest of what otherwise seemed entrancing to him. For the next two hours he wandered the city streets, letting his legs lead him wherever they would, caught up in the sights and sounds of the perpetual motion around him. Out of necessity, he found himself often dodging a variety of transport: horse-drawn omnibuses competing with the new, rattling streetcars on rails; buggies and carriages; goods carts of all different sizes; and individuals riding horses in every direction at the same time. Lost in the commotion, it was not until dusk descended that he gave any thought to where he would spend the night though he should have done so much earlier if he had not been so preoccupied.

Only able to say a few words in English after his short time in America, Peter stopped in front of a newsstand where the seller stood holding single copies of two different newspapers in each hand. Both were in German as were the words he used in shouting out his sales pitch. When Peter drew closer to the man, he could see the title of one paper was the *Anzeiger des Westens,* the other the *Westliche Post.* Since he was hearing his own native tongue spoken, this might be the right person to approach to ask a question.

"Excuse me sir, is there somewhere in this city where they might have information on securing accommodation? I'm looking for somewhere to stay tonight."

Sizing up the young man standing before him by his dress and demeanor, the vendor correctly took Peter to be a newcomer. "You're a bit too late, I'm afraid. Almost everything is booked for the day by now," he replied in a businesslike tone while keeping his eyes peeled for real paper customers. But Peter's body language and worried facial expression began to play on his emotions; this might be a person in a truly precarious position, someone who really doesn't have anywhere else to go. So he took pity on him.

"You're new to Saint Louis then?"

"That I am, sir. I've only just come today by train. I saw your German newspapers and my English is not very good. I guess I became distracted in just believing I'm really here and forgot I have no place to stay. I forgot about eating as well. That's the next thing I'll do after finding a room."

The insouciance of youth brought out a chuckle from the vendor. Placing down one of the newspapers he held on a large stack of others with the same title, he rubbed his chin in thought. "I think I have an idea of what might be best for you to do at this time of the evening young man. You may not yet have heard of *Turnverein* societies that are in many cities. They're like cultural centers for German speakers and non-speakers with German ancestry. Of course, the Saint Louis Turnverein closed during the war with German-American citizens having a few more important things to do then."

"I knew that German-Americans fought in the war. In fact, I even have relatives that were soldiers."

"Many did serve in the war. In the spirit of fighting for liberty in Germany, society members put on the Union uniform and fought for the abolition of slavery too. Taken together, the Turnverein societies form part of the Nordamerikanisher Turnerbund organization. Now that the war is over, our Central Turnhalle here in Saint Louis has reopened again this year. And now they have expanded their activities beyond physical training and political purposes to teaching English and cultural activities for our German community. Physical education in schools still remains a strong component of our Turnverein, however."

"I think I have heard a little about them. My aunt and uncle were in Saint Louis about ten year ago. In one of the letter's they sent back home they mentioned there was a network of special clubs just for Germans in America."

By now, having struck up a conversation with Peter, the newspaper seller had begun to take a genuine interest in the likable young man standing before him. "Look, in ten minutes my partner will be replacing me here. If you're so minded, I can walk with you over to the Turnhalle on 10th Street. I'm certain there will be a lot going on there and we can ask about somewhere to stay for tonight. You can have a bite to eat there as well. By the way, my name is Herman," he said in offering his hand to shake.

"Mine is Peter, Peter Reither. And I would gladly wait for you to go together." Punctually, ten minutes later Herman was replaced by Wilhelm to whom Peter was also introduced. He was already beginning to feel less alone.

"Off we go then. It's not far away."

Alive with early evening activity, the hall was an exception to the rest of the city which appeared to have gone to sleep when the downtown streets had emptied soon after the dinner hour. Before long Peter had met several more people, all speaking to him in German, two of whom even in the Low

German dialect of his native Holstein. The last person to introduce himself was a man named Frederick Lange.

"So you have just arrived and need a place to stay? Herman has just told me about you. What is it that you plan to do for work, if I may ask? City life here is much different from the farm work most are used to in the old country." Frederick's authoritative voice spoke with experience in making the transition between rural and city living.

"That's exactly why I've come here—to try my hand at working and living in a city. My aim is to be a carpenter by trade; that's what I want to do here. At home, I worked on framing several buildings and have done some replacement roofing as well, but finishing work is really what interests me most, cabinet-making and other interior woodworking. I have a little experience in doing that as well."

"The reason I ask," Herman began to explain, "is that there are some changes that have been going on for a while here in this city. And they may affect on which side of town you choose to live. Most people in our German community have stuck together and settled in the central downtown area, at least until recently. This is the way it has been for a long time because most of the jobs were down near the river. If it's something on a riverboat, dock-related labor or other riverside work you were seeking, living close to the Mississippi would be the place where you'd want to be; the Hyde Park district, for example. Soulard would be the quarter for brewery-related employment. Then there's also Bremen and Dutchtown.

But over the past couple of years our once centralized community has been spreading out, leaving the traditional areas to follow the rail line expansion that started in the early 1850s. Once the Pacific Railroad arrived, growth in industries further along the riverfront and to the north and west was quick to follow. There're plenty of employment opportunities everywhere and finding suitable housing shouldn't be a problem either wherever you choose to go. Construction of additional lodging for workers and families has been a priority for awhile now."

"Thank you for taking the time to let me know about the current situation. It helps a lot to know the options. For tonight, though, anywhere indoors with a bed would do fine." Signs of weariness had begun to show in drooping eyelids "If you have any suggestions, I'm more than ready to take them."

"Well, we live in Hyde Park," Frederick responded without a second thought, "My wife and I have an extra bed you can lie your head on for few nights, just until you get your feet under you, that is if you don't mind having three rambunctious children in your midst. There's so much need for craftsmen I'm sure it won't take long to find work. As long as you keep your expectations reasonable, you should have no trouble in getting something within a few days. What do you say? Would you like to stay at our home?"

Perhaps it was because he was overcome by drowsiness or perhaps of the kindness of someone who was a complete stranger only moments ago, but Peter suddenly felt himself overwhelmed by *gemütlichkeit,* that quintessentially German expression for a very warm welcome. Even though it flew in the face of relationships built on generations of tradition and family ties back in the old country, he did not skip a heartbeat before accepting the offer. It was a new life he was learning to live and he was going to let it lead where it would.

Frederick Lange's caretaking of his new roomer did not end after what turned out to be a handful of nights at his

227

house. His connections with local tradesmen landed Peter's first job working with a small crew on a house only a few doors away that had just started on the remodeling of the kitchen and dining-room. So a room was rented in a boardinghouse close by. He soon proved to be a worthy craftsman, with exacting measuring skills and a steady hand, capable of expertly guiding tools in shaping whatever species of wood into its proper contours. He also had a deft eye for making minor changes that made major improvements in functionality without sacrificing aesthetics. His next job was on a small development of three houses. From there, his reputation for reliability and quality work grew and there was no dearth of jobs to tackle in the future. The months flew by working six days a week while his pockets filled to the top with coin.

At the end of an entire year of single-minded focus—come and gone like the summer breezes—on an afternoon following Sunday service at the Lutheran church, Peter sat down on bench in a nearby park to relax and reflect. A lot had been accomplished in a year: confidence had been gained in his craftsman's skills, not a day of work had been missed, new work connections and friends had been made. And he had taken every opportunity to become acquainted with many of the cultural and material things Saint Louis had to offer, walking the streets in every direction in all types of weather when he had a day off. Some of the time left over after long hours of labor was always filled with routine chores necessary to survive, but he was not one to sit back on his laurels when they were done.

In balance, though, he knew his personal life had suffered, especially in the area of companionship, something which he found himself thinking more and more about these days. Instead of just enjoying a day of rest, watching young couples walking side-by-side or sitting on a bench for awhile like he was doing at the moment, he was again reviewing his own situation. There were his brother Johann and all of these others who had found someone to make their life better, someone who made them happy. What of himself? Wasn't it about time he got off his duff and did the same? If the kind of life he was leading in Saint Louis left no time for the most important things, then maybe he should think long and hard about making another change.

A letter he had received the day before from his father in Davenport had mentioned a cousin who had taken up residence in the state of Kentucky. Kentucky, now that was a word with a romantic ring to it! Young and with ample savings to strike out again, it might be the right time to make his way back to the family he left on the train over a year ago but only after a detour to Kentucky—say for a few weeks at most—on his way to Iowa. Later that same afternoon, Peter wrote and posted a letter to John J. Reither, the wayward middle son of his grandfather's brother who had for some unknown reason gone to live in Elizabethtown, the seat of Hardin County in the state of Kentucky, instead of going to Iowa like the rest of them. He had moved there soon after the June 2, 1865 ending of the Civil War and after serving almost five years in the Union Army.

The reply from John J. included an invitation to visit, and to come sooner than later, if he could: "I married a year ago and we are expecting our first child in about two month's time. It would be best if you were to be here before the birth while things still aren't too chaotic. We have room for the

229

moment, but after the baby it will be a little tight. We are already thinking of moving to a larger place later." Peter thought they should have a lot in common since John J. was only five years older than he was, and there was an additional incentive in meeting a new family member; so he made his decision to go before placing the letter back into the envelope.

Yet, he couldn't help feeling regret when he stopped by the Lange house a few days later to inform his former advisor and father-like friend of his plans to keep his promise of rejoining his own family. The regret was mutual. The Lange family had come to view the young man as one of their family by now, their young children becoming particularly attached to someone whom they looked up to like an older brother. He could easily be persuaded to engage in one of their games, and stories he told them of the old country were devoured.

He had already packed clothes, a few tools and other belongings he had accumulated when he stopped by once more at the Lange's home before departing on the train the next morning. Wooden toys he had made himself were given to each of their children, the parents receiving a large box of the Mound City's best chocolates. How ironic it was that his former home scattered with ancient man-made hillocks as flood-safe living places matched the land on which he now stood strewn also with mounds of varied shapes built long ago by indigenous peoples. Although the mounds around the city were disappearing one-by-one as they were flattened for population growth, there were still many to behold just across the river in Cahokia. He couldn't wait to tell the others in Iowa when he saw them of their pre-Columbian mound-making Native American cousins in Saint Louis!

After putting on a light coat, although it was still some

months before Christmas season would begin, a freshly-baked, tightly-wrapped stollen was placed in his hands by Frau Lange to share with his relatives in Kentucky over the holidays.

"It will keep for months if properly looked after. Keep it tightly wrapped and stored in a cool place if you can."

"I'll think of you often but especially when we have a slice on Christmas Eve," he said in tucking the solid loaf of German bread under his arm before leaving.

***

Elizabethtown, Kentucky, June-November 1867

It was during the last leg of his journey to Elizabethtown on the Louisville and Nashville Railroad that he began to have qualms about possibly imposing on his cousin at an inconvenient time when John J. and his wife were expecting their first child. He needn't have worried. A telegram he had sent two days before to them had been received in time. And just now it looked as if someone was making his way towards him as he placed his foot on the last coach stair before stepping onto the platform. Although most people would not have seen the two men as relatives without spending some time with them together, for Peter and John J. there was recognition of kinship at first sight. Without saying much more than each others' name to begin with, a hand placed on Peter's back led him out of the station. All of Peter's reservations had dissolved in an instant.

"It'll be just a few minutes' walk to where we live. Let me carry your bag; you sure do travel lightly. It's been such a long time since we've had a visitor who was a relative. By gosh it's good to have you here, Peter."

"And it's good to be here, cousin. With the war and now a wife and a child on the way, not to mention the distance between here and Iowa, I can see why visits from relatives were not foremost in your mind."

They soon came to a small house on a side street and John J.'s wife was waiting at the door.

"*Willkamen*," was the only word she spoke at first. The smile to go with it made it seem like a speech.

It was the familiar and simple greeting spoken with a Low German accent, the very same accent as if they were at home in Dithmarschen and had gone to visit the neighbor next door. It was unexpected for he was sure that she was not of German birth. In fact, she had been born and raised in the very state in which they now stood, but she had been taught well by her husband. She immediately took him by the arm and brought him inside. The first thing he noticed was the table already laid; then the smell of home-cooked food set his stomach growling. As soon as he was shown where to put his belongings, he was seated at the table. A prayer of thanks was given then the eating began with relish. He was starved from the long train trip. The few words exchanged had mostly to do with meal complements and the grateful acceptance of second helpings. Other than that there were only a few pauses between bites to look across the table at each other with satisfied faces. When the dining had finished the real conversation began.

"You mentioned my coming to live in Kentucky instead of Iowa. I think I'm officially known as the black sheep of our side of the family. It looks like I may not be the only one though," he added in looking Johann up and down. "You may soon join me as the black sheep of your side, breaking away as you did to work in Saint Louis and then coming here. We must be cut from the same cloth!"

"But why did you choose Kentucky? And why especially Elizabethtown?"

"It's a long story. Unlike you, Peter, I did go to Davenport at first along with the rest of my family, including my brother with the same name as your own. But unlike you and me, my Peter is a dyed in the wool farmer and all for making a good life there; except for one thing—he's lacking a good wife!"

"I've heard a little about this cousin Peter too. The different branches of the Reither family must have all liked the name Peter. And there are certainly enough Johanns and Hinrichs to go around as well!"

"I knew in my heart I didn't want to start a life in farming there, and maybe a family also," John J. continued. If I'd let that happen, I'd probably never would have gotten around to what I really wanted to do. No, it just wasn't for me. Like you said in your letter, about your passion for wood—well, the carpentry is what I wanted to follow as well.

"As for choosing Kentucky, I heard a little about Elizabethtown from people who were visiting my parents in Davenport but lived here. So as soon as I was able to get away from the farm in Iowa after harvesting season, I did. I went directly to Elizabethtown to see what it was like for myself for two reasons: climate and fruit orchards.

"I thought, if you are going to start over in America then why not live in a place where the weather is supposed to be milder than the old country, where the temperature is better for outdoor work year around, and where there is supposed to be an abundance of black walnut, hickory and other hardwoods.

There would be a constant supply of the kind of wood from which I could make a decent living right in my own back yard. So I came here when I still thought of myself as Johann Jacob Reither. To make it easier, I changed to John J. for those I met over the next three years. But all this happened before I enlisted."

"You didn't want to go to Iowa to try out living there again after the war either?"

"I didn't think twice about it. After my three years of soldiering were over I went right back to Elizabethtown. It was the place where I had gotten used to and had been happy before the war—even if it meant not seeing family living far away."

"I didn't mean to pry by asking so many questions. Sometimes my curiosity gets the better of me. But you have made some hard and different choices. I'd like to hear more about your experiences in the war sometime. Of course we knew a little about what was happening here when we were in Dithmarschen, enough for our father to decide to wait before immigrating until the fighting had ended. Our mother died, as you probably know. My older sister married and stayed behind so it was only the four of us that left—my father, my brother Johann, my sister Christina and me."

"My brother Peter was also a soldier in the war. He was not mustered out until the very end in 1865. All those years in the thick of so many battles yet, amazingly, he made it through without a major injury. As far as wounds go, I was lucky, too, but I was not so fortunate in avoiding a different form of attack. While on duty during the winter of '63 at Missionary Ridge in Tennessee I came down with what was diagnosed as an exposure disease. When I first experienced the symptoms, I didn't know what had hit me. I had no idea there was something called rheumatism until the doctor told me about it later. It felt like my right knee was on fire and at the same time it locked up in a swollen knot. Each little step I took, as much as a stiff knee would allow, my leg was shot through with burning pain. The inflammation continued to worsen and build each day for weeks until I was unable to walk at all."

Peter winced in sympathy, almost as if he could feel his cousin's pain.

"What happened then? Did the troop have to leave you behind? Were you taken to a hospital?"

"We were bivouacking for a few days while resupplying and resting, or they would've carried me to where I could have received better care. The knee slowly began to calm down and loosen up a bit during the next two weeks as we moved on. But I had another bout when we were marching through Georgia to a town called Adairsville. I had enlisted for three years in '61, as I said, and wanted to carry on until the war ended, like my brother did. But because I was becoming a real burden to the rest of the men, the rheumatism coming and going on its own accord, I knew it might not be possible. Then it started to affect other parts of my body as well, with less intensity but still painful. I was eventually discharged in October of '64 in Nashville. From there, coming back to this Edenlike place was like a tonic, and I almost immediately started to feel better."

"You're not bothered anymore by rheumatism now, then?"

"I wish that were the case. It still seems to have a mind of its own about when and where it decides to flare up. Not so bad that I can't work, though. I take medicine from the pharmacy and have to go now-and-then for a doctor's visit when I have the more severe attacks. But it's never been as bad as when we were constantly marching, eating and sleeping day-after-day in the cold, wet weather of Tennessee. I've been told to expect more attacks in the future—that it's the type of disease that will never completely go away—so I just start taking the medicine as soon as I notice the first signs coming on again. It's what doctors call a chronic disability. But that's more than enough about me."

While John J. had been telling his story, his wife had cleared the table.

"Come and sit yourself down with us, America. I've been talking the ear off Peter. America Reither, my good wife, is the best reason of all for coming back to Elizabethtown. We hadn't met each other yet before the war and even if we had, she would have been too young then for an older fellow like me. But we did meet soon after I returned when she was nearly twenty-one, and married right here in this town.

Peter looked towards the expectant mother wanting to know more about her background as well:

"Has your family been in Kentucky for a long time, America?"

"Yes, I think you could say that it has. My mother's side goes back generations. Not so for my father. He was born in North Carolina. Some of his relatives were farming here in Kentucky where there was more open land to be had so his parents left the Carolinas and moved our whole family to Elizabethtown."

"Were there many children in your family?"

"Quite a few. I have an older brother and six younger sisters and brothers. It was a good thing we were a farming family with ten mouths to feed!"

Peter would have liked to have asked her about Kentucky's involvement with slavery before the war and afterwards but refrained. It would be out of place to bring up such a sensitive topic with someone he had just met, he thought. But almost as if reading his mind, America answered his question without it having to be asked.

"My parents have just a small farm and never used slave labor to work it. However, other relatives with larger farms did own slaves before the war. It's taking some time for them to get used to the idea that you can't "own" people any more—you never really could, actually."

Peter's first day in Elizabethtown ended when the last rays of sunlight finally disappeared during one of the longest days of the year. Daylight was finally exhausted and so was he. A faint glow still hung in the warm evening air, but he was more than ready to put his head down on a pillow. He was glad he had come to Kentucky.

LIPPE DETMOLD

Lippe, North Rhine-Westphalia, Germany, Spring 2013

Grandmother Alma Gerhard was born in the state of Illinois as was her mother, Louisa. The place of birth of Henry Meier, Louisa's father and Alma's maternal grandfather, had earlier been established to be the village of Brakelsiek in the region of Lippe Detmold. Already designated as a principality, Lippe had become one of the states of the German Confederation five years before Henry's birth by virtue of the Congress of Vienna of 1814-1815—and remained so at the time of his immigration to America in 1847.

Several of the major cities in Germany had been visited over the years without knowing much about family history. A more recent trip to the much less touristic place of origin of the Reither family in Holstein had been followed by a second to see firsthand the Gerhard family homeland in the East Brandenburg region of Germany, lands now belonging to Poland. Visiting the place where Meier ancestors had lived became the next objective on the agenda.

The village of Brakelsiek in the *Nordrhein-Westfalen* region had not been heard of until it was seen written down for the first time in documents. It was in one of the smaller states

238

of the historical German Empire which had never been incorporated into Prussia. Hanover, the closest large and well-known city with an airport was only about a fifty-five mile drive away. But we were nowhere near Hanover; in fact, we were on our way to the Belgian town of Bruges. In any event we had already passed time in Hanover on a previous trip many years ago. A modern city completely rebuilt after carpet bombardment during the Second World War, it had presented little historical interest. So taking a series of trains from Bruges to Detmold, the most important German city near Brakelsiek, seemed preferable to going to Brussels and from there flying to Hanover.

A transfer to a regional train was necessary in Bielefeld, a substantial town on the edge of the *Teutoburger Wald*, before reaching Detmold. Out the train window a glimpse of a very large monument peculiarly set in the middle of a forested area stirred our curiosity about what it could be about. A few days later, while passing through the heart of the Teutoburg Forest by car, we came upon this huge statue of a warrior with a winged helmet and holding a long sword pointed high towards the heavens. Its impressive size and setting atop a Classical dome base in an exceptional location must have been to commemorate something of major importance; it needed to be explored up close. Erected in 1875, the *Hermannsdenkmal*, or Hermann Monument, was of Arminius, the chief of the Cherusci tribe who led the defeat of invading Roman legions in 9 AD. Obviously, a long remembered and revered hero, Arminius, or Hermann in the German equivalent to his Latin name, had managed to secure cooperation of other local Germanic tribes in fighting the Battle of the Teutoburg Forest. Roman legions were dispatched again in succeeding years, but the allied tribes stuck together thwarting the enemy's patented divide and conquer strategy. To many natives Hermann is still considered to be the liberator hero of Germany, and the Hermann Monument their Statue of Liberty.

Erroneously believing the city of Detmold to likely be a rather inconsequential place to visit and accommodation thus fairly easy to come by, the number of people on the streets and tables taken at outdoor cafes signaled what was soon to be learned the hard way; we were in a very popular summertime destination! Still early in the day, there was a vacancy in a small hotel directly across from the train station. But before booking a room there, the town was scoured in search of a more tranquil and central locale. There had to be other places available where the noise of local trains arriving and departing would not be a concern, right? Not so. Everything else was already taken.

Finally giving up and racing back to the station in desperation, we had the gut feeling that it would be gone by now too. Mercifully, we were wrong and it was immediately secured for the night with any noise qualms totally forgotten. Another party had stopped in and expressed interest in the room we were told, but they had not returned or it would have been booked as well. By now, it was already late in the afternoon and we had become the lucky ones this time around. Additional nights in what turned out to be a surprisingly quiet hotel were unavailable. So early next morning a sprint dragging luggage behind us was made to the largest modern hotel in town to beat the crowd; and a happy result was achieved in reserving accommodation for the remainder of our stay.

The old section of Detmold, the former capital of the

Principality of Lippe resting at the edge of the forest, is centered on a restored castle of 13th century origins called the *Fürstliche Residenzschloss Detmold*. Counts and princes made the Princely Residence Castle of Detmold their permanent residence and its ownership was still retained by the current Prince of Lippe at the time of our visit. Most of the castle was much more recent construction, but sections having beginnings in medieval times still existed. A crowded public park formed part of the grounds surrounding the structure.

Detmold per se was not our main objective in travelling to the area, but the fact that it was only about seventeen miles from the village of Brakelsiek meant that it must have been frequented by Meier ancestors on market and other special days or for official business or possibly even to visit relations living there. Since the *Landesarchiv NRW*, the National Archive of Nordrhein-Westfalen, office was housed in the city, stopping there to see if any family listings could be found in local records was a convenient must-do. Computerized indexes were searched and Meier entries were identified. Yet, staff shortage made waiting time for retrieval of the actual documents prohibitive so the research attempt was abandoned.

Upon leaving the archives a wide dirt and gravel tree-lined road-like path beside the river *Berlebecke* was stumbled upon purely by accident. An ideal chance for a promenade, the *Allee* was a straight shot from the town center to the outskirts through a wooded area called *Bismarckhain*. Closer to town but still in a southwesterly direction, the *Hochschule für Musik Detmold* was passed followed by the *Detmold Konzerthaus* just another hundred and fifty yards away. Something seemed to be happening since both the Europe-renowned music university and concert hall were humming with activity; scads

241

of mostly young people were milling around on surrounding lawns. In no particular hurry, we stopped to enter the lobby of the attractive and very modern concert hall where we able to hear and watch musicians playing inside the main room on a big screen. We were joined by many others also viewing the concert's sold out student performances remotely.

Greater Detmold was a combination of flatlands, hills and forests as well as half-timbered houses and modern buildings. The atmosphere was calm and casual, the music school and an applied sciences university lending the youthful vitality of a college town. Before shifting to a car as means of locomotion for the next three days of our journey, the *Lippisches Landesmuseum* was toured. One of the most prominent traditional buildings in terms of scale and location, the museum housed an array of traditional and eclectic collections on several floors under one roof. Originally founded as a natural history museum in the 1830s, over the decades it had evolved to include a wide variety of cultural artifacts from different time periods: there were swords, shields and spears from the middle ages, ethnographically-costumed mannequins and entire room representations of life in more recent centuries, objects of folklore, modern interior architecture and furniture.

Bizarrely, the oldest mummy in Europe, reputed to be that of a Peruvian child and estimated to be over six thousand years old, was also a featured exhibit. Also very much a highlight, a magnificent glowing painting depicted the warrior Hermann—our old friend of monument fame—bountifully muscled and handsomely armored in a scene dripping with golden romanticism took center stage. Assisted by his wife, Thusnelda, in preparation for the all-important battle to come, the work hung on a wall by itself separated from the other artwork displayed for emphasis. Exhibitions were spread over five floors, including narrow and slanted attic spaces with exposed beams and rafters requiring careful attention because of the cramped headroom.

Brakelsiek, the ancestral home of grandmother Alma's paternal grandfather, was reached in less than forty minutes drive after leaving Detmold the next day. The compact village of not much more than a third of a mile from side-to-side was set to one side of the bottom of a long hill, undisturbed by a highway running nearby. No sign of activity could be seen or heard after the car was parked and we began to walk around a mini-web of very short streets—none of which was straight and only a handful over fifty yards in length. One was even named *Kurze Strasse* or Short Street. The only relatively longish street ran through the village center, effectively splitting the village into two halves. It was, of course, labeled *Lange Strasse* or Long Street.

Each of the curvy little streets was fronted by picturesque houses and barns with gabled roofs, perhaps around a hundred in all in the southwest and oldest part of the village. There was an assortment of traditional styles built with a mix of wood and stone—many roofed with red tiles again—along with dwellings of more recent architectural design. There was no telling yet in which of these dwellings the Meier family had resided before they left for America in 1847—a mystery that lasted only until one of those magical genealogy moments happened!

In taking one more tour up and down each of the little streets by car this time a wooden box containing a flyer looking like an advertisement of some sort was spotted in one of the few spaces still left open in-between buildings after centuries of habitation. Behind the glass door a black and white drawing on a sheet of paper appeared to be an advertisement with an image from a pamphlet or book cover. The stark black lines depicted men with pails of water fighting a fire consuming a house or barn; it was entitled *Der grosse Brand in Brakelsiek vom 10. Mai 1848.* High school German proved sufficient to understand the subject matter was a big fire in the village.

Just the date of 1848 alone, the year after the Meiers had emigrated, made it an instant object of curiosity. There was just enough additional information on the sheet to know it was published locally and that it was for sale. But there were insufficient details to know where and by whom. Not wanting to miss what might be a once in a life time opportunity, a knock on the nearest door of a house across the street was made to inquire about who the responsible person might be. Two smiling women who answered the door were able to instantly provide the phone number and address of the man in the village from whom a copy could be obtained.

A quick phone call and an arrangement for meeting him had been made, the proprietors of the house waiting to greet us when we rang the bell. Within a few minutes we had in our hands a publication of more than a hundred pages describing the history of the houses in Brakelsiek. Newspaper and magazine articles reporting on the incident at the time and afterwards throughout the years were reproduced in their entirety. From their doorstep our particular interest in the village was transmitted in broken German. And upon hearing our family connection to Brakelsiek, we were invited inside for apfelsaft and to talk further.

As luck would have it, we had entered the domain of the village's local historian and no ordinary genealogist as well! After he had looked over our documents showing how we were related to locals of the past, we gathered around the computer containing detailed family files. His records held information for both houses that had survived the fire and for those which had been destroyed. **Vollmeierhof Nr.7**, the house in which my ancestors, the Meier family, had lived— each village house had its own name and number—was one of the many that were burnt to the ground. In total, fifty-one families comprising two hundred and twelve villagers, around half of the village population, were left homeless. How fortuitous was it that great-great-grandfather Henry and his family had escaped the disaster by emigrating from Lippe the year before! What must they have thought when they heard the news at their new home in Illinois—their old home as they remembered it now gone forever?

According to the May 21st, 1898 issue of the *Lippische Landes-Zeitung*—the fiftieth anniversary of the fire—in a newspaper article recapitulating the events of May 1848, the loud sound of the fire bell was heard sometime between noon and 12:30 p.m. Voices were soon heard on the streets and all eyes were directed towards the northeast end of the village. Dense smoke and brightly burning flames announced that a house had been consumed by fire. Started by two very young boys playing with fire in a small adjoining building serving as a shed and stable, it had immediately spread setting the main house at Number 54 ablaze too. Six years after the Great Fire of Hamburg had burned nearly one-third of that city's old town in May of 1842, fire again had wreaked havoc, consuming an even greater percentage of the structures in

Brakelsiek. First to report the catastrophe a few days afterwards in magazine articles appearing on the 11th and 16th of May 1848 was the *Vaterländische Blätter lippisches Magazin*.

But even more informative documents were gleaned from the records of one of the Brakelsiek school teachers. Otto Tippenhauer had been born nearly fifty years after the fire, but in May 1949 he presented his meticulous study of the event on its one hundred year commemoration. The fire had occurred in the midst of an especially bleak period of local area history and had been one more adversity in what had reached a crisis stage by 1846; that was the year when ongoing drought caused a failure in essential grain crops. The price of a bushel of wheat grain to make bread flour had risen to five thalers—the name for a silver coin that still exists in some dollar currencies—a bushel of rye was not much less, and the price was still rising from month to month.

To give an idea of what that meant back then; the fare for sailing from the port of Bremen in Germany to New York at that time was between thirty-five and thirty eight thalers, or approximately the equivalent of seven bushels of wheat! And, if things could get any worse, the year 1847 became known as the Hunger Year. Although the government had made efforts in providing cheaper grain and by using local labor to build roads to reduce unemployment as well as by supplying fabric and other materials for children to produce shirts, gloves, aprons and other clothing items while attending school, desperate needs were still unmet and it was not enough.

The increase in advertisements for forced sales of houses, land and entire estates was therefore not surprising. Also unsurprising, given the circumstances of the time, was the decision to immigrate to America made by many of the inhabitants of Brakelsiek and other villages and towns of the Lippishe southeast. But what was alarming was the sheer number of emigrants from the area during the hardship years, and the village of Brakelsiek was at the top of the mountain among those places most affected.

In 1847 alone, the year when the Meiers set sail for America, the official government gazette reported twelve families plus ten individuals who left. The exodus continued in 1848 when thirty-four persons, including a wife with her children, departed from their homeland for good. Otto Tippenhauer stressed in his account that these permanent departures were one of the saddest chapters in the village's history. So it was already the toughest of times for a community dependent on agriculture and the whims of weather when the devastating fire made them victims again.

The opportunity for a better life on fertile farmland in the northwest corner of the state of Illinois must have irresistibly beckoned even after generations of living in one place. It had been a community where familiarity was paramount and where intermarriage among villagers was more common than not. Vollmeierhoff No. 7, the house the Meiers had vacated, had been part of their family at least from the time of its first mention in the 1529 register at the official office in Schwalenberg, the slightly larger town just down the road. At that time it was in possession of a man named Cordt Ridder who called the house Meier Cordt, or Meier Kordt, to distinguish it from another already Ridder-named household in the village; later it was shortened simply to Meier. According to the register, along with the house there were thirty-one acres of arable land, two acres of grassland and area for a kitchen garden.

After centuries of families living in the same structure, the name of the house took on a life of its own, becoming more important than the surname of any current inhabitant. This is evidenced when in 1829 Franz Heinrich Niedermeier married the widow of Wilhelm Meier of Brakelsiek No. 7, moved into her house and took the name of Meier for his surname thereafter. A similar circumstance happened even much earlier, in 1763, when Johann Conrad Lessmann, a man from a neighboring house, bought No. 7 following the mysterious and unaccounted for disappearance of Johann Jürgen Meier, the last of the Meiers living in the house. Lessmann immediately assumed the surname of Meier for himself as well.

It almost seems unfathomable that Grandmother Alma's grandfather, Henry Meier, would simply pull up stakes and abandon a worthy house of such a lengthy history, but that was what he did. In October of 1846, he announced, again at the office in Schwalenberg, that he wished to emigrate then asked the government office in Detmold for permission. Almost without question that permission would be granted, the property was soon offered for sale by auction through the notice section of the official government gazette.

Publically and properly announced, a top offer was made by a resident of Schwalenberg which was accepted. When the Detmold government asked what his intentions were regarding Meier Cordt because of concern over speculation during a volatile property market, the new owner replied that he wanted to lease the farm at first then manage it himself afterwards. Based on these statements, he was awarded the purchase. However, by the following year, in June 1847, the farm was sold to the daughter of an old Brakelsiek neighbor of Henry

Meier living at Nr. 20. The selling price of seven thousand represented a gain of seven hundred and seventy thalers over the government agreed purchasing price of six thousand two hundred and thirty in less than a year. So much for government control of speculation by wealthier land owners!

Ironically, it was less than a year later when the fire of May 1848 ended the life of the venerable structure. It was not to remain an empty lot for long; rebuilt a few years afterwards, Brakelsiek Nr. 7 regained its proper place in the community. With help in finding its exact location both present and past, the wooden façade on the "new" house contained the translated inscription:

My God, it is well known to you - I build out of need and not from lust - The previous house Lord Jesus Christ has become dust and ashes - God give our hearts to be better in Your love - I pray thee my Lord and God keep this house from the peril of fire, even for those who make use of these buildings, defending me from my defects - Lord God in your loving grace give happiness and blessings – Amen

Since the small village of Brakelsiek had neither hotels nor bed and breakfast accommodation, a room was sought in the bigger, sister town of Schwalenberg. It was easily reached by driving only about a mile and half down the highway. Still serving as the seat for local vital records as it had in the past, the population was about fourteen hundred persons compared to Brakelsiek's nine hundred. There was an atmosphere of importance in its hillside vantage point, an impression

Schwalenberg must have given off in the past as well in accordance with its official role. A museum, an ancient Ratskeller, cafés and several restaurants were complemented by lofty black and white half-timbered houses in and around the town center.

Disproportionally seeming for such a small place, there were also a good number of buildings devoted to art. A holdover from former times, it was learned that Schwalenberg had once drawn artists from other parts of Germany after gaining a reputation as an art colony. Indeed, during the late 19th and early 20th centuries it had been called the Painters City. Although no longer a full-fledged habitat for artists, recipients of the Schwalenberg scholarship for young artists still spent time in the little town, living and working in the *Künstlerhaus* for up to six months at a time. In the *Werkhaus* the Schwalenberger summer academy offered courses and workshops in painting, sculpture, old master techniques and other art forms. Exhibits and galleries presented examples of artwork representing the whole region.

For eons the parish church serving worshipers from Brakelsiek had been in Schwalenberg. And it still was. Meier family members along with their fellow villagers on foot or in horse-drawn carts attended Sunday service, and were baptized and married in the Johanneskirche Evangelical Church. As the heart of the surrounding farming community, Schwalenberg's market square and businesses saw locals from other villages make purchases, trade or sell their goods there.

Another factor in accounting for the town's prominence had to do with the *Burg Schwalenberg*, the castle first built by the Counts of Schwalenberg in the 13th century. Since then this hilltop castle overlooking the town has been rebuilt more than once, has changed hands several times and has even been a hotel with a restaurant. No matter what its circumstances were at any given point in time, an imposing edifice with a town beneath bearing its name lent an importance to Schwalenberg greater than similarly sized villages in the area.

Of more recent history, due to North Rhine-Westphalia territorial reforms of 1 January 1970, the self-governing structure of a number of small towns and villages was dissolved. Schwalenberg, Brakelsiek, Schieder, and five other municipalities plus part of a sixth, were merged to form the new city of Schieder-Schwalenberg. Old municipalities were now referred to as communes within the new city configuration. Losing part of their unique identity through incorporation into a single governmental entity must have been a shock at first after centuries of independence. Perhaps a newly-formed representative-based block of more than eight thousand inhabitants served to calm traditional attitudes to some degree in creating a more cohesive and powerful voice in dealing with wider governmental and political matters in their rural region.

Two hotels in Schwalenberg provided most of the visitor accommodation in town. Little was known about the history of the Schwalenberger Malkasten at the time of reserving for a stay of three nights. Later it was learned that it was first built around the same time as the castle in the 13th century but at the bottom of the castle hill. By 1214, the large and colorfully-painted building housed and acted as a court for the Schwalenberger Burgmannen knights; a contingent of the free aristocratic Knights of Eblinghusen, they were charged with guarding and defending the castle. Initially paid for their services with houses and farmland, the knights were later

251

rewarded with money instead.

In 1559 the building became part of Lippe domain and, after the Lippe merger with the Paderborn domain, it was sold. Centuries later, in the 1940s, it was reconstructed as an inn called the *Lippischer Hof*. During the artistic colony period and after transforming into an inn, it became the temporary abode of artists. The interior walls remain adorned to this day with legacy murals. Fanciful renditions of artists at work have since been painted on the exterior as well. A sign on the outer facade of the building reading "Schau Dir Bitte Die Historischen Gemalde In Der Galerie An!" invited visitors to "Please take a look at the historical paintings in the gallery!" It was no wonder the house was aptly named *Malkasten*, because it truly was a paintbox.

A mile and a half east of the village of Brakelsiek were the remains of the *Wallburg Rodenstatt*, an Iron Age hill-fort settlement. The thirty acre site was partially ruined when the old stones were used for building purposes and the creation of a brickyard and pottery operation but is now protected as a historic monument. Portions of the ancient ramparts could still be seen in the middle of an encroaching forest cover. Across the main road and just behind the village of Schwalenberg, sheep avoiding the intense sunshine grazed in shady areas. Hiking access into the Schwalenberger Wald was found just beyond. A walk through Das Mörth, a hillside moor wooded with larch and spruce trees instead of the typical beach tree coverage surrounding it, offered both a welcome canopy shelter from the heat and overviews of Schwalenberg and Brakelsiek.

Rolling countryside just beyond the two places could be held in a single sweep of the eyes, including armies of omnipresent German wind turbines. Formerly a bog, where efforts in making and transporting peat bricks were made before it was drained, the Mörth exhibits only the wonders of nature to the hiker today. Mörth, a word derived from Lippe Low German, belonged to the same language three ancestral families had held in common; the Meier family of Brakelsiek in North Rhine-Westphalia and the Gerhard family from Bärfelde in East Brandenburg, both settling in Illinois; and the Reithers of Marne who went to Iowa—all were speakers of Plattdeutsch.

On a small side street and up an embankment at the edge of the village of Brakelsiek, gravestones of a well-kept cemetery faced the heavens. Each grave was placed in a rectangular frame of stone that enclosed flowering plants and green shrubs as well, a typical practice of German Protestantism. Like a well-manicured boot hill on a raised plot of land exposed to prairie winds, there were views towards a backdrop of open fields to the south and west. A tour of the graveyard found no tombstones inscribed with the name of Meier. But there seemed to be way too few graves to be the only burial place in the village over so many centuries. Perhaps there was another, older one elsewhere in or near Brakelsiek, or possibly many villagers had been buried in Schwalenberg instead? And then too, because burial plots in Germany are often leased for a block of years due to land availability issues, disinterring occurs when maintenance payments cease, the plot then becoming available for reuse for the next departed soul.

A region often dubbed the German Switzerland actually did resemble the lower elevations of its neighbor to the south in many respects; scattered villages separated by agricultural fields and rolling hills, patches of forest groves, lush meadows and lakes. An afternoon was idled away at the nearby lakeside community of Schieder, the largest component of the Schieder-Schwalenberg grouping. Schieder See shimmered in the bright sunshine while sunbathers and boaters enjoyed the relaxing spot; joining them on the beach was not to be resisted. Next stop was Barntrup where we stayed overnight before going on to Blomberg, Horn and other towns. By the time the tour was finished, a fair sense of the Lippe district had been gained.

Outside the boundaries of the Lippe district, less than thirty-five miles away from Detmold and situated between the larger cities of Bielefeld and Hanover, the famed city of Hameln was easily attainable. With the Pied Piper legend hanging over it, Hameln—better known as Hamelin to English speakers—might be imagined as the quintessential tourism destination, overrun with tourists instead of rats. Not so. Other than a rodent-related street performance and a Piper-themed statue, the wandering of streets and squares was as normal as any other town. Buildings displayed consistent medieval architectural style on a grand scale, many painted in varying shades of white, pink, yellow and beige offsetting the grayness of winter months. Their number suggested a town of wealth, and Hameln's placement on a curve of the river Weser only added to its enchantment.

It was with fond memories that we left this part of northern Germany after returning the car to Detmold to board a train to our next destination. The opportunity to experience a new region even for a few days, especially the off-the beaten-path village of Brakelsiek, had satisfied the urge to see things firsthand. It was an achievement made all the more timely because only three years earlier, in 2010, Brakelsiek had celebrated its five-hundredth year anniversary. Barring fire or other catastrophe, the handsomely rebuilt ancestral home of Alma Gerhard's grandfather will hopefully take its rightful place in the village for another five hundred years!

DAVENPORT

Davenport, Iowa, March 1895

Maria Reither had a few minutes to herself which was unusual for the mother of nine children. When a bit of free time rarely came about, she first had to shake herself to believe it was really true then usually started right up again on the long list of things she had put off. Today, it took extra self-persuasion to sit down by the wood-burning stove to warm partially frozen hands for a few moments. A thin layer of snow already covered the ground and dark-clouded skies shaped the horizon, signaling yet another storm heading in their direction. It would have to pass before there would be any chance of rising temperatures to end a late winter season. It was still very cold in the heartland of America even more so than her fading memories of the frigid winters there had been growing up in Dithmarschen. But it was a different kind of cold here in Iowa, crackling dry with a bite to it, unlike the bone-chilling dampness so much a part of living by the sea.

She had just been out to the woodshed to carry an armful of firewood back into the house. Only a few moments outdoors had been enough to turn numbed fingertips a shade of blue. But it took more than harsh weather to keep Maria from the chores needing to be done—or to hold her children back from going to school, for that matter. Most of her children were still living at home except for the two eldest: Sophia and Emil. Born in Iowa as they all had been they were use to the climate and were actually thrilled when the first winter snow fell from the sky but fed up with it by winters end. The school day almost over, they would soon be back to their home in Cleona, only a handful of miles down the road from Hickory Grove Township with the unincorporated community of Plainview squeezed in-between. Davenport itself was only about fifteen miles from the farm acreage on which their house stood.

Julius would get a firm chiding for his negligence in filling the wood storage bin this morning before leaving for school. It wasn't the first time. As the eldest of her children still in the household, he needed to be more responsible, an example to the others. Maria now recalled how he had seemed to be in hurry to dash off. He had torn out the door so quickly she had failed to notice that some of his chores had been left undone.

Not yet fifty, she wasn't too old yet, she thought, to allow herself to be remiss in paying attention to a well-run home. But the drain of lengthy winters and an abundance of mouths to feed sometimes made her feel tired beyond her years. The passing of time and life's complications had added a weight upon her shoulders, and a tendency towards stoutness even when she was younger had been somewhat unkind to her waistline as well. But she was as sure of herself and her beliefs as she had been when she first met Johann Reither back in Holstein.

Now the warmth of the fire replenished by the fuel from

her arms began to affect her and she slid down deeper into the old armchair. It should be quiet for another hour until her first child returned and shutting her eyes her mind began to drift backwards to days gone by:

For a while she had been uncertain whether she would ever find the kind of husband she imagined; there may never have been the children that were necessary in making a real family. John's father had made his disapproval of her perfectly clear. He had told her it was because his father thought she was too young to be involved with him. He had said she shouldn't think it was because his father didn't like her; in reality he knew little about her at all. But she had believed his attitude towards her went beyond just age differences. It had to do with something else, something much deeper that was disagreeable to him, she thought. Perhaps there had been a quarrel of some sort between their two families in the past.

When Maria asked her mother if she knew of any grudges or feuds, she could not recall that there were any. But grievances could be one-sided too, passed down and kept alive for generations. Whatever reasons behind his disdain for her, they had only intensified during the crossing to America thirty years ago. After they had gone separate ways in New York before heading for Iowa, she had prayed that any differences would be set aside, forgiven and forgotten before reaching Davenport. Lingering disagreements of any kind would have only added to the struggle of starting over in a new land.

Her eyelids grew heavier now and she began to doze off. But just when Maria's mind had left the trail of old memories and slumber was almost upon her, a sharp crack of splitting wood snapped her back once again to the shadows of the past:

She saw herself standing on the dock on the banks of the

Mississippi looking across at the city on the other side as it appeared when she first arrived. She had just stepped off the train from New York along with the rest of her family in 1866. It had been a much simpler time then, and she had been naïve when she thought of the changes she had seen over the years since. She saw it so clearly; it was as if past had now become present.

Satisfaction from safely surviving the ordeal of passage to America then onwards to their final destination of Iowa should have been enough. It was to a point. But the ache in the pit of her stomach could not be ignored; Johann had not been there to meet her as she had hoped. She had dreamed of sharing together her first few moments in their new home. They had left each other at the port in New York after a voyage of highs and lows, her family beginning the trip westward before his did. All the same she wished it had been the other way around, and he had been in Iowa before she arrived to greet her. To have seen his welcoming face again at the station would have meant the world to her.

It was after the fact when she first heard from her mother that his family had also arrived in Davenport a few days later. Maria's father had known earlier when the train had arrived, but for fear of meddling where he shouldn't, he had kept it to himself. Even though he had gotten over any misgivings he had harbored at first about their relationship long ago, any involvement with the irksome father of Johann was a risk not worth taking. So left uniformed, she had not been at the station when it was his turn to arrive either.

But her father's wishes for her best interests, for the best interests of both families really, could not stop them from discretely meeting a few days later and whenever possible

259

thereafter. As careful as they tried to be discrete, there was no such thing as a rendezvous kept secret in their German community. Eyes and ears were everywhere. They were aware of the impact of gossip but taking a chance on undue attention was the only thing they could do if they wanted to continue seeing each other. If her father knew about it, he hadn't mentioned it to her. His silence was good enough for her.

It had been fortunate that during their first few weeks in Davenport, when the two families were staying at the same hotel, the Germania House catering to newcomers fresh off the train or steamboat, there had been no incidents. By the time Johann had left and moved to a leased farm a few miles away, he had already taken John for his new American name. Maria's family soon dispersed in city and countryside as well; the oldest son hired out as a laborer on a nearby farm, a daughter taken on as a servant in another, and others secured jobs or attended school in Davenport.

Maria suddenly awoke for a moment from her reverie. She poked at the embers before closing her eyes once more:

The conversation she had with John on a late Sunday afternoon many years ago began to unfold. They had met to stroll down the paths of Central Park, one of their favorite places to go in Davenport. She was at his side as the scene replayed itself.

"It's already been nearly two weeks since we've seen each other, Maria. I hope we're finished with all the snow after the storm last Sunday so we won't have to wait so long next time. It kept everyone indoors for days, although you couldn't tell by the weather we're having right now. Look around. It looks like there's someone in every corner of this park!" his arms reaching skywards towards the sun for emphasis. "A single dose of March sunshine and you'd think everyone believed we're in the middle of summer again. Your father must have been happy last weekend, though, when no one dared leaving the house for fear of freezing to death."

"Let's not mention my father now, John. It wouldn't do any good anyway. He just doesn't want to be the one to cause any more trouble with your father. Hopefully, there'll be a time when all of this is behind us."

"I guess you're right. Sorry I brought it up on such a perfect day. I really don't want to spoil it. I just wish my father would come to be more accepting like yours, and sooner rather than later." They turned down the central tree-lined promenade arm in arm. The popular park had been recently expanded and was set to grow in size again within the next two years. "There's a dry bench free ahead on the left. Are you ready to sit down yet, Maria?"

"Yes. Just for a few minutes. It's too cold to sit still longer than that." Sure enough, the iciness of the wooden slats started to penetrate their clothing almost immediately.

John leaned forward and twisted his body to face her as much as he could while still keeping his feet planted on the ground in front of him. "I think it's time we take the next step together," he began seriously and nervously at the same time. "I'm tired of waiting and I'm tired of worrying about what others think about us. We're old enough to make our own decisions, don't you agree?"

She looked up at him as he spoke, a hint of a smile forming on her lips. "Why John Reither if I'm hearing from you what I think I'm hearing, are you asking me to...?"

"...to marry you. I am. That's exactly what I'm saying. I know it's not a very romantic way to go about proposing to

261

you, but the words just needed to come out now. Even though we've known each other forever, there still may be doubts in your mind. Even if there are, please don't say no immediately. I'd much rather have it be a maybe, or let me think it over answer if can't be a yes now. I can understand if you're not quite ready."

"You should know there are no doubts about you. There never have been, never will be."

"Shall I get down on one knee then, Maria, and ask you properly?"

"It's much too damp to do any kneeling. You know I'm much too practical for that. The answer is yes. Yes and double yes. Of course I will marry you. I would have married you in a minute even on the ship, if we could have arranged it."

It was his turn to let happiness filter through, anxiety having evaporated completely. He raised her to her feet, and circling arms around her waist they slowly resumed their walk through the park; it was time to let the world know. Sunlight was about to lose any warmth it yet had, but before it did they had set a wedding date in May, only two short months away. Why wait any longer?

In front of the fire glowing much less than her heart had at that time, her fond recollections began to fade as the embers died down. Still, she managed to pick up where she had left off once again:

Two days after returning from the park, her father gathered the family together in the kitchen. He placed two pieces of paper in front of him on the table.

"Yesterday, I've had a letter from our relatives in Chicago. They've invited us to come for a visit as soon as we can. I think this might be the last chance for a man who has nearly reached his sixtieth year to board a train and make such a trip so I've said yes. I'll need someone to go with me, and Maria, I've decided it's you, my dear. You are the best one to take of those still at home. We will leave on Saturday week. It's not a very long trip, but it will be long enough for me at my age."

She felt as if she were about to faint, her face turning as white as the undisturbed Iowan snow blanketing the ground. Even though she realized it would probably be useless, Maria collected herself in an effort to dissuade him.

"But why not wait till the weather is better? You must remember, I'm supposed to talk to the Bentz family next week about helping them with household chores. Maybe one of my younger sisters would be better to go with you?"

"I thought it all over before and the decision has been made. Let's not mention it again."

It wasn't until after they had been in Chicago for a week that her father said he would be returning to Davenport— without her! She was needed to stay a while longer to lend a hand in watching children and with keeping house while their daughter was away. Maria hadn't seen this coming, but later she realized that it had been carefully orchestrated to temper her relationship with John—perhaps time and distance would make it go away, maybe even forever. She later learned the two fathers had met on a single occasion to talk about them. Seeing no reason to hope for John's father ever changing his mind, her father was convinced the pair of them would be doomed from the start without his blessing. He had seen it happen before; disagreeable parents could cast a shadow on any chance of happiness for the long run.

But he was shortsighted in understanding his daughter's

determination. Although a short excursion to Chicago would lengthen into a stay of more than six months, it deterred neither Maria nor John from reaching their objective when she reappeared in Davenport. Married in 1868, two and a half years later the birth of Sophia brightened their lives. She would be the first child of many more to come.

Years and memories sped by faster and faster behind her drowsy eyes:

Her father had taken his last breath soon after the birth of Maria's second child in 1872. He had lived long enough to realize it had been wrong to tamper with his daughter's affections. He had underestimated both the strength of her will and her commitment to John. This wasn't the case for John's father, however. Two months later in the same year, he too passed away never giving an inch, stubbornly clinging to the belief of a disobedient son and leaving their relationship unmended.

But there were so many good things to mark the years gone by. How exciting it had been to take possession of their first farm together in 1869, rented and managed for a share of production; three hundred and twenty acres of fields and fifteen more of pastures. And then there was the unforgettable taste of their first crop of homegrown American potatoes. John had watched with hungry eyes as Maria peeled off their musty-smelling skins and set them to boiling for the evening meal. The sight of oats and wheat shimmering wavelike in the early summer breezes always took her breath away. Of course stalks of Indian corn reaching for the sky—grown taller than she was—had brought back to her the old folktale of Jack and the Beanstalk. Only two at the beginning but increasing upon the birth of two more, their "herd" of cows had grown to twelve altogether, along with two horses and a few pigs. Yes, there had been many good times, even if a waterfall of tears had been shed for Maria's tenth child, Alfred, who had died at the age of three months.

A move to a second and smaller leased farm in Cleona—the town in which she now drifted along in the comfortable chair—had been necessary after the owner of the Hickory Grove farm had sold all of the acreage to a buyer with a large family. With the aid of a few hired hands, the new owners managed the acreage by themselves, no longer needing tenant farmer help. It had been one of the worst days of their lives to have to pack belongings and leave the home they had loved. It was where they had first dropped anchor in a new land, where they had come to know each corner of every field, every tree and bush—the place where American roots had been deeply dug into the soil.

The family continued to thrive as the children passed into adulthood on the Cleona farm. But they had been unable to establish the close friendships made over the years in Hickory Grove. Sophia had already left the family to take-up employment as a servant girl in Davenport. As the eldest child she knew it was up to her to do her part in making ends meet. Davenport itself had changed a great deal over the years, never stagnant, ever becoming larger. Even now, when national development had almost come to a standstill during wide-spread economic depression, Davenport had continued to prosper and expand. One had to look no further for evidence than the nearly completed city hall which would be opening in the next few months. The majestic building had been financed primarily by revenues acquired from a tax on saloons—the town was laden with a wealth of such establishments, good or bad as that may be. Davenport had managed to buck the economic doldrums affecting the rest of the country and news of its favorable circumstances had rapidly spread to other cities and towns, stimulating another onslaught of migration. This time it came from other parts of the country rather than overseas.

Maria conjured up one last memory before Adelia, her youngest, entered the house in letting the screen door slam shut behind her as was her daily habit. She never minded the banging because it let her know that her youngest was safely home. But this time it was a picture of John sitting at the kitchen table only few nights ago. He was nervously drumming his fingers:

"I've been running this over in my mind for many days, Maria. We've made it through a lot of things together throughout the years. And even though we haven't been long in Cleona and maybe haven't given it the chance it deserves, I believe we can do better for ourselves. There's talk of good land to still to be had in Iowa out west. What would you say if I were to look into it? If it's too much to consider right now with all of the children so involved here, or not a good idea at all, just say so. It's just that I still feel unsettled. I think you feel the same way. It's never felt quite like home here, like when we lived in Hickory Grove. I see our family starting to go separate ways and I don't want to leave it until it's too late."

For John, a man of usually few words, it was one of the longer speeches of a serious note Maria had ever heard from him. And using carefully measured words, he never spoke recklessly. To suggest making yet another move was not something to be taken lightly as if it was a fleeting thought off the top of his head. And she didn't. In fact, she felt the same uncertainty as he did about Cleona. Up until now she had given no serious thought to another change, or had heard of any prospects coming their way, but she had often wished life had taken a different course after leaving Hickory Grove.

"It would be good to look elsewhere while we can, before too much more time goes by. You should go ahead and look into it, Johann, do whatever is necessary," she advised in reverting to the German version of his name as she sometimes did when they were alone. "But before we go too far, we should talk to the children, at least to the older ones—to see what they think about it."

"Yes, the children need to know although for the moment it's only an idea. I don't want to stir things up or alarm anybody without good cause when another move may never happen. Even if it does eventually come about, it could be a long time off. And who knows for sure if what I've heard about this land is true or not."

"You never know when another opportunity will come along, Johann. It's better to at least let them hear what we're thinking. Sooner is better than later so there'll be no complaints from not being told. The older ones would need time to consider where they want to make their lives; it will be a big decision for them. No, it's definitely better now than later."

"Then let's talk about it tonight, if we can get them all together."

That same evening the family had gathered around the kitchen table again. While there had been questioning looks on the faces of the younger generation—not another change upsetting their lives again—without concrete specifics of where and when, the idea had been tenuous enough there was no reason to become overly concerned. In truth, they had not been inclined the slightest to be bothered by such a remote possibility.

Who would really think of leaving the Davenport area when they had so many relatives living here? Take Aunt Christina, for example, their father's sister. She had years ago married someone having the same surname. She hadn't waited long, only one year after arriving in 1866, before wedding Jacob Reither, a first cousin. He was the son of her father's older brother, Uncle Henry, whose family's immigration to America had preceded Christina's by almost ten years. A child had followed the next year and there were three more to follow over the next decade; four daughters in all, and all bound to their lives in Davenport. It would be hard to leave this family with whom free time was shared so often together. So much so it was almost as if the two families had been blended into one.

Only Peter, the carpenter who had gone to Saint Louis to live and work before visiting his cousin John J. in Kentucky had seen fit to live elsewhere before finally settling down in Iowa. And when he did, it wasn't with the rest of them in Davenport. He had opened a cabinetry business in the town of Manning, west of Des Moines and very far west of Davenport. It was seldom they heard much about Peter, and even more rarely had they seen John J. who had eventually made Indiana his home.

So a move to a new place leaving close relatives behind seemed farfetched. Sophia, Emil, Herman and Ida, the four oldest of nine children, were established and content with the farm and household jobs they had. Even John Reither, the middle child whose passion for horse and other livestock trading had been flamed by the profit from the sale of his first cows, was committed to a life in Davenport. Stock trading know-how had been taught to him by a friend and neighbor who had noticed John's aptitude for the buying and selling business where the forming of many good relationships was the key to success.

The sound of footsteps drawing closer ended Maria's daydreaming. Her rest over, she gave a final shake of her head to erase the cobwebs of events past, then rose from the chair and walked to the kitchen where Adelia was sure to be by now. Life was a rocky road for immigrants, and their lives had been no different. But for the present, with her daughter home and her brothers and sisters soon to follow, there would be one thing in common; they would all be clamoring for a slice of the cake Maria had baked that morning. It would have to tide them over until their father came in from the fields to sit for the evening meal.

DNA

Central Coast, California, 2017

It's ubiquitous, in the daily newspapers, the focus of television shows, on the tongues of friends and family; DNA, the three letters standing for deoxyribonucleic acid, a person's genetic makeup. The substance of a genome, the unique set of genes and chromosomes belonging to an individual, it plays a critical role in health factors and medical conditions, biological parent identification, locating missing persons, criminal investigation and questions of cloning. The importance of DNA in today's world is hard to ignore.

DNA tests are also the scientific backbone for family historians wanting to learn more about their heritage, ethnicity and potential relations. These tests are currently attainable by most people in terms of cost and ease of self-administration and they have become a critical tool in solving ancestral questions. Complementing traditional genealogical research focusing on the paper trail retained by official institutions and often available online in digitized form, DNA tests can sometimes confirm or refute family stories.

However, even with improving accuracy, test results must be taken with a degree of skepticism when breaking out ethnicity percentages and identifying regions of origin. Lacking refinement in pinpointing specific ancestral countries, they seem to be best when used for broad projections of African, Middle Eastern, European, Asian, Ashkenazi and American roots. As the number of people taking genealogical DNA tests increases, geographical narrowing and ethnic detail is expected to become more precise. The major competing test companies all offer up a list of names or user identities of test takers who match chromosome relatedness to some degree. Matches can range from nuclear family members to very distant cousins, and a method of contact is usually provided.

Taking the plunge, a basic autosomal test analyzing DNA from both parents was taken from one of the competing companies. Later, two more companies were added for test comparison. Each of them interpreted ethnicity differently and provided unique sets of matches. Expecting to find a figure of around fifty percent for German ethnicity along with a map highlighting Germany, or maybe even northern Germany, or even better Schleswig-Holstein, as one of the primary places of origin, outcomes were both disappointing and eye-opening at the same time for all of the companies. Only one of them even included German as an ethnicity category and even then it was grouped together with French origins.

Germany and France as a group was broad enough to create doubt, but results from a third company were even more inexact in lumping Germany into a Europe West category also comprising Belgium, France, Netherlands, Switzerland, Luxembourg and Liechtenstein. For people with little knowledge of their ancestry it would be a hopeless task as to where to start. For those without these ancestries, ethnicity percentages fell into other European categories, such as

Europe East, Broadly European and British and Irish, each composed of different country groups. The pairing Finland/Northwest Russia was one of the narrower groupings in focusing more on specific countries than regions. Scandinavia was another one with Swedish ethnicity even further delineated. And it was the southern Nordic region that was the most surprising and puzzling in my case: the amount of personal Scandinavian ancestry, whether it was Swedish or Norwegian, ranged from twenty-six to thirty-three percent among the three companies.

The only verified place of origin for my paternal ancestors going back to the late 1600s was Germany. But two out of three companies with ancestor location maps had skipped over Schleswig-Holstein as a target area altogether! At this point it looked like existing algorithms were sorely in need of reconfiguration, conflating the northernmost part of modern Germany between Hamburg and the Danish border with the even more northern Scandinavia. Could it be that earlier Viking raids and Danish rule of Schleswig and Holstein for over three hundred years had skewed the results in favor of Scandinavia? Danish censuses from Dithmarschen testify to families with Scandinavian surnames living as neighbors beside German-surnamed families, and intermarriage between Germans and Danes before and after these censuses were taken in the 1800s would have been more than likely.

From the time the tests were originally taken segregation of German ethnicity has improved and percentages have been adjusted accordingly. A truer picture has emerged supporting traditional genealogy knowledge, and reduced numbers for Scandinavian heritage—nearly by half—could reflect a more accurate ethnic component. Meaningful autosomal DNA tests are supposed to be valid no further back than about three hundred years in time, or ten generations. After that point the amount of DNA transmitted from multiple times great-grandparents would be so small as to be negligible.

If ancestors had brought their DNA to Germany from Scandinavia more than ten generations ago it would have been watered down by now, literally almost washed out by the more dominant ethnicity in the area in which they had settled. Even five generations back would find ethnic percentages to be very low numbers if there had been no marriage between individuals with divergent ethnicity afterwards. Even though it seems certain now that Swedish ethnicity, probably from my mother's side, figures significantly in my ancestry, all of the major companies need more participants and technology development to segregate Scandinavian from German DNA chromosome markers.

The single thread of consistency among the autosomal tests taken was the percentage of ethnicity from the regional category of Northwestern Europe. While each of the three companies termed this region with a different title, the countries included were much the same and personal ethnicity percentages were noted as fifty-five, sixty-four and sixty-six percent of the total tally respectively. An eleven percent difference separated the lowest and highest estimate, but all were over fifty percent. At least the results were clearly distinguished from the other main European categories. Currently, only basic autosomal tests deal with ethnicity, but none of them were sophisticated enough to be able to attribute ethnicity specifically to a male or female line of ancestors. Further analytic progress may yet offer this distinction.

A second type of genealogical test focusing on the female

line only was taken next. The mtDNA test examines mitochondria DNA, which is also found in cells along with autosomal DNA. While used exclusively for tracing a succession of maternal ancestry, both males and females can take the test. Mitochondrial DNA is passed down by a mother, mother's mother, mother's mother's mother, and so on in a continuous line. It eliminates genetic evidence coming from an individual's father. As anticipated, the results were mostly a confirmation of traditional research and personal knowledge. Although this test does not measure percentages of ethnicity, it did include a different group of matching surnames and a map placing their names in respective countries.

Y-DNA, a test for males only, completed the three main testing choices. The Y chromosome is passed on to all male offspring—males having one X and one Y chromosome and females with two X chromosomes—from father to father and so on. Markers, essentially chromosome fragments of various lengths, were compared with those of other test participants for similarity and number and new paternal connections were found through chromosome marker matching.

Of value for contacting close matches and exploring possible relationships through name mapping, it was similar to the mtDNA test in that ethnicity analysis is not a factor in either one. Match distribution broken out by individuals and by specific countries in terms of genetic distance was also of interest in measuring time to most recent common ancestors for both mtDNA and Y-DNA tests. The range of separation was anywhere from four generations to one hundred and three generations for Y-DNA, much less significant than autosomal matching predictions.

Testing Y-DNA is also used for tracing deep ancient

migration routes through male only haplogroups. Again, like mtDNA for female haplogroups, Y-DNA tests purport to place a tester's genetic background into one of several large branches of population that had congregated in different geographic locations thousands of years ago. Since exact ethnicity and location of close ancestors was of foremost concern, both mtDNA and Y-DNA tests, although interesting, were of marginal importance.

MOVEMENT

Cleona, Scott County, Iowa, June 1897

Time marched on again and it seemed like talk about a possible move from Cleona to the northwestern part of Iowa four years earlier had been just that—talk. The young people had mostly forgotten about it by now in the final years of the 19th century, as if the idea had evaporated as winter snow in late springtime. Most of the Reither children, except for the three youngest, had finished with their schooling. Meta, turning twelve last February, and her sister Adelia now just eleven, continued on with their education, while Otto was within days of finishing his final year. The older, unmarried children were either working with their father on the farm, hired as farmhands elsewhere, or had found jobs as servant girls in houses in the Davenport vicinity. Sophia and Ida, the two eldest daughters, though both still young women, had been married for several years now: Sophia, a mother of three children with one more on the way; Ida and husband Adolph Giese, parents of a daughter born two years earlier.

With so many of the Reither children putting down roots in the same place as their parents, life seemed destined to continue unperturbed by thoughts of anything different. On a

276

hot June afternoon, as if was already the middle of summer, the Reither family, including the married couples with children in tow, gathered together to share a meal as they often did after Sunday service at the Lutheran church in Davenport. Out of the blue, their father stood up and clinked a knife against the side of a glass to draw attention to what he was about to say.

"Once again mother and I wanted to have you all here to talk over what we spoke about ages ago. If you recall, we were starting to think about moving to somewhere else in Iowa but nothing came of it then. Now the kind of opportunity we thought might work out before has finally come about on the other side of the state. More reasonably priced farm land not far from the bordering states of Minnesota and Nebraska is still for sale and it's supposed to be some of the best land anywhere in Iowa. We've made an offer on a parcel that was accepted by one of the owners. Since our decision concerns not just your mother and me but all of us, we wanted to let you know as soon as possible. It won't happen tomorrow. But it won't be that long either. Your sister Ida will explain more afterwards, since it involves her family too."

Everyone had remained silent to this point, not knowing what to say, until son John spoke up. "You mean it's not a hundred percent certain yet? What do you mean by one of the owners?"

"There is a second owner who owns half the property. We will know in a matter of a few days if he is agreeable or not. But since the paperwork has already been started, it looks pretty much a certainty. I think he is counting on selling it too.

"Your mother and I are getting on in years so this may be our last chance to be on a property that belongs to us. We'll need to wrap up commitments here and things need to be ready there before we can leave. So it will be at least a month or two before we're able to make a move, that's if everything else goes according to plan. The western half of Iowa is starting to come into its own and there seem to be many opportunities there. If you do decide to join us, I don't think you'll be disappointed; but you're all old enough now to make up your own minds. We know what it means to leave somewhere familiar and how involved you are in this area so we will be happy with whatever you decide."

He paused for a moment to look closely at the faces intently looking back at his own before adding a few more remarks which, when all were said and done, left everyone's heads spinning with possibilities. Sitting back down with his hands clasped together in front of him, he waited for the murmurings to quiet down. It was Emil, the oldest son, who began to speak for the group.

"We agree. We will need some time to talk it over later. It's a big change to consider, and since you're not leaving right away, we don't need to decide what we want to do today even if we are all here in one place. But we would like to talk it over a little more today before going our separate ways."

"There's one more thing you should know then mother and I will leave you alone to discuss. There'll be time to continue the conversation later. Ida, it's almost your turn now. But I'll just finish by saying our good friends Claus, Adolph's father, and his wife Anna have recently finished purchasing one hundred and sixty acres of good farmland in O'Brien County, the same place in which we are buying.

"Their land is in Lincoln Township in the northeast corner of the county. Adolph and Ida have been working hard to help realize their dream of migrating across Iowa with their parents to a less crowded area, the same dream your mother and I have had ever since Davenport became a victim of its own popularity. Scott County land prices have gone through the roof and rural families like ours cannot afford enough acres to call our own and still make a living.

"Good land that could be purchased at an average of thirty dollars fifteen years ago is now a hundred dollars an acre and increasing every month. Out west in O'Brien County land prices are much lower for now, but we can't wait forever or they'll be out of reach there as well. But pardon me Ida, I may have taken too much of your turn to speak already."

"Claus Giese and Anna just signed the purchase contract a few days ago so Adolph and I haven't had much time yet to sit down to discuss details with his parents, or to tell you all about our plans. Of course, without us working together on the purchase, we wouldn't have been able to take advantage of such a good opportunity." Ida sounded almost apologetic, her voice quavering a bit. Her nervousness seemed to trickle down to the rest of her well-rounded body, heavily pregnant as she was with their second child, when she continued.

"But this may be the most shocking part to all of you; we're going to be leaving Cleona within two weeks! You can pretend we're the advance guard; we'll see how it goes there then let the rest of you know. We think that if we can be a little settled there before the baby is born, it would be so much easier for us," she explained in placing a hand on her belly, "and it will probably be less than two months from now."

The Giese family, about to be leaving before you know it, and the Reithers not so long afterwards, it seemed like the younger generation were being deserted before they even had a chance to mull it over. It was like breaking up the clan-like living arrangement they had taken for granted for so long. Ida wriggled in her chair and wished she could wipe away confused looks in all of their faces.

"To repeat what father just said, we don't want our choice to leave with Adolph's parents to influence the rest of you in making your own decision. Like he said, many of you have already made good lives here in Scott County. So if we stay around now while you have your discussion, Adolph and I promise to keep quiet and just listen to what you have to say."

"Are there any cities like Davenport near this Lincoln Township?" John piped up again. Ida's outspoken younger brother seemed never to be at a loss for words no matter what.

"It's true; most of us don't know anything about that part of Iowa," his brother Emil added. "It's so far away from where we live. What if it turns out to be there's no need for our farming skills in this new place, Ida? What would be able to do then once we're already there?"

"I don't think you have to worry. After all, Claus and Anna and our parents made the journey to America from Holstein. The other side of Iowa is only a stone's throw away in comparison. And Claus gave up his occupation as a miller in the old country to reinvent himself as a farmer only few months later. I think we know how to adapt and get whatever needs doing done wherever we go by now."

The smallest ones, Meta and Delia, started talking among themselves, not yet daring enough to join in a grown-up discussion. Their elevating voices soon caused sets of eyes around the table to fall upon them unhappily.

"C'mon Delia, I think it's time we go outside. I'll ask if it's okay to leave the table." Their loud voices becoming a nuisance anyhow permission was willingly granted.

The girls had a lot to say to each other; but what they were most worried about was losing friends at school and their freedom to move about the community. As the youngest of the brood they had managed to escape the scrutiny of distracted parents a good deal of the time.

It was beginning to look like the discussion intended to be held later without parents present had taken on a life of its own in present company. Ida began talking again.

"But to answer John's earlier question; no, there aren't any cities like Davenport nearby. There are two small towns, though: Hartley and Sanborn. Both of them, from what we've learned so far, were founded less than ten years ago after the local railroad was completed. But you know more about these places than we do, father."

"The Milwaukee railroad passes through both Sanborn and Hartley. It started operating in 1878, only a dozen years after we arrived in Davenport but long enough ago to be well-established by now. Easy access to the railroad for trading purposes is one of the main reasons—that and value for money in terms of farmland size—why we were looking at these two prairie towns in the first place. Both towns are deeded townships without homestead claims on them, which makes them even more promising. Claus and Anna are only a little ahead of us and are itching to go. We'll hear from their experience in the next month or so before we are able to leave as well."

"That's what Adolph's father says about the railroad too," Ida agreed. "He thinks having it there makes it prime territory because the next closest east-west rail connection is over twenty miles away to the north."

Questions and attempted answers swirled around the table until the long daylight of the June evening was nearly at its end. Finally it was their father who called a stop to the conversation; he was tired and it was time for bed. They could continue with their ideas in the forthcoming days. Nothing needed to be decided that evening.

***

Lincoln and Hartley, O'Brien County, Iowa, May 1899

"John Hofmeier, Fred Gerhard and Christian Tolle loaded their household goods, farm machinery, etc., and started for Spencer, Iowa from Rock City today," an article reported in the *Freeport Weekly Democrat* on 18 March 1895.

After twelve years of struggling to realize the dream he had kept since arriving in Stephenson County in the northwest corner of Illinois, Friedrich Gerhard had taken the gamble to pull up stakes and move his family to a neighboring state. It meant giving up one rural county for another—O'Brien County in Iowa. For Fred and his two old friends, the lure of someday owning their own farms had beckoned too strongly to be resisted.

In moving to Iowa with Louisa and their three children it would be going into the unknown for none of them had ever been there before. Would the soil in Iowa be as fertile as the ground under plow in Stephenson County? Would they be able find an affordable house large enough for the whole family, a place that would keep them warm during the harsh winters and cool in summers? And would Alma, their seven year old daughter, ever get over the tears shed in having to leave good

282

friends? Equally traumatic for his wife, would she be able to adjust to separation from her parents who were among the first German settlers of Rock City? There would be so many other relatives that would be missed as well.

Earlier settlement was a good deal of the problem facing more recent immigrants like Fred. The first wave of German immigrants to the area during the 1840s and 1850s had purchased plots of farmland at low prices from an even earlier proprietor. Conrad Epley, new owner of the Epleyanna Mills, and his sons had acquired large plots of untouched land in the vicinity of the mill. His land clearing prowess and other developments had made him an institution; various places of importance in the community bore his name, ensuring his lasting legacy even after the eventual splintering of his holdings.

By the time Fred Gerhard had arrived with his parents in 1883, it was already too late. German pioneers had sewn up the best land nearest to town. It had been years and would likely be many more before newcomers like the Gerhards could break the lock they had on farmland ownership. Even his wife Louisa—one of ten children and daughter of one of these prosperous landowners—could not expect to obtain a piece of land threatened with division into parcels too small to sustain a living. Fred was much too impatient and ambitious to bide his time to wait it out. Why should he waste his energy treading water in the prime of his life when there was the promise of better prospects somewhere else?

So with his 31st birthday during the same month of March, they left for Iowa, excited but with plenty of qualms as well. But soon, with bended backs, field hardened hands, mud-encrusted overalls and sweat streaked faces, the worries they

283

had were laid to rest but not also without brows furrowed like the rows in the fields they plowed. It took some time, but four years on, in 1899, they found themselves living in a house large enough for another child born in 1896, almost one year to the day after their departure from Illinois. Although it was not free from mortgage or in Spencer where they had at first resided, they were now owners of their first farm on the outskirts of the town of Hartley. Fred's long held wish had become a reality. Even Alma, the daughter whose tears had copiously dropped before leaving her home in Illinois, had gotten over it with time. From her dried tears had emerged a self-assured eleven year old, someone on the way to becoming a young women with a serious and steady nature seemingly content with her life.

Alma Gerhard felt at home at her school too. The German Evangelical Lutheran church had been founded in Hartley during the same year they had moved into their new home and the school had later become part of the church. Fluent in German, she was, of course, completely conversant in English as well. But classes and playmate conversations were mostly in German and provided an important continuity with her early educational years in Illinois. Her mother's birth to German immigrants in northern Stephenson County meant Alma was second generation American. On her father's side, however, she was first generation and German still predominated in their household. Moreover, why shouldn't it be the main language of their small community since Hartley was mostly comprised of inhabitants with German heritage? The pockets of Dutch, Irish and Scandinavians would just have to fend for themselves!

Even at her young age Alma was seen as a force to be

reckoned with at a school where ages of the children ranged from five to seventeen. Her essays were a cut above even those who were three or four years older than she was and her recitation exercises almost never failed in being faultlessly delivered. Above average in everything else that was taught in the one-room school, she had begun to realize her aptitude for learning. With this awareness, devotion to studies had only intensified in becoming a main source of personal fulfillment. She had even taken it on her own to emulate the practice of the schoolmaster in taking under her wing some of the younger children who were in need of help—there were a couple of older ones as well—and informally tutored them whenever she could.

A more telling quality, one of future importance that she had demonstrated on several occasions, was her sensitivity to the children who were outsiders. Maybe it was almost a flaw in her character, but when she felt others were left out or badly treated, she felt she had to intervene—sometimes to the point of over-reaction. She hated to see classmates teased or made fun of for whatever reason. Whether they dressed differently, talked more slowly or lacked basic social skills, she made it her mission to support them, to show them they were not alone. For belittlement and harassment she had no tolerance and would not let it stand.

In recent days she had been closely watching one of the new girls, another transplant from Davenport, who was often by herself standing on the playground sidelines at recess. Adelia Reither appeared to be on the shy side and without any friends yet. Her shyness carried over when called upon to speak in front of the class; there had been giggling between classmates, which had only made her more self-effacing and tongue-tied. Two days before Alma had watched her tumble to the ground when one of the girls sitting on a bench whispering to another had stuck out a foot, tripping Adelia as she ran by. At thirteen, the new student was two years older than Alma but not too old to receive an offer of help.

"Hello. My name's Alma. I already know your name."
At first, Adelia looked to the side, trying to ignore the younger but taller person who had come up to her; timidity had gotten the best of age superiority. But Alma didn't give up. She wasn't about to let this girl remain alone. She wanted her to join in, to become part of the screams and chatter coming out of the loud mouths of the others running around the playground.

Children could go an entire school year isolated, if it went unnoticed and was not caught early on. She had already seen it happen when she was younger. Teachers wanted everyone to participate, of course, but they were preoccupied with the curriculum and in keeping classroom control. On the playground, it was a blur of many bodies of different ages, sizes and levels going in all directions at the same time and hard to pick out potential problems.

After a few seconds of silence and eyes still avoiding hers, Alma went closer and put her an arm around Adelia's shoulder tight enough so she could not pull away; together she started her walking slowly around the playground. They stopped now and then to engage classmates Alma considered to be her own friends and friendly towards others as well. With each introduction, Adelia seemed to be a little more open and responsive to any questions asked of her. By the time recess was over, an observant person would have seen a change starting to take place. She found a few more words to say and a flat demeanor was visibly transforming into a hint of cheerfulness. She could now actually look someone in the eyes instead of elsewhere when speaking to them.

Alma knew she had achieved a smidgen of success when Adelia began speaking first, even if it was just hello or saying her own name. No longer did she feel restricted to a simple shake of the head as a response. Then when one of the girls invited Adelia to join them in a game of tag, it was certain things were going in the right direction. Pausing for just a moment before reentering the school room and returning to their seats, Adelia nudged Alma's shoulder with her own.

"You know when I was in Davenport no one called me Adelia. It's my real name, but Delia is what I usually go by. I hope you'll call me Delia—and the rest of the kids too."

Alma placed a hand on Delia's back to shepherd her into the building for everyone to see. A steely look was cast on staring children around the room just to make sure they understood what was meant from now on. An especially lengthy glare towards the two girls who had tripped Delia said it all. As weeks turned into months a deeper friendship was formed between them.

When another, this time self-initiated, fall to the ground at the end of the school day resulted in a torn dress and skinned knees, Alma offered to help carry the smaller but older girl's books home for her. Wounded, she gratefully accepted and the short trek was soon made together. Shortly after entering the door, Alma found herself swarmed by Delia's siblings. When they had heard the voice of their sister along with another unfamiliar female one chatting like song birds, the boys had been drawn to see for themselves. To the Reither brothers she was a new person of curiosity. Nonchalantly looking Alma up and down, they next began to pepper her with questions until Delia decided enough was enough and it was time for them to make an escape. She asked if her friend would like go to the kitchen for a muffin she had helped her mother bake.

"Can I join you? I'm hungry too." Not so easily dismissed, John Reither, the persistent nineteen year old and oldest of the Reither children still living at home had been bold enough to wedge himself between the two girls. There was something interesting about this new friend of Delia's and he was not about to let it pass.

Warning sparks darted from Delia's eyes, "Only if you let us talk without interrupting—and limit yourself to eating one muffin only!" Turning towards Alma, she continued, "I've seen him eat four of them at one go before stopping to let the rest of us have a chance." At home, Delia didn't seem reserved at all, handling her siblings with a confidence that had been missing during her first weeks at school.

Actually, it took no effort at all on his part for John to fade more or less into the background. He was content just to watch Alma's gestures, her small, delicate movements, the various expressions crisscrossing the face of the new very slender guest. It may have been his first encounter with her, but without realizing it, he was already locking the memory away. He wished she had been able to stay longer when she left a half hour later to go home.

John Reither had already finished with schooling and had been working as a farm laborer for over two years. So it was only occasionally after their first meeting that he had the chance to see Alma Gerhard again. But because the lands the families tilled were side-by-side he often talked to others in her family, sharing with them knowledge on the latest farm implements, worrying about the state of the crops, discussing the weather and local news. Several times he had been sure to make a stop by her house after Sunday service. Well-liked and respected for his stock buying knowledge in the wider agricultural community, John had passed on several opportunities to pursue serious female relationships. Each time something had held him back from going too far down a path that never seemed quite right to him. But this time it was different.

JOHN AND ALMA

Hartley, O'Brien County, Iowa, March 1904

Two memorable events took place over the years that had elapsed since the Reither family had moved from Davenport to O'Brien County in 1899, and both of them had served to reinforce John's feelings towards Alma Gerhard. In 1900 the German Evangelical Church had bought the old Methodist Episcopal Church building and had it moved intact to a new location in the northeast part of Hartley. And in 1903 the interior was completely remodeled, almost unrecognizable from its former state.

Sixteen years old and verging on adulthood, Alma Gerhard and the new church were now both ready for her to receive confirmation, and the ritual was performed on the 27th day of March in 1904. On the certificate handed to her by Reverend Wilhelm Vehe, just above her name, the word *Denkspruch* was written. Below the German word—meaning an adage in English—was a verse from the bible. Delicate hands belying their strength gripped the colorful sheet of paper as she slowly read each of the words before leaving the church. They would prove to be prophetic, as if they had been selected with care to encapsulate the life that lay ahead:

Solches habe ich mit euch geredet, daß ihr in mir Frieden habet. In der Welt habt ihr Angst, aber seid getrost, ich habe die Welt überwunden. Johannes 16:33

According to the English rendering of the King James Version, it said:

These things I have spoken unto you, that in me ye might have peace. In the world ye shall have tribulation: but be of good cheer; I have overcome the world. John 16.33

In attendance at Alma's confirmation were all eight of her siblings, including the spouses of those already married and their children. A score of friends were also present, including the twenty-five year old and still bachelor, John Reither. Each time spent with Alma over the years as she grew into womanhood his attraction to her had only become stronger. Other people, other places disappeared, as if they no longer existed, when she was present; a shining star to his eyes wherever they met, his attention fastened only on her. And it was the same on this special day inside the holy walls of the church.

All but a few of the well-wishers had just exited the handsome shiplap-sided wood structure through the same front door they had entered, each one heavily wrapped to ward off the chill of an overcast spring day. After an older couple had finished commenting on the inspirational steeple redolent of old country architecture, John approached her.

"Congratulations, Alma. It was a very nice ceremony."

"Thank you, John. I'm glad you were able to come today.

It's taken me a very long time to get to this point. There were so many preparations and lessons over the past few years I thought I might never get there." Turning to her left to receive the good wishes from a few others who hadn't left yet, she looked back in his direction afterwards to find him still there and standing in the very same place; he had waited for her to be finished, immovable. An awkward moment it could have been, but Alma's adept social skills were not about to let that happen.

"Would you like to join us for a slice of cake and a glass of punch at our house, John—to help us celebrate? My brothers and sisters would love to see you. It's been a while since you've been over to see us with work taking up so much of everyone's time nowadays." She had been cognizant of the attention John had paid to her on past occasions. But it was dismissed as habit when she had also noticed several of the local girls giving him extra attention of their own only to have it returned in kind. However, that was some time ago, when they both were younger. Could an older man really be interested in a girl still in her teens? She didn't really think so. However, he was always nice to be with, and funny at times. And since he was an old friend of the family, why not invite him to join them in adding to the celebration.

"I would very much like to come over. Thank you for the invitation," his words sounding much too formal when he thought about it later.

"We're all walking back home together. You can come with us now if you like."

In the sitting room, with conversations starting and stopping as Alma mingled among the group, there really wasn't an opportunity to talk to her one-on-one. Although he would have liked to, it didn't matter that much since she still held the same fascination of just watching her move about and talk with ease to everyone. And when she finished talking to everyone else and came over to him to share a few words before saying goodbye, he felt especially gratified. So much so that after pocketing hands against the cold he left to go home with a new bounce to his step and beaming.

***

Lincoln and Hartley, O'Brien County, Iowa, July 1907-August 1908

In 1907, three years later, another gathering had brought younger and older folks together, this time at the Giese farm. Ida and Adolph and his parents had led the way in migrating across the state from Scott to O'Brien County. Now they were about to celebrate the harvest of three acres of fruit trees with family and friends. Adolph himself had set out the orchard soon after taking possession of their good-sized chunk of farm land. Ladders were placed up and down the rows of trees and local neighbors and friends invited to empty pickings of mostly plums into the buckets provided. A hardier and more plentiful crop of apples would be ready by late September or early October.

The Gerhards' were among those joining the Giese family on a temperature-climbing July morning. In the middle of summer starting early to avoid intense afternoon heat was the only way to enjoy the outdoors. Adolph had taken over much of the labor on the farm some eight years before, not so long after their arrival at Lincoln. The two townships of Lincoln and Hartley shared a border, the former dependent on the more developed downtown of the latter for basic amenities. A few Reither family members were there as well. By now old friends with the Gerhards, they had started out in O'Brien County during the same year. Alma, a svelte and rather ethereal looking nineteen year old, attracted the eyes of many at the gathering but none more so than by one particular admirer.

Picnic lunch under shade trees for the sprightly ones and on the long wooden porch for the less limber seniors had come to an end. Adolph, who had been circulating among those resting on the lawn and the seated guests, stood midway between them waving his arms.

"May I have your attention for a moment, please? For anyone who might be interested and hasn't been here for a while, I'd like to show you what we've been doing on our farm. I promise not to go into too much detail and bore you, but I think you'll find it worthwhile."

A short tour of the layout of grain crops and a visit to the graded livestock was offered to anyone who could tolerate the withering rays of the sun. Profits derived from the sale of agricultural production during the early years had been reinvested, and it showed in the extensive land improvements and modern farm equipment. The Giese family farm was thought to be one of the most progressive in the farming community.

Alma Gerhard was among the first to get up from the grass, and keeping a sharp eye out, John Reither immediately followed suit. He couldn't help but remark to himself the willowy grace to her movements. She hadn't changed. It didn't take long, just a few hundred yards of walking from pastures to fields then onto barn and stable, before what had been brewing now for many years to finally come to a boil. It was definite—Alma Gerhard was the only one for him, the one he wanted to be his wife someday. Now, if she could only feel the same way about him. To make that happen, he resolved to set his cap in earnest for her.

But he was unaware that Alma's affections had already been led in a different direction; she had been quietly seeing someone else, someone much younger than John and almost her own age. She was under the illusion that her parents were still in the dark about the relationship, but she was wrong. They knew but had decided to keep their opinions to themselves so far. He was the son of the Fischers who ran the dry goods store on Main Street. Unlike John, whose height followed the above average pattern that ran in the Reither family, Jurgen Fischer was a shorter, more compactly built man. He had kept the blond hair that sprouted as a toddler, and his neat appearance and occupation were a good part of why Alma was captivated by him. He was different from her own family and from so many others surrounding her where dirt-smeared faces and calloused hands were all they had to show from a hard day's work behind horse and plow. His carefully pressed shirt and well-kempt looks seemed like features that fit perfectly with her own calling of becoming a school teacher in the near future.

So when John began to engage her in a clearly interested way as they walked side-by-side around Adolph' farm, she tried to respond without emotion and focus only on what they were there to see. She wanted not to encourage him in any way, so when they came to a small muddy patch between pens to be crossed over to continue, she was on guard.

"Let me give you a hand getting past this sticky spot. Lean your weight on my arm and I'll help you around it."

"It's all right, John," she countered, "I'll just step on the lower fence rail and swing a leg over. But thanks, anyway."

She had sensed a few times in past meetings that he liked seeing her; and even more so today. She liked John but not in the same way as Jurgen; with him she was smitten just in his presence. It would be a fine balance maintaining a friendship with John without letting it go beyond that. She would need to choose her words carefully and control her gestures to make sure they were neither hurtful nor promising in any future conversations with him. When they had finished viewing the grazing cows and hearing about grain types and seed varieties, she broke away to be join the others as soon as she could; it had been a bit like walking on egg shells.

Afternoon socializing came to a close and thank-yous were exchanged, each visitor going home with a bulging bag of fruit tucked under an arm. John came up to Alma once more to tell her that he was very glad she had been there too then took his leave without submitting to an urge to look back. He is nice, and certainly attentive, she thought, before thanking Adolph and Ida for their hospitality and leaving herself. Then her mind switched over to Jurgen and the summer outing they had planned for next Saturday after he was finished working at the store.

Saturday couldn't come soon enough. When it finally did, Alma decided to surprise him by coming early using the back door to enter the storeroom. She knew he would come there to change out of his apron and into street clothes and she would be there waiting for him. But it was she who was surprised to hear raised voices as she passed under an open rear window just before reaching the door. It sounded like a heated discussion between Jurgen and someone else, a female voice that seemed vaguely familiar.

"But you promised we'd be able to go to my parents' house tonight. You couldn't have already forgotten that, Jurgen? This was the evening you were going to talk to my father. We've put it off already several times because you thought it might be too soon. Now you want to wait even longer?"

"Something's come up that I have to do here at the store. Anyway, I think we still need a little more time before we say anything to them, you know, to ask permission and let them know we even have a date in mind. I think you and I should talk it over again first and be a more prepared for what their reaction might be. For sure, your father will want details about when and where. But most of all he'll be expecting to hear why you are the right one for me."

"We've already gone over everything many times before and now you're saying we have to do it all over again? And all of a sudden you're doing something else tonight so we can't see them, or each other? Maybe you are having second thoughts?" More agitated by the minute, an already reddish face deepened in color.

Nah, I just need to do something for a short while. Then I'll come over later. I won't be too long. I just have to finish up here. There's some tidying up and organizing that needs to get done before the store opens again early in the morning. So it's better not to take on your father tonight when he'll probably be tired anyway. Besides, we just want to be absolutely sure that talking about marriage to him at this point is the right thing to do."

"Sure! What's that got to do now with...you just, oh never mind."

Alma had heard enough to know whose voice it was by now. It was Trudy! She didn't know her that well but apparently Jurgen did. Trudy indeed! It wasn't even necessary to find something to stand on to take a peek through the window to make sure it was her. Her ears sufficed for picturing the two of them standing there alone in the back room. She paused for a minute to gather herself. Then she hitched her skirt up just high enough to free her long legs for a hurried retreat from the scene. Taking the shortest route, she made her way down Main Street lined with horse and buggies parked on an angle, staying as close as she dared to the hitching posts to avoid bumping into passersby. So she was being two-timed! Who cares about that lout anyway? Let Trudy have him then. Pride had overshadowed hurt—at least for the moment.

Later on, after a few days had past, when the immediacy of the scene she had witnessed had faded somewhat and while she was routinely cleaning house, a mind freed from the fatigue of overthinking suddenly latched onto a conclusion. She was actually glad she had heard what she did before letting herself in for a big mistake. Perhaps a good deal of her attraction to Jurgen had not been for the right reasons anyhow. How easy it had been to convince herself with preconceived notions that a satisfying life was in store for her if she married a townsman from a family of standing. In fact, when you came right down to it, it was almost as much her fault as it was his in that respect. Well, she was now taking the first steps in getting over it.

Nevertheless, she definitely wanted nothing more to do

with Jurgen despite his attempts to contact her. But an accidental meeting eventually could not be avoided while shopping in town. She wanted to just keep on walking when he came up to her; he caught her by the arm and said that he could explain everything, but could he ask one question first. Her reply was short and to the point: "Ask your questions of Trudy, let her answer them." Then she did walk off around the corner and out of sight. She could accept that he liked someone else more than her, but sneaking around, hiding another relationship obviously more important than the one with her, could not be abided. Did he think he could dangle the prospect of a life together with two different women at the same time and get away with it forever?

Summer heat had from one day to the next evaporated into the chilly winds of autumn in late September. For Alma, the change in temperature was welcome. A new season meant the recent past was receding, so what made others shiver felt like reinvigorating breezes to her. What's more, autumn of 1907 marked a milestone for her; Alma Gerhard had begun her first year as a teacher at a school in East Hartley. By Christmas, she had mastered delivering a balanced curriculum to a range of ages in a one room schoolhouse. Her no-nonsense demeanor and practiced voice cadence were great assets in creating a relatively calm learning environment. So she was good at maintaining class discipline—most of the time. It was a natural progression for her, innate talent and dedication during her own school days paying off as far as realistic expectations went, and the first four months of a new career passed without regrets.

All the same, holiday celebrations at home would be a welcome break from the stress of planning, preparing and delivering the first iteration of a raft of subjects to so many students at so many different levels of knowledge. It had been more taxing than she thought. And there would be adjustments to be made when she returned to the classroom, nothing major as far as academics, rather a larger focus on comportment—social skills, good manners and basic etiquette—and extra emphasis on the golden rule. But at least for the last weeks of December and the beginning of January, it would be a time to put all that aside and just enjoy being home with her family and restored by winter's diversions.

After the holidays were over, locals were looking forward to going to the first major function of the New Year, Alma as much as any of them. The Masquerade Ball at the Grand Opera House in Hartley had been scheduled for the end of January. It was not every year that the dance and dining occasion was held and it had become the talk of town and farm. Alma and her old friend, Delia had already decided to go, as Indians. Alma had suggested it in honor of the native peoples who had lived and hunted on the same land that they now farmed. It was part of the Iowa history curriculum taught in her classroom. The Indians were gone before Hartley was founded, but towns like Sioux City and Cherokee carried the names of local tribes. Only the old-timers could recollect the retaliatory massacre of 1857 at Spirit Lake. A starving renegade band of Sioux had travelled down from the north to within thirty-five miles northeast of Hartley and five miles from the border with Minnesota to avenge the killing of the chief's brother. At least thirty-five settlers were killed and several women were taken captive. So long ago now, it was told almost like a folk tale to the younger generations.

The day before the January 28th ball was to take place, the

two young women got together to put the finishing touches on their costumes.

"Will you be able to have the Oyster Supper they'll be serving in the hall, Alma? I'd like to, if it's not too expensive."

"The entrance ticket price for the ladies is only ten cents. That's a real bargain, Delia. Tickets for the gents are a dollar, though. The girls are getting off easy, I guess, while they get stuck with making up the difference. So the dinner must be reasonable as well, I should think."

"Then we ought to do the dinner too. There'll be music by a professional band, which should be good. It's supposed to be Moore's Ideal Orchestra. They're the musicians from over in Estherville who play at a lot of dance dinners around our corner of the state nowadays."

Pausing for a moment to reflect, then recalling, "I think I do remember who they are—three brothers. The oldest one plays the violin, I believe." She started to adjust her headdress. "Yes, I have heard about them and they are supposed to be quite good. Do you think there are enough feathers? Are they going in the right direction?" she wondered in spinning around.

"It looks fine just the way you have it," Delia reassured while placing the borrowed buckskin top over her own head and onto her shoulders.

By the end of the afternoon outfits had been sorted out and they felt ready for next evening's festivities. And when that evening came and they entered the hall, it seemed like at least half the town was already there before them. Stopping to talk with friends and exchange costume compliments, they moved about as well as they could, considering the number of bodies they had to squeeze by. Suddenly, Alma grasped

Delia's wrist and pulled her to a halt. Not ten paces ahead were Jurgen and Trudy talking to another couple. Frozen to the floor by the shock of it, only firm tapping on her shoulder broke the stupor and she turned around. The pair of sky blue eyes looking squarely into hers belonged to the familiar face of John Reither.

"Hello, Alma. I saw you and my sister as you were coming in, but it took a few minutes to get through all of the people here. Would you like a glass of punch? I'll bring one over for you both if you can wait while I dodge the crowd."

Never had a distraction unwittingly caused been more welcome. "No, don't go by yourself. We'll go with you. C'mon Delia. Let's all get some punch. It's so nice to see you here, John."

"I've just spotted cousin Christina over in the corner and it looks like she might be all alone. I think I should go over and see how things are with her." Throwing a quick regard Alma's way, Delia quickly left the two of them together to talk. Grateful as Alma was for John's rescue from the chance of an awkward encounter, she had not expected what would happen next. Any thought of rejoining Delia and meeting other friends was put on hold when a young man dressed in Western garb bumped her arm causing a goodly amount of pink liquid to be sloshed onto her legs. Without speaking, John motioned to her to wait while he returned to the punch bowl table to retrieve a pile of napkins. She dried herself off while he bent down to wipe splashes up from the floor. When finished, they looked at each other rather seriously then broke into laughter. From thereon, a conversation began that lasted until they were called to supper. It didn't stop for long even then, starting up again as soon as they seated themselves side-by-side at the table.

When the music recommenced, Alma actually found herself hoping he would ask her to dance with him, although she hadn't yet grasped just why her feelings had changed. So when he did ask, she was quite pleased. Left hand clasping left hand they twirled around the floor dance after dance, until the music stopped; the winners of the costume contest were about to be announced. Moving closer to the stage to get a better view, Alma Gerhard was stunned to hear her name called out along with Delia's. Their outfits had been judged winners of second place and they were called forward to the stage. Their prize: one dollar apiece! First prize winners, a group of four young men representing soldiers, received five dollars each. This time when she returned to her partner and had her hand taken in congratulations she didn't let it go, pulling him instead to open space on the dance floor.

"Let's keep dancing forever. I can't believe it; we actually won! And when he wrapped his arm around her waist, he realized something was different with her. She seemed to be no longer seeing him as just John Reither, one of Delia's brothers and a friend but actually wanted to be held by him until the music stopped. When the evening was over and John walked the two young women home, it was a brand new world filled with possibilities.

Ten days passed as the calendar pages turned from January to February 1908. During that time Alma often reverted to what had happened at the ball. What was it about John that was affecting her now? Had the magic of that evening somehow intoxicated her, bewitched her into believing he was someone more than he had been all along until that night, someone who really cared for her—and even more strangely—she for him? Was it just a momentary feeling, soon to be over before it really started? Why had she not paid more attention to him when they had been together in the past? If he was really interested in her, would he make an effort to see her again? And most of all, why was she even asking herself these questions at this time in the first place? Finally she told herself she must stop thinking about it—at least for the time being—and concentrate on preparation for the next event of the winter season.

The luncheon to raise funds for her school was to be held on the 14th of February—Valentine's Day. With help from her pupils, Alma would be organizing and hosting a basket social at her school in District 7 of East Hartley. Young, unmarried women in the community, often older sisters of current students, were assembling food baskets containing meals to be eaten on the premises as well as preserves to take home at the end of the affair. They would be brought to the school to be auctioned off to male bidders, the winners having the privilege of dining with the ladies who had made them. Alma herself had been seen with an overflowing basket to show her support for the school. Almost all of the district school teachers held similar activities during the school year, but coordinated planning had been careful to spread them out so no more than one auction occurred on the same weekend. Alma's was the first of 1908 to be held in Hartley.

On the day of the event, desks had been moved towards the rear of the classroom for seating and eating purposes while work tables were set-up to display food baskets in the front. Bidding was to be done by a number attached to a ribbon hanging over the side of each basket. The many chefs were already standing behind tables waiting for the bidding to begin. But warmly bundled supporters were still trickling in, many of them pausing just long enough to remember a special number before sitting down. The room was soon filled with young men who had shed farmer overalls for their Sunday's best. Fear of bad weather had not deterred a good turn-out, even though snow was beginning to fall again when Alma peered out an ice-cornered window just before the auction began.

"Your attention please, everyone; the bidding is about to begin," she announced in ringing a bell for emphasis. Talking ceased, although there were still a few furtive looks around the room to pick out possible bidding competitors.

"I'm sure you all know by now that all of the proceeds will go to our school. The winning bids will help to buy necessary supplies and new equipment which will help to give our children the kind of education they deserve. None of your generous offers will go towards administrative expenses or teacher salaries, I can assure you.

"These ladies standing before you have spared no effort in putting together food baskets to tantalize your appetites. You've all had a chance to see the variety of jams and jelly jars and other delectables on display today.

"This is how it will work. You will need to remember the number of the basket you have won. When the auction is over I will call out each number. Please come to the table under the blackboard and pay the amounts due. Then the basket maker will join you at your desk for a delicious meal. Don't worry, there's plenty for two in each basket! Now let's start the bidding. Who will be the first to make an offer of one dollar on bountiful basket number one?"

Immediately the hand of Karl Voss shot high in the air,

but he would not get off so lightly. Other bidders chimed in and Karl's purchase ended up costing him three dollars and fifty cents. He would have gone even higher for he had long been waiting for an opportunity to get to know Anna better. One-by-one they were all sold until only Alma's remained. More hands were raised at each new bid level, but when five dollars was reached and then seven shouted out by John Reither in the back, all eyes turned towards him and the bidding was over. Alma had noticed when he had entered the school but had become too involved to keep track of where he was in the room. She thought he was still there but had kept the possibility of seeing him in check if she didn't.

She needn't have worried because they spent the rest of the afternoon into early evening eating and talking together. All the time snow continued to lightly fall outside. At his suggestion to take a breath of fresh air, Alma and John buttoned up coats, put on hats and stepped out the door. They circuited the building several times before stopping under a bare-leaved white oak tree. The winds had died down and the temperature actually felt warmer as large flakes softly fluttered to the ground. By the time it took for a white mantle to form on shoulders and hats, they knew they had gone well beyond the point of being good friends. When John took her hand in his to go back towards the schoolhouse, life had taken a turn. Alma stood by the door to thank each person as they left at the end of the day while John waited alone to walk her home later. He didn't mind. He didn't mind anything now.

A nearly disastrous experience brought the Reither and Gerhard families together again later that year. A late winter storm of deluge proportions had begun to cause anxiety for everyone. In spite of the bad weather, Alma and her parents had decided to go ahead with plans for a Saturday visit to an old friend on the other side of town who had been feeling poorly. To their great good fortune, a light shone down on the bridge they needed to cross to get there. What came into their vision was a structure on the verge of collapse, swaying back and forth in the wind as if it was a toy, rising waters pounding the pillars. They had stopped in the nick of time, turning back in the direction they came to return to home.

The May 1908 issue of the *Hartley Journal* a few days later reported on how Emil Reither, John's brother, had been the person whose light warning had been life-saving:

> "Emil Reither, living on the east side of town, did the act of a hero last Saturday night during the heavy storm. A stream runs a short distance from his home and realizing the approach to the bridge would be taken out and that parties were liable to pass that way during the night, he faced the storm of wind, rain and hail to the bridge and hung out a lantern. It was a good thought put into action."

When the weather cleared, the Gerhard and Reither families descended in mass on the childless home of Emil and his wife. In their arms they carried enough food to feed the whole town as a way of thanks. When John sat down next to Alma, he couldn't help thinking again of what might have happened. Although he hadn't been there, he reran the imagined scene over and over again until a plate of food was placed in his lap. Of all the grateful folks sitting in the room, his gratitude towards his brother had reached a level above all the rest.

Two days later, John was behind the reins of a buckboard

laden with supplies from town and bound for home. Turning a bend of the road he saw Alma Gerhard walking in the same direction and pulled up beside her.

"Can I introduce to you the best horse in the world? Dolly meet Alma—my favorite girl in the world!" He extended a hand to help her up to take a seat beside him on the wooden bench. In the short time it took before arriving at her home two good things had happened: a formal marriage proposal was made and accepted, and a wedding date was set. After the bridge affair neither of them wanted to wait any longer. And two months after the end of the school year in June, on August 27th, 1908, they were married in Hartley.

The Reverend J. Fischer—the new pastor who had come only the year before—conducted the ceremony. He was the first to live in the recently constructed parsonage next door to the Lutheran church, but the marriage did not take place there. The home of Alma's parents was chosen instead, and it was Dolly that brought John's buckboard up to the front door. Truly a family affair, parents, brothers and sisters, nephews, nieces and cousins witnessed the bride and groom take their vows. And to appease growling stomachs, a bounteous supper was served afterwards.

IN THREES

Iowa, California, Oregon, 1911-1944

> If tears could make a staircase,
> And heartaches make a lane,
> We'd walk the path to heaven
> And bring you home again.

Until We Meet Again, Unknown

Alma continued to teach at the same school for the next two years. In 1911 came the birth of her first child, a son, followed by a second son in 1913 then two more boys, twins, in 1916. Finally, a female child made an appearance in 1919, but even then she was not alone; a brother had joined her to make a second set of twins. One last addition—making seven children in all—came as an unexpected gift, a second girl arriving sixteen years after the birth of her eldest sibling.

In raising such a large brood towards adulthood, Alma could find little time to do what she most loved doing—teaching children, whether professionally at a school or tutoring at home. The years before the outbreak of the First World War were prosperous ones for the Reithers, and John's reputation as an honest and smart stock buyer solidified with his years of experience. An important relationship formed with the major livestock farm of Ray Dale of Hawarden in Sioux County during the war had been instrumental to success and his family's well-being. With the help of the Sioux City Association of Credit, much of their surplus income had been prudently invested in lands in and around Hartley.

Then, in 1922, life in Iowa became more difficult when it took a reverse turn. When the madcap pace of wartime industrial production had quickly retreated at the end of the conflict, and before it picked-up once again during the economic boom of the Roaring Twenties, the Reithers were caught in the middle of a nightmare lawsuit. They had been charged along with another group of defendants for outstanding loans called in for immediate payment. The loans had been secured when things were on the upswing, but now they were about to lose all of the land acquisitions in which the borrowed money and their life savings were invested . On an overcast day matching the somber mood of those who sat in the Primghar courthouse in O'Brien County, they watched their properties be auctioned off one by one.

The resilient Reithers would see their fortunes rebound, but never to the same degree as before. The family would break apart and disperse when financial reserves dried up again during the years of the Great Depression. Still, Alma found solace in the time she devoted to serving the community in becoming a leader in the local Women's Relief Corps. The WRC, an auxiliary of the Grand Army of the Republic, was tasked with remembering and assisting war veterans and their families. In her role of vice-president she returned to her educational roots in helping hospitalized children, children of widows and widowers, and especially orphans. Her commitment to the Relief Corps remained constant through decades, right up to her death in the 1960s, serving as the Hartley Unit president for many of those years. Her civic involvement did not stop there. The Republican Party had become another of her interests after the First World War at a time when the German language and Germanic associations were viewed negatively. When the family's religious involvement shifted from the German Lutheran faith to the Hartley Methodist Episcopal Church, her obligations grew once again.

In 1967, under the auspices of the WRC, Alma Reither received the local Friday Club nomination for Mother of the Year in Iowa. What figured most prominently in her nomination was her early training and experience as a teacher. After her own children had left home, she had taught pupils who were struggling academically for short stays, tutoring them as part of their educational preparation. A town club she belonged to had made the nomination and together with women selected throughout Iowa, the nominees were then entered into a state contest, the Iowan winner competing against winners from other states for American Mother of the Year.

***

Things often come in threes, they say—good and bad. Superstition, old wives' tale, utter nonsense, certainly scoffed at and dismissed by those with scientific backgrounds.

As with almost all families, life did not follow a natural progression without undergoing its sorrows. Birth, childhood, adulthood, work, marriage, and finally a peaceful demise at a venerable age, a story book pattern repeated for each successive generation, would not be the lot for John and Alma either. Any expectations that it might have been so came literally crashing down in the space of a single year.

It began with Louis, twin to Louise and youngest of their five sons, on a clear spring Thursday afternoon that still held enough warmth in it for an adventure. Perhaps a borrowed motorcycle had been calling to be taken out for a spin. Feel the wind tousle your hair as you speed along; the freedom of the wide open road; lean into every bend wherever it may lead. That may have been the plan for a last ride before dark. So Louis and a friend climbed astride the powerful machine and happily set off.

But what the two young men had failed to notice in time was the car in front of them slowing down to cross a wooden creek bridge; slamming into its rear bumper, they were sent hurtling into space. Louis had been chief A&E mechanic at the Pella airport, having been deferred from the draft because of his work with air frames and engines for military purposes; his friend had been visiting the area near Oskaloosa.

The nearest hospital to that town was some twenty miles away from where the wreckage of bodies and machine lay. In the time it took for ambulances to deliver them to hospital care, their conditions had worsened. The gravity of his wounds had left no question of transporting Louis to the hospital in his home town of Hartley several hours further away. Within two days, they had both succumbed to their injuries. In April 1943, at the age of twenty-three, his family never had the chance to see Louis again before his death.

A second cause for grieving came less than two months

later during the first week of June. Max, one half of Alma's and John's first set of twins, was destined to meet a similar fate. While working for Man Construction Company as a carpenter on the upper story of a new building, Max Reither tripped and fell all the way to the ground. He had been working alongside his twin, Maurice, and an older brother at the Alameda Naval Air Station across the Bay from San Francisco. Three years older than his brother Louis when he died, he was twenty-six when he passed away the following day at Alameda Hospital.

A grudge kept to herself from family for most of her life, his twin sister eventually admitted to blaming the older brother for Max's untimely death. Louise had left Iowa to live with her brothers in San Francisco before her marriage set to take place less than a month after the accident. In her mind the older brother had failed his responsibility to look after his siblings and his negligence was the cause of the death. He should have made sure no object was lying on scaffolding planks that caused Max to stumble, whether it had been a length of coiled rope or power cord or a tool left behind. He had been derelict in his duty as a big brother and would be held accountable forever.

Merritt Reither, oldest of the seven siblings, was the third member of the family to die during a year marred with triple tragedy. In 1930 the depression was in full swing, families struggling to survive; the Reither family had not been spared. So at the age of eighteen Merritt packed his bags and hitched a ride on the Burlington railroad for his first excursion westward taking up an offer of road maintenance work in the Black Hills town of Moorcroft in Crook County, Wyoming. Four years later, on a trip to Mankato, Minnesota, again for work purposes, he met and soon afterwards married his wife. Returning to his Iowa home, four children followed in quick succession for the couple, each one separated by a single year only and all born in that state. A year later, a last son was born in 1937, but this time in Minnesota. The following year, however, did not see yet another child born. To the contrary, the annual birth cycle ended as did their marriage in divorce.

During 1938 Merritt left Iowa once again, this time for good, to travel even further west, to Alturas, California, to pursue his passion for ranching, especially anything to do with horses. Now in northern California and in his late twenties, his cattle wrangling and cowboy rodeo skills could be indulged with abandon. Known as "Slim" to his western compatriots and friends, a second woman from the northwestern state of Washington entered his life. Their time together was divided between a ranch in Fort Klamath in the Wood River Valley, a little north of Klamath Falls in Oregon and close to Crater Lake, and their house in Alturas. Cattle transported by train from Chiloquin in Klamath County were wintered a bit further south in the town of Willows in California.

Merritt gained local fame and prize money for his bronco busting prowess in Klamath Falls and elsewhere on the rodeo circuit. When his premature death occurred in April of 1944, you had expected to read that this ranch hand had been kicked by a horse, or had been killed when thrown to the dirt during Klamath Buckaroo Days at Modoc Field, or even trampled in a cattle stampede. So it was more than a little ironic when he was crushed to death beneath a passenger car while it was being unloaded from a truck. The brakes had failed and the car slid down the truck bed pinning him to the ground, breaking his neck and killing him instantly. His faithful blue Australian shepherd dog, once lost and found again days later, had stayed by his side until the ambulance carried his body away. Three brothers gone in the space of a year: April 1943 to April 1944.

They say things come in threes—good and bad.

WHERE BLUE BUTTERFLIES FLUTTER

Hartley, Iowa, July 1958

All was not sadness for Alma and John as the years scudded by like clouds in a stormy sky. When three of their children had left to go to California, they hadn't felt alone with the youngest child still at home. Even with the departure of their remaining daughter just after the death of Dolly—the beloved horse that had been part of so many of their memories—there were still other relatives and old friends to enjoy life with in Iowa. John and Alma were not the type to travel far very often, but as grandchildren began to arrive they made the long trip west to meet the newest family members while reuniting with their own children. After all, they had survived three wars, a depression and the brink of the poor house, so leaving daily routines in Hartley during the winter months was a snap in comparison.

Maintaining mental equilibrium was essential through it all. Alma had always kept close to her heart an old German proverb spoken by her father whenever a crisis had touched their family: "Man muss die Dinge nehmen, wie sie kommen." It literally meant: "You have to take things the way they come". Although the habit of speaking German for her own generation had stopped after the war as did German-language church services and schools, and even though her own children were never taught the language, it did not keep her from thinking and dreaming in her father's native tongue at times.

Now, only two days before the first guests were to arrive to join them in celebration of their golden wedding anniversary, they sat by themselves on a muggy August evening. Their elbows resting on the large family table in the old two-story wood-framed house, they looked across at watery eyes, not a word needing to be said. The family tradition in gathering around the venerable table when important decisions were discussed and sometimes even made brought back memories of those who were no longer with them. Stories told by their parents of the old country when it was still the Duchy of Holstein and long before it would be called Germany, their first farm near Davenport on the eastern side of Iowa, and the move to O'Brien County often besieged their thoughts.

In the twilight of fifty years together, the table before them transformed into living rooms, houses, gardens, churches and the people that were in them—a collection of life's memories. Soon they would be welcoming family and friends from near and far for one last gathering. Alma's childhood had been dominated by a strict mother who had vacillated between generosity and unkindness, almost seeming like resentment at times, towards Alma and the other children. Since she could blow hot or cold on any given day they had prepared themselves to expect anything. It was remarkable that none of the negativity had rubbed off on her. The love for her own children, grandchildren and the orphans she taught had strengthened her resolve to remain consistent in the face of a changing world. It was as if the lessons taken from her own upbringing had been turned on their head in shaping a person whose concern for the young had become a life's calling.

It tickled her to recall how her children used to believe they had gone unnoticed when, instead of asleep in their beds upstairs as they should have been, they flitted around like blue butterflies on the first days of spring before huddling around the cast iron grate placed between the first and second floors. From their second story vantage point they had listened in on conversations that were supposed to be for grown-ups only. Through the Victorian lacework vent, intended to let heat from the lower floor rise to the rooms above, a simple amusement had been found in snatches of sounds and glimpses of shadowy movements below.

Throughout the post-depression years John's trade in buying and selling cattle and horses had continued, providing a steady source of income and allowing for a comfortable middle class life. His knack in handling and judging animals was only surmounted by his ability to close a trade deal. He had come upon his calling early in life and he was one of the fortunate ones to be able to do what he loved for the remainder of it through good times and bad.

The number of friends he had made travelling the county and even further afield could not be counted. Great wealth as an outcome had neither been sought nor obtained, but neither had the trials of the 20's and the Great Depression years come knocking at their door again. Possessions had never been a priority; children, horses, dogs and livestock—that was different. That and the backyard garden where his hands and fingernails soaked up dirt digging potatoes had given him all that was needed. Surely they were among the best ever grown in Iowa even when they had been brought up from the musty outdoor cellar after many months of cool storage.

They were the same worn and deeply lined hands that now reached across the table taking Alma's into their own. It had been by far the best thing that ever had happened to him in his life when he had pulled his wagon up to a halt along the old dirt road and she sat down beside him. But soon familiar faces would be all around them. The hour had grown late and the time for bed had come before the big day would soon be there; it was as if fifty years together was no more than the space of a day as their eyes closed shut.

www.ingramcontent.com/pod-product-compliance
Lightning Source LLC
Chambersburg PA
CBHW050011120726
47903CB00006B/1729